The Survivor

James Herbert is not just Britain's No. 1 bestselling writer of chiller fiction, a position he has held ever since publication of his first novel, but is one of our greatest popular novelists, whose books are sold in thirty-three foreign languages, including Russian and Chinese. Widely imitated and hugely influential, his nineteen novels have sold more than 42 million copies worldwide.

Also by James Herbert

JAMES HERBERT

The Survivor

PAN BOOKS

First published 1976 by New English Library

This edition published 1999 by Pan Books
an imprint of Macmillan Publishers Ltd
25 Eccleston Place, London SW1W 9NF
Basingstoke and Oxford
Associated companies throughout the world
www.macmillan.co.uk

ISBN 0 330 37616 0

1 3 5 7 9 8 6 4 2

A CIP catalogue record for this book is available from
the British Library.

Typeset by SetSystems Ltd, Saffron Walden, Essex
Printed and bound in Great Britain by
Mackays of Chatham plc, Chatham, Kent

The Survivor

Prologue

The old man tightened his scarf and pulled the lapels of his heavy overcoat up around his neck. The warm air from his lungs became visible as it emerged from his mouth and was instantly chilled by the cold night air. For a few seconds, he allowed his feet to beat a soft tattoo on the hard concrete surface of the iron bridge, then stopped, settling his ageing frame more comfortably on the unyielding bench. He looked up at the dark October sky, enjoying the feeling of smallness its deepness gave him. There was a half moon, crisp and clear-edged, hanging flatly and remotely, as though added as an afterthought and playing no important part in the dark empyrean.

Sighing inwardly, he lowered his gaze to the river, black with sudden splashes of reflected light constantly joining and parting in a dazzling display of effulgence. He looked towards its banks: at the small boats and launches stirring smoothly in its easy flow; at the bright shops and restaurants, and the public house at the end, all night-lit clean, their middle greys of the day concealed in contrasts of uncompromising light and dark.

Beautiful, he thought. Beautiful, this time of night, this time of year. The lateness meant fewer people used the bridge as a thoroughfare; the coldness meant less people would linger on its unshielded length. Most of the tourists had left

1

Windsor by now, their season having sighed to a halt. The day-trippers had scurried back into their coaches and cars and departed with the short autumn dusk. Now there would be fewer pilgrimages across the bridge from Windsor to see Eton, his town, to visit the famous College with its Tudor schoolyard and beautiful fifteenth-century chapel, to admire the eighteenth-century shop fronts and half-timbered medieval buildings, to browse through the numerous antique shops crammed into its narrow High Street. He hadn't quite appreciated the beauty of his birthplace himself until he'd read the official guide-book for Eton a few years before; it had become lost to him through a lifetime of familiarity. But now that he'd had a few years to pause, to look around him, to take stock of himself and his surroundings, he'd taken a deeper interest in the history and the uniqueness of his native town. For the past four years, since his retirement and after his illness, he had made a study of Eton, becoming an expert on the subject. Any tourists stopping the old man in the street to ask for directions would suddenly find themselves with a knowledgeable and seemingly tireless guide, who would not let them go until they had grasped at least a fundamental history of the place. But towards the end of summer, he would grow tired of the tourists and the bustle they brought to his normally peaceful habitat, and he would welcome the arrival of the cold weather and the darker evenings.

Every night now, he would leave his tiny terraced house in Eton Square at about 8.30 and walk down to the College, then back up to the High Street towards the bridge where he would spend at least twenty to thirty minutes, regardless of weather, staring downriver to where the Thames divided around Romney Island, never particularly deep in thought, just enjoying the mood of the night. Occasionally, mainly in summer, he would be joined by others, some strangers, some acquaintances, and he would chat with them for a while, but soon fall into his own reflective silence. Then he would walk back, stop in at The Christopher Courage for a single brandy, one of the few luxuries he allowed himself, and afterwards return home to bed.

Tonight, he imagined, would be no different from any other. Then, the drone of an aeroplane's engines reached his ears. It was nothing unusual – Eton was on a direct air route from nearby Heathrow Airport, a cause of much complaint to the local people both in Eton and Windsor – but for some reason he peered up into the sky to find the source of the noise. He saw the tail light first and then the huge bulk of the plane became visible as his eyes adjusted to the inky backdrop.

One of the big 'uns, he thought. Damn nuisance, all these planes. Especially those big ones. Noisy brutes. Necessary evil, I suppose. He wanted to avert his eyes, the tension in his neck muscles now becoming an uncomfortable strain as they stretched upwards; but for some reason, he was unable to do so. The huge body – quite low – the red light, the droning noise, had suddenly become fascinating to him. He'd seen too many of the monsters for this one in particular to hold any real interest, yet he found he could not tear his eyes away from it. Something was wrong. He had no idea how he knew, but there was something wrong up there.

It seemed to be turning, which in itself was unusual because most other aircraft flew directly across Eton in a straight line. The right-hand wing seemed to be dipping. Yes, it was definitely turning. And then, he saw the plane split open. He heard the muffled explosion, but his senses barely registered the noise. They were too entranced by the horror of the spectacle, for the aeroplane hadn't quite broken up and the whole body was now plummeting towards the earth. He

3

could see objects falling from it as it plunged; objects that could only be seats, cases – and bodies!

'Oh God!' he said aloud, as the noise suddenly penetrated his brain. 'It can't be! Help them, God, help—' The whining roar drowned his cries as the falling plane passed over him, skimming over the High Street, its four engines and the rushing of wind combining to create a terrible sound, the force of the engines preventing it from merely dropping from the sky. The old man could see that the windows in the front section were lit up by a red blaze, and tails of fire were emerging from the huge crack in its body, flattened by the rushing wind. The aircraft was hardly held together, the rear section dragging downwards, about to break away from the main body at any moment.

The plane disappeared from view, the boathouses mercifully hiding the inevitable and final destruction from the old man's vision. There seemed to be a pause – a moment of silence, a moment when it appeared that nothing had happened – but then came the explosion. The sky shone red and he saw the flames in the near distance reach up from behind the boathouses. He fell to his knees at the sound, and the blast appeared to make even the bridge tremble. It filled his ears and he clapped his hands to them, leaning forward from the waist so that his face almost touched his knees. But still the noise penetrated and reverberated inside his head, the shock of what had happened held in abeyance for the moment whilst his brain dealt with the physical pain. At last, the sound seemed to diminish. It had only taken seconds, but they were frozen seconds, timeless.

Slowly he raised his head, his hands still tight against his ears, his eyes wide with fear. He saw the pulsating glow, the rising palls of smoke, but everything else was still. He saw other figures along the High Street, their faces just white

blobs in the strangely red-hued night light, standing transfixed, afraid or unable to move. The shattering of glass from
a restaurant window at the foot of the bridge broke the
stillness, and the old man observed the whole street was
littered with glistening shards of glass. People began to
appear at windows and doorways; he heard voices calling out.
Nobody seemed sure of what had happened. He staggered to
his feet and began to run towards the fields where he knew
the plane had come to rest.

As he ran past the boathouses, the old man noticed they
were ablaze at the rear. He reached a small lane that led into
the long fields beyond, his breathing becoming more painful
with each step. He glanced back over his shoulder and saw
there were several small fires in the buildings behind him.
Turning a corner, he stopped at the edge of the field, one
hand clutched to his chest, his shoulders heaving with exertion and the effort of breathing.

He stared aghast at the wrecked aeroplane lit up by its
own fires. Its belly was crushed, its nose pushed up and
squashed flat. The only wing he could see was lying alongside
the rear end which had finally broken off completely from the
main body. Only the tail rose majestically from the mangled
wreckage, almost untouched, but somehow obscene because
of it, glowing red in the light from the flames, defiant, but
now ugly in its sleekness.

The area appeared to be covered with twisted metal,
material that had been scattered and flung wide on impact.
The old man reluctantly entered the field, aware that there
might be a possibility of helping someone. It seemed unlikely,
but it was the only thing to do. As he moved forward, he
heard the sounds of shouts and footsteps behind him. Others
must be arriving on the scene; he prayed that they would be
of some use. He carefully skirted around glowing pieces of

metal, some that burnt the grass they rested on. And then came the smell. He didn't recognize it at first because it was mingled with smoke and the odour of melting metal. Then he realized its source. It was burning flesh.

He retched and almost fell to his knees again. How many passengers did these big planes take? It was more than three hundred, he felt certain. Oh dear God, no wonder the smell was so strong!

Suddenly the old man felt faint. It wasn't just the odious smell; the heat was intolerable, and up till now he hadn't realized how fierce it was. He had to move away; it was no good, no one could have survived this carnage. He looked around in desperation just in case, and was repulsed when he discovered that some of what he had imagined as being twisted metal was, in fact, twisted bodies. They were scattered all around him; he was standing in a field of maimed, torn human beings. He ran his hands over his eyes as though to dismiss the sight, but he couldn't shut out the vision he'd already seen. Slowly, his hands ran down his face and again he looked around in some faint hope that he might find someone alive. He closed his mind to the sight of dismembered limbs, to blackened bodies, to bodies that seemed to move – tricks of the unsteady light. He saw something small and pink, naked and seemingly unmarked. Small enough to be – a child? A baby? Oh God, please give this one a chance! He ran towards it, avoiding obstacles, human or otherwise. The child was facing downwards, its body stiff. He prayed aloud, his words emerging in choking sobs, as he knelt down beside the body and turned it over.

Huge, sightless eyes stared up at him. Its small mouth grinned and moved in the flickering light. One side of the doll's face had melted away, giving it an ugly, scarred appearance, the grinning lips adding to the obscenity. The old man screamed and threw the object down and, in his confusion, stumbled towards the fire and the main wreckage. The intensity of heat didn't warn him of his direction but, fortunately, a large fragment of smouldering metal tripped him, halting his progress. He lay flat in the churned mud, his body shaking, his fingers digging into the soft slime. The shock was beginning to hit him: he was an old man; he was no longer strong enough to bear a punishment such as this. The earth filled his mouth and he began to choke, and it was only this physical discomfort that forced his frightened mind to function properly again. He raised his head and lifted himself to his elbows. He stared up at the flames and was forced to close his eyes quickly as they became scorched by the heat. But before he'd closed them, something had registered. A shape, a silhouette against the bright glare, was coming towards him. He looked again, this time shielding his eyes as much as he could with one hand.

It was a man! Coming away from the aeroplane! Away from the fire! It couldn't be. No one had passed him. Yet no one could escape from a disaster like that. At least, not on his own two legs!

The old man squinted and peered more closely at the figure. Even his suit seemed undamaged. It was dark, or was that just because of the brightness behind? It looked like a uniform. The figure walked slowly and easily towards him, away from the flames, away from the destroyed aircraft, away from the dead.

The old man's vision began to swim before him and a lightness ran through his head. Just before he fainted, he saw the figure stooping down towards him, one hand outstretched.

1

Keller drove the car steadily along Pococks Lane, resisting the impulse for speed, trying to enjoy the multi-browns of autumn in the surrounding playing fields. But his mind rarely wandered far from his objective: the small town that lay not too far ahead. He turned left into Windsor Road, crossed a small bridge then found himself among the tall, dignified buildings of Eton College. He hardly paused to admire them, driving on into the High Street where he stopped to get his bearings. He still found it difficult to concentrate for too long.

Drawing away from the kerb again he continued on down the High Street until he reached the bridge at the end, its iron posts preventing traffic from crossing it. He turned right and drove past the burnt-out boathouses, and right again led him towards the fields he sought. There was a more direct route avoiding the High Street according to his map, but he had wanted to see more of the town itself. He wasn't sure why.

The policeman watched him park his midnight-blue Stag. Another one, he thought. Another bloody sightseer. Maybe a souvenir hunter. The trouble they'd had since the accident; mobs of 'em flocking to the scene of the crash. Ghouls. It always happened after any major disaster – particularly with an air crash – they turned out in their thousands to see the gore, blocking roads, getting in the way. He'd send them all packing if he had his way. The worst of it was when the vendors had arrived, selling peanuts, ice-creams, soft drinks; that had really sickened him. Trouble is, it's so near London. It was a nice day out for the city-dwellers.

The constable adjusted his chinstrap and set his jaw more firmly. Well this one is going to get the rough end of my tongue, he thought, but as Keller emerged from the car, he changed his mind. He looks like a journalist. Got to watch what you say to them. Mind you, they were worse than the thrill-seekers, probing and inventing stories when they couldn't find one, just to sell their bloody newspapers! He'd had a few run-ins with them over the past month. But you'd think they'd let it die down now; after all, it was nearly four weeks since it'd happened. No, they wouldn't let anything rest, these reporters; at least, not while the investigation was still going on. He hadn't realized it took so long to find out the cause of an air crash; you just located the Black Box, or whatever it was called, and that told you exactly what had happened. That's what *he'd* thought, anyway. But they'd been poring over that field for a long time now, taking bits and pieces away, searching every corner of the big field, the South Meadow, that was just behind the High Street; even dragged the small river that branched off from the Thames and ran through the South Field. They'd found a few bodies in there, bodies that must have been thrown clear on impact, right across the road over The Brocas, and into the river. Others that had been sucked out before impact. God, that had been horrible. Three days it had taken to find and collect all the bodies; or what was left of 'em.

'You can't go in there, sir!' he told Keller gruffly.

Keller stopped, but ignored the policeman, looking past his shoulder into the field beyond. He could see the remains of the aircraft, or the main bulk of what they'd left. It stood, a huge blackened shell, cone-shaped because of its flattened belly, broken and ashamed. The guts of it would be back in the laboratories being reassembled, analysed, tested. He could see figures carrying clipboards moving about the field, stooping, picking up objects, examining grooves in the earth, their grim purpose contrasting with the bright, cold day, the greenness of the field, the quiet in the air.

The constable examined Keller closely. He looked familiar. 'I'm sorry, sir, but you're not allowed to go in,' he said.

Keller finally tore his eyes away from the field and looked at the policeman. 'I want to see Harry Tewson,' he told him. 'He's one of the investigating officers.'

'Oh, yes. Mr Tewson. Er, I'm not sure that he can be disturbed just now, sir. Was it for an interview?' He raised his eyebrows at Keller.

'No, I'm a friend.'

The policeman looked relieved. 'Right then, I'll see what I can do.'

Keller watched him walk across the field. He stopped and turned when he was only forty yards away. 'Oh, what name shall I say?' he called back.

'Keller. David Keller.'

The policeman stood still for a few seconds, as though rooted to the spot. Keller could see the puzzled look on his face. He turned and resumed his journey across the field, his rubber boots squelching in the mud. When he reached a group of figures crouching by the broken and emptied shell of the aircraft, he bent down to speak to one of them. Five faces turned and looked back at Keller. One of the figures stood up and broke away from the group, plodding quickly towards him, giving a brief wave of his hand. The policeman followed five paces behind.

'Dave! What the hell are you doing here?'

Tewson was smiling, but it was a slightly nervous smile. His handshake was warm enough though.

'I want to talk to you, Harry,' Keller said.

'Of course, Dave. But you shouldn't be here, you know. I thought you were on leave?' He removed his glasses and began to polish them with a rumpled handkerchief, his eyes still peering intently into Keller's face.

Keller grinned wryly at him. 'I am – officially. Unofficially, I've been laid off.'

'What? Well, I'm sure it's not for long; you know how soon they like to get you lot back into the air after this sort of nasty experience.'

'They've already tried, Harry. It was no good.'

'Well they tried too bloody soon then.'

'No. It was me. I insisted.'

'But after what you've been through it's bound to take a bit of time before your nerves settle down.'

'It wasn't nerves, Harry. It was me – I just couldn't fly. I couldn't think straight.'

'It's the shock, Dave. It'll wear off.'

Keller shrugged. 'Can we talk?'

'Yes, of course. Look, I can get away in about ten minutes. I'll meet you in the High Street, in The George. It's about time for a spot of lunch anyway.' He clapped a hand on Keller's shoulder, then turned and walked back towards the wreckage, a worried expression on his face.

Keller returned to his car, locked it and began to walk back to the High Street.

The policeman watched him and scratched his cheek thoughtfully. Keller. Yes, David Keller. Thought I recognized him. He was the co-pilot of the plane – the Jumbo. This one.

And he was the only one who walked away from it. Without a scratch on him. The only survivor.

Keller ordered a beer and found himself a table in a quiet corner. The barman had barely given him a second glance, and for this he was grateful. The past four weeks had been a nightmare of questions, innuendoes, staring faces and abrupt silences. His colleagues and bosses at Consul, the airline company he flew for, had been mostly kind and considerate apart from the few who had viewed him with strange suspicion. And then, the newspapers had played up the story; the crash, dramatic and catastrophic though it had been, wasn't enough for them. That a man could walk from the terrible carnage, unscathed, even his uniform unmarked, was proclaimed a miracle. Intensive medical examination found no internal injuries; there were no burns; his nerves appeared to be stable. Physically, he seemed to be perfect except for one thing – amnesia. Indeed, he experienced total amnesia as far as the crash and the events leading up to it were concerned. It was the shock, of course, the doctors told him and, in time, when his mind had healed enough to remember – to allow him to remember – then it would all come back. But there was always the possibility his mind would never heal.

The 'miracle' story had persisted, though gradually he had become aware of a resentment against him, not just from the public, from some of his own colleagues. Not many, but enough to cause a feeling of guilt within himself. In the eyes of the public, he should never have lived; he was a pilot, he represented the airline – it was his duty to die with the passengers! Incredibly, he sensed the same feeling amongst some of his fellow pilots. He had no right to live when innocent men, women and children – three hundred and thirty-two of them – had died so tragically. As a member of the crew, as part of the airline, he was to blame. Until the cause of the crash could be discovered the pilot must take the blame. And he was co-pilot; he had to share the responsibility.

He had taken a test flight in a private aircraft less than two weeks after the accident, but it had been hopeless. He froze as soon as his hands touched the controls. His pilot, the veteran who had played such a large part in his training, had taken the aircraft up in the hope that, once in the air, Keller's natural instinct would take over. But it hadn't happened; his mind just would not concentrate, wouldn't apply itself. He just didn't know *how* to fly any more.

His company, very sensitive to public opinion and aware they had a pilot on their hands who, in their view, was liable to crack at any moment, decided to send him on 'leave' for a long period. Dismissal, apart from being unjust, would only stir up more public clamour, arouse more publicity, which could only damage their reputation as a national airline. His record was excellent and they took great pains to emphasize this in every public statement, but it was felt he deserved a long rest after such a shocking and traumatic experience.

His brooding was interrupted by Harry Tewson's smiling face appearing before him. 'What'll you have, Dave?'

'No, let me . . .'

Tewson stopped him with an upraised hand. 'I'll get some food, too,' he said, and disappeared through the crowd in the direction of the bar.

Food, mused Keller. I've hardly eaten since the accident; just enough to keep going. He doubted whether he'd ever have an appetite again. Tewson laid a mound of sandwiches down on the table, disappeared again, then returned with the drinks.

'It's good to see you again, Dave,' he said, as he settled into a chair. He, too, had been a pilot and gone through basic training at the same time as Keller, but suddenly, and inexplicably, his vision had begun to fail and resulted in his need to wear glasses full time. His experience and above-average technical knowledge had been too valuable to be wasted, so he had been drafted into the Board of Trade Accidents Investigation Branch (AIB), a body of pilots and engineers set up to probe all serious civil flying accidents in Britain, as well as overseas crashes involving British aircraft. He had soon proved his worth by uncanny insight into the causes of crashes; by making skilful guesses, then working backwards to prove them correct, a method not wholly approved of by his peers. So far, however, he had not often been wrong.

He took a huge bite from a sandwich, then a gulp of his light ale. 'How can I help you?' he asked, having swallowed both the food and the drink.

Keller smiled. No messing about with Harry. Straight to the point.

'I want to know what you've found out about the crash,' he said.

'Oh, come on, Dave. You know it's all got to be collated then submitted to the official inquiry. And you know everything comes under the Official Secrets Act until then.'

'I need to know, Harry.'

'Look,' Tewson began, not unkindly, 'it's nothing to do with you now, Dave ...'

'Nothing to do with me?' Keller's voice was calm, but he fixed Tewson with a stare that chilled the investigator. 'D'you know how I feel, Harry? I feel like a freak. An outcast. People resent the fact that I lived and all those others died. I feel like a captain who's deserted a sinking ship, left his passengers to drown. They're blaming me, Harry. The public, the airline, and . . .' He broke off and stared at his drink.

After a brief, stunned silence, Tewson spoke. 'What's the matter with you, Dave? Nobody's blaming you for this. Certainly not the airline. And the public will know the cause of the crash just as soon as we publish our findings – not that I think you're correct in your morbid assumption that they resent you being alive! As for anything . . .' he paused, 'or anyone else – well, you're just suffering from an overdose of misguided guilt and melancholia. Now, get a grip on yourself and drink your bloody beer!'

'Finished?' Keller asked mildly.

Tewson lowered the glass again just before it reached his lips. 'No, I'm not bloody finished. I've known you a long time, Dave. You were a good pilot and you will be again – just as soon as you forget about all this and start to think of the future.' His voice softened. 'I know you had your own personal loss in the crash, Dave, but she wouldn't have wanted you to go on like this.'

Keller looked at him in surprise. 'You knew about Cathy?'

'Yes, of course I knew. It was no big secret was it? It's not unusual for a pilot to have a stewardess as a girlfriend.'

'It was a bit more than that.'

'I don't doubt it, Dave. Look, mate, I don't mean to be rough on you, but the word is going around that you're finished, you'll never be a good flyer now, and the way I've heard you've been moping around, I'm not surprised. But I know you better. You've got a lot in you, Dave, more than most, and I think within a few weeks you'll be back to normal. Now, do you mind if I get on with my drink?'

Keller sipped at his own beer, feeling Tewson's eyes studying him from over the rim of his glass.

'I appreciate what you're trying to do, Harry, but it's not necessary. It's true I feel sad, but it's got nothing to do with nervous depression; it's more like a great weariness at the back of my mind. It might sound crazy to you, but I feel there's something I've got to do, something I've got to find out, and the answer lies here in Eton. I can't explain it and I can't resist it – not if I'm ever going to be all right again. There's something more that I can't put my finger on. Maybe it's a memory, I don't know. But sooner or later, it'll come through, and then perhaps I will be helping you. For the moment though, I'm asking you.'

Tewson sighed heavily and laid his glass back on the table. For a few moments he was deep in thought, his chin almost resting on his chest. Abruptly, he straightened, his decision made.

'Okay, Dave,' he said, 'this is strictly between you and me – off the record. If Slater ever found out I'd told you anything, he'd get rid of me like a shot. We don't get along at the best of times.'

Keller nodded. Slater was the investigator in charge of the air crash and responsible for the organization, conduct and control of the investigation. It was his job to establish the working groups covering the various phases of the inquiry. A dour, methodical man, Keller knew he had little time for Tewson's rash and cart-before-the-horse method of working.

'Right,' Tewson began, taking a huge swallow of beer as though to fortify himself. 'As you know, the first thing we look for in a disaster of this kind is the Flight Recorder. We found it all right, but the entire outer metal case showed signs of melting. The main damage was in the front, and the aluminium foil strip, on which all the information from the different flight instruments is recorded in code, was exposed.

'It was covered in soot, but not too badly damaged. We removed it from its outer covering and sent it off to the labs for decoding. Well, although the recording of your take-off was mostly destroyed, we can assume that you, as co-pilot, went through the normal check list with the flight engineer as soon as the Control Tower gave Captain Rogan permission to start engines at the apron.'

'I just don't remember, Harry,' Keller said worriedly.

'No, I know that. But as switching on the recorder was part of the check list, it's a fair assumption you went through the lot.'

Keller nodded. 'Go on.'

'The recorder keeps a note of five aircraft parameters: the positive or negative gravitational forces as read by one of the aircraft's gyroscopes; the magnetic heading from the compass; the indicated air speed; the altitude at which the aircraft is flying taken from the pressure altimeter dials; and the time in seconds, not related to the time of day on a clock. This was all graphed and then compared with a chart of another 747 that had taken off in similar conditions – time, weather, load, that sort of thing – a few days before. From that, we learnt everything had been normal except for one detail: the HDG – the magnetic heading – had begun to differ from the other 747's before it had even reached cruising speed. In other words, Captain Rogan had changed direction. Possibly he was turning back for Heathrow. There's no way of knowing because that's when the instruments began to malfunction.'

'But he must have called Control to let them know of his change of course,' Keller said, leaning forward across the table, his eyes fixed on Tewson's face.

'He tried to, but whatever happened, happened fast. He had no time to relay the message.'

Keller was silent for a moment, desperately trying to remember. But his mind was a blank. He sat back in his seat again.

Tewson continued: 'Our systems people had already begun an examination of the cockpit which had been nearly completely destroyed, but they were still able to establish the positions of quite a number of the aircraft's controls and switches and, although some of them were burnt completely away, they were still able to determine whether they were "on" or "off" according to the positions . . .'

'Were the bodies of the crew still in the cockpit?' Keller interrupted.

'Er, yes, they were. Impossible to identify absolutely, of course, but . . .'

'Then how did I get out? Why wasn't my body there? Why wasn't I killed?'

'It's obvious you must have left the cabin before the crash, Dave.'

'Why? Why should I leave the cabin so soon after take-off? I . . .'

A sudden flash. A memory almost breaking through. A picture. A frozen picture of the skipper's face, his mouth open, shouting something at him, alarm in his eyes. Fear.

And then it was gone. As his mind had rushed to meet it, the memory had evaded him, hiding itself away in some dark recess.

'What's up, Dave? You look ghastly – have you remembered something?' Tewson's voice broke through the emptiness that remained.

Keller ran a trembling hand across his eyes. 'No, it's okay.

For a moment, I thought I *was* going to remember. But it's gone. I can't . . .'

'It'll come, Dave,' said Tewson softly. 'Give it time. It'll come back.'

'Perhaps I don't want to remember, Harry. Perhaps it's better that I don't.'

Tewson shrugged. 'Maybe. D'you want me to go on?'

Keller nodded.

'It took five days to trace and note all the available cockpit instruments. Fortunately, many indication dials are designed to retain an imprint of what was being displayed at the time of impact and, once it had all been plotted, nothing was found to be in an incorrect position, nor was there any evidence of any major electrical fault that could have contributed to the cause of the accident.

'All the aircraft's maintenance records have been impounded and they're being sifted through at this moment. So far they've found nothing of any importance except for a strut bolt on the bogie trim cycling unit that was found to be missing on the last check, and that was immediately replaced, of course, before the Jumbo was released again for flight.

'The technical entries up to the day before the accident, and dating back to the previous year, reported no serious problems with the aircraft. The engines have been recovered and stripped and, as yet, nothing has been found that indicates any were malfunctioning prior to the crash. In fact, if my theory is correct, it was the engines that prevented the Jumbo from dropping like a stone.'

'Your theory?' asked Keller, well aware that Tewson's 'theories' often and uncannily proved to be correct.

'Well, I'll get to that in a moment. Nothing's been proved yet.' He took another long swallow from his glass, and pulled a face at the beer which had begun to lose its bite. 'It was a cold night, so the anti-ice system had been checked. Again no fault. The remains of the fuel systems are still being checked. So far: no fault.

'Now, the "human factor". You, as the only survivor, have been of no help at all.' It was typical of Tewson that there was no hint of apology in his bluntness; he was too absorbed in technicalities at the moment to concern himself with human sensitivity. 'Flight-training records of all the crew and their complete medical history have been inspected. You, yourself, were subjected to a complete medical examination immediately after the crash. This wasn't just to see if you'd sustained any internal injuries. Blood and urine tests were included in the examination. Just how much work the captain and yourself had been doing over the past few months was also ascertained, and whether you'd both had sufficient rest prior to the fight. The remains of your flight bags were retrieved from the cockpit and enough was left of them to establish that neither contained any drugs or medicines. No problem. All your proficiency tests – both your own and Captain Rogan's – had been excellent over the past year. Everything, so far, has checked. Except you couldn't have been in the place you were supposed to have been at the time of the crash.

'Right. Let me go on. Positions of the dead bodies, both inside and outside the aircraft, have been charted. We even found some poor souls at the bottom of the river that runs near the field. The interesting thing is that a large concentration of *overlapping* bodies was found inside the aircraft: burnt beyond recognition and, because of their mutilated condition, they had obviously been subjected to a tremendous blast of some kind.'

Keller shuddered and wondered at his companion's lack of feeling for the unfortunate victims but, by now, Tewson was too carried away by his own intense interest in the investigation to concern himself with the human element.

Tewson went on: 'Now, I've been involved on the Structures Group side. We've mapped out the whole area, using aerial photography and charts, and have exact positions of the wreckage site as well as the crash path. It shows which parts of the aircraft broke away first from the fuselage and the positions they were found in. This roughly determines the order in which the 747 broke up, and we can tell which area or areas played a part in the cause of the accident. The initial area of damage was somewhere towards the front of the aircraft.'

He was smiling now, and Keller had to avert his eyes; the urge to wipe the smile from the investigator's face was becoming too strong.

Oblivious, Tewson continued. 'I was examining the port wing when I discovered some barely visible scratches running down its full length. Under a microscope, I saw that in the grooves were bits of blue and yellow paint.' He sat back smugly.

'So?' said Keller.

'So what colour is your airline's logo?'

'Blue and yellow.'

'Right. And it's painted on the fuselage, beginning near the nose and ending quite near the wing-span. The paint is being chemically analysed right now, just to confirm, but I know I'm right.'

'But what does it mean?' asked Keller impatiently.

'It means, old chum, that the cabin wall had been blown out with terrific force. An explosion. And the kind, because of its strength, that could have only been caused by a bomb.'

He grinned perversely at Keller's pallid face.

2

The little black car bumped to a rough stop as close to the hedge as Ken Paynter could get it.

'It won't get stuck in the mud, will it?' the girl sitting beside him asked, nervously peering out of the side window into the dark night.

'No, it's all right,' Ken reassured her, jerking up the handbrake which he knew to be useless anyway. 'The path's wide and solid enough. We won't get stuck.'

He turned off his headlights and the sudden, complete darkness startled them both. They were silent for a few moments while their eyes became accustomed to the gloom. Ken was pleased with his little Mini, a second-hand car he'd had in his possession for just over three months now. In his job at the garage, you had to keep your eyes open for the bargains that now and then came along, and this little job came along just at the right time. He didn't earn much as an apprentice mechanic – not yet, anyway – but his governor had agreed to take a slice off his wages each week to pay the couple of hundred the car had cost. Yes, he was pleased with the car; it could take him down nice little dark lanes like this and if you didn't have your own place, a car and a dark lane was the next best thing.

What he wasn't too pleased with, though, was Audrey. She was becoming a pain in the arse. He had plenty of girlfriends who enjoyed his little detours off the beaten track but Audrey was always twittering on about romance, saving yourself for the right person, the seriousness and true meaning of making love – all that bollocks! Well, tonight was her last chance; if she didn't come across, she could just piss off. He had it too good to worry about a scrag-end like her. Good legs, though.

Audrey looked across at him and tried to discern his features in the darkness. She knew he loved her, she could tell. It was that chemical reaction all true lovers felt, the thumping of the heart, the spreading glow that ran through their bodies each time they met. True, he was a bit gruff at times, but that was just his way and it didn't mean anything. She'd kept him at bay for a long time now, and there were times she thought she'd lost him, but he'd come through the test! He really loved her, otherwise he'd never have stayed around. Now she was sure, perhaps it was time to give him some reward. Just a little. Enough to keep him interested. Enough to keep him attentive! She leant across to his seat and aimed a small kiss at his cheek. It missed because he was advancing towards her at the same time, one hand stretched forward so that it would rest casually on her thigh. He stopped to rub his damp eye.

'Sorry,' she said solemnly.

He muttered something inaudible and stretched forward again. This time their lips beamed in on one another's and they kissed, she rapturously, he using the contact as a show of strength.

After a few crushing seconds, she pulled away. 'You're hurting me, Ken,' she complained.

'Sorry, darlin',' he said, 'but you know how I feel about you.' Horny, he thought.

'Yes, I know, Ken. You really love me, don't you?'

That's right, he thought, kid yourself ''Course I do, babe,' he said. 'I think I always have, ever since I've known you.'

She sighed, and snuggled down to his shoulder. Give her a few minutes, he thought, don't overplay your hand.

'I'm cold, Ken,' she said. He pulled his left arm free and draped it over the back of her seat and around her shoulders.

'I'll warm you up in a minute,' he said, slyly tentative. He heard her giggle. Christ, it's getting hopeful!

He suddenly felt her stiffen. Oh, no, here we go! He began to relax his grip on her.

'Where are we, Ken?' she asked him, sitting up straight, and rubbing at the windscreen that was becoming misty.

'Eh?'

'Where are we?' she repeated.

'We're in my car.'

'No, I don't mean that. We're near South Field, aren't we?'

'Yeah, at the back of it. What about it?'

'Ooh, how could you bring us where that plane crashed?'

'Oh, Christ! That was weeks ago! Anyway, we're nowhere near where it came down.'

'All the same, it's a bit creepy. I think we ought to go. It's morbid.'

'Don't be daft, darlin'. I can't go drivin' about anyway; I 'aven't got much petrol in the car.' And I'm not tearing about the countryside looking for a quiet place just for a piece of *your* arse, he added to himself.

'Well, I'm cold. We're too near the river.'

'Well, I told you I could warm you up,' he said, pulling her towards him.

Her rigidity left her, and she pressed close to him. 'I do love you, Ken. It is different with us, isn't it?'

'Yes, Aud,' he assured her, and began to kiss the top of her head. She turned her face upwards towards his.

'You'd never leave me, would you, Ken?'

He could just see her wide searching eyes in the dark. 'Never,' he told her, and shifted his angle in his seat so he could reach her mouth more easily. He began to kiss her forehead, her nose, and then her lips. The passion had already risen in him, but now he could feel it come surging through her. Here came the test. His right hand, which was closed around her arm, began to move slowly and cautiously towards her breast. He'd reached this point so many times with her only to be thrust forcefully and tearfully away. But tonight, he felt it was different – she'd finally got wised up to the permissive society! His fingers were trembling excitedly as they found her breast, soft and pliant beneath the woolly jumper.

'Ooh, darling,' he heard her moan softly, and her fingers dug into his shoulder. 'Say you love me.'

'I love you.' It was easy to say.

'You won't leave me.'

'I won't leave you.' At the heat of the moment, he almost meant it.

'Yes, darling,' she murmured, as his hand began to pull at the bottom of her jumper. Just the word 'yes' sent his blood rushing frenziedly, and the contact of his cold fingers on the bare flesh of her stomach caused Audrey to squeeze her thighs together in exquisite excitement. His groping hand reached her bra and quickly passed over it to loosen the strap at her shoulder. It slid down her arm easily and his hand raced back to what was now his possession. He cupped her breast and enjoyed for a few moments the sensation of its fleshy softness and hard little centre, but his greedy mind was already racing ahead to other regions.

And it was at that moment that her body went rigid again.

'What was that?' he heard her gasp.

He froze, wondering whether to kill her or just dump her into the hedge and drive away. Instead he said woodenly, his hand still grasping its prize: 'What?'

'There's someone outside. I heard something,' she said in a hushed voice.

His hand reluctantly retreated and he turned away to look through the steamed-up windows.

'Well, they can't bloody see anything, can they, with the windows like this?'

'Listen, Ken, listen!' she pleaded.

He sat there, staring at the blank windscreen, and tried to listen, but the torment of his disappointed passion slowing down overruled his other senses.

'There's nothing there,' he said wearily, but at the same time trying to remember whether he'd locked the doors or not. He began to wipe the mist from the windscreen with his coatsleeve until he had cleared an area big enough to look through. He bent forward, his nose only inches away from the glass.

'No,' he said huffily. 'Can't see a bloody thing.'

'Let's go, Ken. It's so cold, can't you feel it?'

He could. It wasn't just the coldness of autumn. This was a chill that seemed to reach deep down inside him. And then he heard something.

It was like a whisper, similar to the stirring of the leafless branches in the hedge, but somehow he felt it couldn't be a natural sound. It had a human quality; and yet it didn't sound human. They heard it again, a low, breathless whisper.

Audrey clutched at his arm, her eyes not leaving the windscreen. 'Let's go, Ken. Let's go now!' Her voice was unsteady and her body shook slightly.

'It's probably someone messing about,' he told her unconvincingly, but he reached for the ignition anyway. His heart sank as he heard the engine rattle, then whine to a stop. He felt Audrey turn towards him in alarm, but he refrained from looking at her in case his eyes gave away his own trepidation. He turned the ignition again. This time, it seemed that the engine would catch, but once more it coughed, then faded into a pitiful whine. After the third attempt, he knew he would have to give the weary battery a brief rest before he tried again. They sat there in the still, black silence, straining their ears for the slightest sound, and inwardly praying it wouldn't come. But it did. A low, murmuring whisper. Close. Close, and it seemed to be from the girl's side.

Ken stared past her at the blank side window; the steam from their bodies had created a dark grey opaqueness. But he thought he saw a lighter shape just beyond the window, getting slowly bigger, like warm breath on glass, its edges undefined, an approaching oval of greyness. His mouth opened, but he couldn't speak. The top of his spine and shoulders became locked rigid. The hair on his scalp and down his back bristled. The shape stopped growing, and the boy knew it was just outside the window, inches away from Audrey's turned head. The girl suddenly realized he was staring past her left shoulder and her heart lurched at the expression of terror on his face.

Slowly, as though her head were moving mechanically, she moved her eyes away from his face and turned fearfully towards the side window. As a sheer reflex, she raised a hand and wiped it in one stroke across the glass to clear the steam. She screamed immediately, a cry that rose from her innermost being, a screech that filled the small car in the same way it filled the boy's head.

Two large, dark eyes were staring at her through the glass. So intense was their gaze that she could not wrench her own eyes from them; they seemed to bore through her, as though searching her mind, reaching for her soul. And in her horror she knew – her senses screamed it – the thing that was out there was not human, it wasn't a living thing. Even in her panic, she realized what it was. The large, staring eyes, the small, white face, the tiny smiling lips, the strange blemish on the cheek – it was the face of a doll! But the eyes were alive, burning into her. She heard the whisper again, now echoing through her mind, but she didn't understand the words, they had no meaning.

It was her scream that broke the paralysing spell Ken was under. In complete panic, he lunged for the ignition key and turned it, his foot hard down on the accelerator pedal. The car began to rock, gently at first, and then harder, more violently. His foot slipped from the pedal and the engine whined to a stop just as it was about to roar into life. He was tossed towards the middle as his side of the car was completely raised off the muddy path it stood on. Audrey felt herself slam against the window, and the terrible dark eyes were only separated from her own by the thickness of the glass. But in that moment she saw the misery, the utmost despair that shone from them. And she saw the malice.

She was thrown to the other side of the car as it rose up on her side, and this time she clung to Ken, crying hysterically. The rocking reached a new intensity and then the car began to vibrate, to shake and quiver with a rage of its own.

'What's happening, what's happening?' the girl screamed, but the boy would have had no answer even if the words had penetrated his terror-struck brain. Abruptly, the car fell to the ground with a crash that threatened to shake it apart, and then there was silence except for the sobbing moans of the distraught girl. Moving instinctively, Ken tore himself away from her and reached for the door handle. He pulled it and jerked the door open with his shoulder, then stumbled out into the cruel branches of the leafless hedge. The sharp wood tore into his flesh but he ignored the pain as he beat through the narrow path between vehicle and hedge. He felt the branches tugging at his clothing and, in his fright, imagined they were hands trying to hold him back. He cried out and his struggling became wilder, frantic, until he had scrambled free from the narrow space.

Without looking round – he didn't *want* to see anything – he ran down the dark lane, oblivious to anything but his own blind terror. Only in the deep recesses of his consciousness did the pitiful screams of the girl register, the screams that pleaded for him to come back for her, not to leave her there alone.

He ran on, stumbling and falling in the dark, away from the little car. Away from the malevolence he knew was back there.

3

Keller inhaled, drawing the smoke from the cigarette deep into his lungs, and then allowed it to escape again in a long, steady stream. He sat in the dark, his body slumped into his only armchair, his eyes gazing sightlessly at the ceiling.

He had returned to his London flat earlier that evening, his mind buzzing with the information Tewson had given him. He had thrown off his coat, loosened his tie, then poured himself a stiff Glenfiddich. He rarely drank heavily – flying and drinking were not a good blend – but over the past few weeks he had come to appreciate the nerve-dulling effects of alcohol. He had sunk into the armchair, placing the bottle on the armrest whilst he unbuttoned his shirtcuffs and rolled them up to his elbows, then lit a cigarette. And there he had remained for over two hours, lost in confused and uneasy thought.

A bomb! Could it be possible? The rules were so stringent nowadays; luggage and hand baggage were thoroughly screened, and each passenger was quickly but expertly searched before boarding the aircraft. And yet it still happened; bombs were *still* found on board, men *still* produced guns from somewhere once in flight. Security could never be a hundred per cent perfect.

But why should anyone wish to blow up this particular aeroplane anyway? The passenger list, as far as he remembered, had given no indication of any political personages being on board, British or foreign, nor had there been any religious groups. The list had comprised mainly British and American businessmen and tourists of various nationalities. Could it have just been the indiscriminate work of a madman? Even so, there was usually a reason, no matter how vague or self-inspired, for an outrage of this kind yet, as far as he knew, the police had uncovered no evidence pointing to this.

He had argued the point with Tewson who had argued back that with almost three hundred and fifty people on board there were bound to be a few with grievances held against them. But then how could the bomb have been smuggled on board? The 747 had been thoroughly searched beforehand, as were all aircraft prior to takeoff, and how *could* a passenger have slipped through the massive security screen imposed particularly on major flights such as this? Tewson was sticking his neck out by even suggesting a bomb and had sworn Keller to secrecy again before leaving him, already regretting his over-enthusiasm for his own cleverness. Even so, there was something more that diverted Keller's attention away from thoughts of explosives.

It was the sudden flashback in memory; the frozen picture which had abruptly focused in his mind. The skipper's face, his mouth open as though shouting something in alarm – or was it anger? The thought jolted him into an upright position. Perhaps it hadn't been fear he'd remembered on Captain Rogan's face; perhaps he'd been shouting in anger – *at him*! They'd argued – fragments were coming back to him now – they'd argued before the flight. Had it been that day, or had it been the night before? No, it had been the *day* before. The pieces were falling into place now; they began to form a picture. The argument had been violent, not physically, he was sure, but verbally. He could see the skipper's face before him now, white, tight-lipped with suppressed fury, his fists clenched, held stiff at his sides as though the effort to keep them from Keller's throat was overwhelming. And his own anger. He remembered he had not stood silent against the captain's tirade; he had struck back, again with words only, but they were just as damaging as physical blows. Maybe more so.

Could that have played any part in the destruction of the 747? Could the feud have carried on once inside the aircraft? Could it have caused an error in pilot judgement? No, he was sure they had both been too professional for that. And yet, the look on Captain Rogan's face just before they'd crashed . . . And now, another fragment had fallen into place.

The flashback was of a moment in time *just* before they'd gone into the dive. He remembered the atmosphere in the cockpit: the glowing instrument panels, the dark night outside and the tiny clusters of light that were towns far below, the skipper's white face, looking up at him, as though he, Keller, were rising from his seat. What were the words, the words coming from Rogan's lips, directed at him? Shouted words. Fear or anger. Which? He could see the picture now so clearly. If only the words would come through.

The picture began to fade, and he knew he had lost it. He felt the warm glow from his cigarette and stubbed it out before his fingers were burnt. He sipped at the Scotch and looked towards the sideboard where the picture of Cathy lay face down. He heaved himself from the armchair and walked over to it, pausing before he picked it up. The photograph had lain like that since the crash. It had been the first thing he'd done when they'd allowed him to return home; he'd gone straight to the picture and turned it flat against the sideboard, not wanting to look at her face. Now he picked it up and looked at the smiling image, feeling no tears, for his crying was done, leaving him with only empty sadness – a strange, calm sadness. He stood the picture up and thought of Cathy, the photograph only a superficial replica of someone who had once existed, giving only a hint of what lay beyond those smiling eyes.

She had moved in with him only three months before the fatal day, but their courtship had begun a year before, casual at first – casual on both sides – but gradually and unavoidably growing into something else; more binding and more enduring than either had thought possible. Their attachment had fanned when she, on her test flight as head flight attendant, had had to deal with a sudden cardiac arrest. He had gone back to help and, between them, they'd managed to keep the elderly passenger alive until they'd reached their destination. He'd met her a couple of times before that particular flight, and had certainly found her attractive, but because of other romantic commitments had not gone out of his way to form a better acquaintanceship. But the mutual involvement, created through the saving of a human life, cut through any other considerations.

They had soon developed an affectionate, undemanding relationship which slowly, as they became more aware of each other's sensitivities and individuality, grew into a deep and unquestioning love. They had kept their affair fairly well to themselves, knowing that their particular airline, although not actually frowning upon romances between members of air crews, did their best to keep such lovers on different flights; emotions of that sort had no place at 33,000 feet above sea level – too many things could go wrong that would need concentration and undivided attention. So they had kept it quiet, not wanting to miss the chance of visiting together so many exciting places on their stopovers. Of course, it was impossible to hide it from their closer working colleagues, especially for Keller, whose sudden lack of interest in other girls was noticeable in itself; but air crews are adept at keeping such matters within their own circles.

She had moved in with him at a point when it had become the only natural move to make, anything else seeming ridiculous and false. Marriage was obviously the next step, and both knew that this would come about naturally and without any urging from either side.

He walked to the window and looked down into the busy Cromwell Road. They had planned to buy a small house somewhere in the country, not too far from the airport. He smiled without humour; they had even considered the area around Eton or Windsor. And that was where their dreams had been shattered; in a quiet field at Eton!

He walked away from the window and lit another cigarette, his mind again in a turmoil of thoughts. Eton! Was that why he felt this compulsion to return there, because they had planned to live nearby? Was he trying to recapture something of the past, their visits to the small town? Or was it because he felt an answer was waiting for him there?

The desire to return to the scene of the crash had been almost overwhelming. He'd fought hard to resist, wanting no physical reminder of the dreadful event that had taken place there, but he'd been drawn to the place, against his will, against his comprehension. He wanted to stay away, but some instinct, some taunting voice somewhere in his mind told him he would not find peace until he returned. It was both inexplicable and irresistible.

Perhaps, by going back, a small nerve in his memory cells would be jogged; perhaps he would remember the crash, and the events leading up to it. And remember, too, how he had escaped without a scratch when everybody else on board had either been burnt to death or their bodies mangled into oblivion. Witnesses thought he had emerged from the broken belly of the aircraft, but their statements had been confused, almost hysterical because of the immensity of the disaster. It was more likely that he'd been thrown clear on to the soft earth and lain unconscious for a few minutes before rising and walking away from the burning wreckage. He knew he had felt no emotion then, that he had accepted the fact that everybody back there was dead, even Cathy, and there was no point in going back into the flames. No, the tears and reprisals had come later, when the shock had worn off.

He remembered clearly the old man he'd found lying in the mud; perhaps he would be able to tell him more. He had been quivering with fear, sprawled flat on the churned-up earth, looking up at him with terror-filled eyes. If he could find him, he might be able to tell him what he'd seen. God knows if it would be of any use, but there wasn't much else he could do.

At that moment, he heard a soft tapping at the door. He wasn't sure at first, his mind had been too absorbed in its own thoughts, but the sound came again. A light tapping, which sounded as though only fingernails were being used. He glanced down at his watch; just after ten. Who the hell could be calling at this time of night? He crossed the room, suddenly aware that all the lights inside the flat were off. He paused before he turned the catch, not knowing why, but feeling sudden apprehension. The tapping came again and startled him into action. He swung the door open. In the dimly lit hallway stood the figure of a man, his features barely discernible because of the poor light. He was silent, but Keller could feel the man's eyes boring into him. He quickly flicked on his own light switch so that light flooded into the hallway from behind.

The man was small and slightly plump. His face was round and he was balding. His hands were thrust deep into a shabby fawn raincoat and his shirt collar was slightly crumpled. In a crowd he would have gone unnoticed, except for one disturbing feature – his eyes. They were strong, penetrating, somehow betrayed by the small body they were housed in. They were of the palest grey, icy in their intensity, and yet, compassionate. Keller absorbed all this in those first few moments of silence and then he saw that puzzlement had crept into the strange and disquieting gaze. The man's face expressed the barest frown, only the eyes showed his puzzlement – and curiosity.

Keller was forced to speak first. 'Yes?' was all he could say, his mouth suddenly dry, his hand clenched tightly on to the side of the door.

The man was silent for a few moments, his eyes never leaving Keller's. Then he blinked and that small action appeared to bring the rest of his body alive. He stepped perhaps an inch closer and said: 'It's Keller, isn't it? David Keller?'

The co-pilot nodded.

'Yes, I recognize you from the photographs in the papers,' the man said, as though Keller's confirmation hadn't really counted. He was silent again while he now appraised the co-pilot from head to foot, but just as Keller felt impatience rising in him like a bubble searching for the surface, the man seemed to snap himself together.

'I'm sorry,' he said. 'My name is Hobbs. I'm a spiritualist.'

4

Ah, the best time of the day, this, thought George Bundsen, a smile of contentment spreading across his face. The water lapped around his small rowing boat, rocking it gently and relaxingly. He lit his pipe and peered into the damp early morning mists of the Thames. Bloody cold, but it was worth it to be alone for a change. He could hear Hilary's shrill voice in his ear even now: 'You make sure you're back in time to open the shop up! I'm not doing it on my own again! You've got too much of it, always down by that stinking river! You'll fall in one day, and with your weight, you'll never get out again!' The urge to throw the cup of milky tea all over her had been almost irresistible, but all he had said, as he held the rattling cup and saucer out towards her, was: 'I won't be long, dear. It's just my little bit of pleasure.'

'What about my bit of pleasure?' she had retorted, sitting up and taking the pillow from his side of the bed and stuffing it behind her back, on top of her own. 'When's the last time you took me anywhere?' She snatched the cup and saucer from him, the tea spilling over and a few heavy drops falling on to the white bedspread. 'Now look what you've done!' she screamed at him.

He scurried off into the bathroom and came hurrying back with a face flannel, and began to scrub vigorously at the light brown stains.

'It's all right, dear, it's coming out,' he assured her.

Hilary raised her eyes heavenwards. What would she do with this great hulk who called himself a man? He was so genial, so *helpful*, to all the customers of their little tobacconist's-cum-confectionery cum-newsagent's shop they'd owned for the past fifteen years in Windsor. It didn't seem to worry him that the days of the small shopkeeper were numbered, that the big combines were taking over. Their sort of shop, the ones that diversified, were the last of the remaining few. The butchers, the bakers, the greengrocers – all were facing stiff competition from the big chain stores. And that great tub of lard – all he could think of was going fishing! Yes, he appeared helpful in the shop as far as the customers were concerned, but who would have to sort the newspaper deliveries out, give the boys their quota and send them packing; who would have to open up the shop, take note of stock, serve the early morning rush, the commuters on their way to the station? Muggins, that's who.

'Go on, get off with you!' she told him frostily. 'But be back sharp at seven!'

'Yes, dear,' he mumbled gratefully, as he struggled into a huge woollen jumper that managed loyally to cover his vast stomach and several chins. He pulled on his wellingtons, kicking the dry mud that flaked off them under the bed out of sight, and tucked in his trousers. He shrugged himself into a heavy fur-lined coat and stood at the foot of the bed as though waiting to be dismissed.

'Well, what are you waiting for? Get off – and try and catch something today!' She pulled a face at the lukewarm tea. Without a word, he made for the door. He turned and puckered his lips, then blew the kiss towards her. She scoffed at his idiocy.

He brought his fishing tackle from the hut at the bottom

of the garden, then made his way down the long, curved hill towards the river. He crossed the small bridge and made towards the partially burnt-out boathouses. His rowing boat, the one Arnold rented cheaply to him for most mornings of the week, was moored by the jetty. Lucky old Arnold, he thought to himself. The old boathouses needed doing up and now he's got that airline company paying for it as compensation for the damage the Jumbo had done. Terrible business, but there you are – out of the worst sort of disaster, there's always someone who comes out lucky, and old Arnold's done just that. Not to mention that co-pilot, of course. How lucky can you get?

He slowly and lazily rowed the boat upstream, round the bend, under the railway bridge and into the reeds of a small island. It was fairly quiet here, apart from the trains that occasionally passed over the bridge nearby, and they never seemed to really bother the fish. They drifted in with the current caused by the bend opposite and his bait acted like a magnet. Hilary hadn't been quite fair when she'd derided him for not catching any. The fact was he often met friends on the way back as they opened their shops, and by the time they'd chatted and exchanged the usual jokes about the one that got away, he'd find himself several fish lighter through his own generosity. And he *always* stopped by the florist's and gave Miss Parsons a couple. Nice, quiet woman, that. Couldn't understand why she'd never married. Mind you, can't understand why *I* did.

He puffed at his pipe and brooded on his favourite subject, his eyes on the small white float that bobbed up and down at the end of his line. They'd been all right for the first eight years – things couldn't have been better – but after that one little indiscretion on his part, everything had changed. It was such a tiny indiscretion, too. Why, he hadn't even bedded the woman – just a quick one, at the back of the shop while Hilary was supposed to be visiting her sister. God, the fright he'd had when he'd heard the key in the latch and then the shop bell ring as the door opened. It was early afternoon closing, and the woman had been his last customer, purposely hanging around till closing time. He'd chatted to her a few times when Hilary had been out, and it had soon become apparent what she was after. Of course, he was a lot slimmer in those days. And he'd always tried to be helpful to customers, especially good ones.

He could still remember his heart freezing with horror as he'd peeped over the counter and seen Hilary striding grim-faced towards him. She'd just had a row with her sister, and had become even more grim-faced when she'd seen who was laying on the floor behind the counter, trying to hoist up frilly knickers over bulging thighs. If only they'd gone upstairs, he might have had a chance to hide her and sneak her out later, but he hadn't wanted to make a big thing of it; just a quickie, in and out in five minutes. But there was no hiding this: he on his knees, trying to pull up trousers which were pinned down under his knees by the weight of his body, and she scrambling around on the floor in a great fluster, naturally unwilling to show herself above the counter top. Both their struggles had ceased as Hilary peered over the counter, her face set in straight lines, which slowly began to waver and break as the rage built up inside her.

The next five minutes had been ingrained on his memory as though the event had occurred only yesterday: the screams, the wild fingers clutching at his hair, the sobs of the poor woman lying on the floor desperately trying to cover her nakedness. He'd bolted for the door at the back of the shop, his trousers at his knees, restricting his movements, then hobbled up the stairs and hid in their bedroom, locking the door from the inside. There had been more screams from downstairs and the occasional loud sob. He had heard the doorbell jingling, then a slam as it was closed hurriedly, the clatter of high heels down the street. He heard movements from downstairs, clomping across their parlour, the sound of the kettle being filled in the kitchen. He assumed it had been the other woman he'd heard scuttering off down the road.

He'd stayed in the room, shaking, crouched by the side of the bed, until it grew dark, then he'd crept over to the door and unlocked it. He'd listened for a while, then undressed and got into bed. There he had lain in trembling fear, the bedclothes up to his chin, until ten o'clock, when he'd heard her heavy steps clomping up the stairs. She'd marched straight in without turning on the light, undressed in the dark, climbed into the bed and lain rigidly beside him. It was three weeks before she spoke to him, and at least two before she even looked at him. The subject of his unfaithfulness had never been raised since that day, but things had changed all right. God, how they'd changed!

He sighed and shifted his massive bulk in the boat, causing it to rock unsteadily. From that day, he had grown fatter and she had grown more shrill. Oh yes – and her body had become sacred. Maybe once or twice a year – around Christmas or Easter, when she'd had a few sherries – but certainly no more. It was fortunate there were quite a number of widowed women living in Windsor who needed the occasional comforting. And that Miss Parsons was an extremely nice person, quite attractive really. Yes, things were developing nicely there. Slow, but at forty-five he had learnt to take things slowly.

He was startled from his thoughts as his float was suddenly jerked under water. Aha, got one! He grinned and clutched the pipe more firmly between his teeth. He began to play the line, but strangely it wasn't jerking in the usual way. Instead, the line was being drawn steadily down, as though the fish was taking the bait to the river-bed. He began to resist the pull and reel the line in. The rod bent and the line stood taut and stiff out of the water. Good Lord, he thought, this is a big 'un! Suddenly, the line snapped, throwing him back heavily into the boat. He sprawled there with his knees over the seat, his elbows on either side of the small boat allowing him to raise his head and peer into the misty waters. Just as he began to help himself into a sitting position again, the float bobbed to the surface.

'That's bloody funny,' he said, taking his pipe from his mouth and staring blankly at the bouncing float. 'It *must've* been a big 'un!'

Cursing his luck, he began to reel the broken line all the way in, deciding he'd had enough for the day. It was at that moment he heard the whisper, drifting over the water towards him. Was it just one whisper, or had he heard several hushed voices speaking together? Or was it just the rustling of the reeds at the water's edge?

He heard it again. A man's voice? Or was it a woman's? It was too low to tell. His spine shivered at the next sound he heard, for it sounded like a chuckle – a quiet, dry chuckle, which now seemed very near, almost at the end of the boat.

'W-who's there?' His voice was unsteady. 'Come on, stop playing games. I know there's someone there.' He glanced around nervously, but all he could hear now was his own sharp breathing. He decided he'd had enough, and just as he was reaching for an oar he heard another noise. It sounded as though something were being dragged through the water; not swimming, for it was a wet, slithering noise, stopping for a few seconds, then starting again, the water gurgling, but no air bubbles reaching the surface.

Frightened, he reached for the oar again and quickly placed it in the rowlock, feeling towards the bottom of the boat for its mate. Abruptly, the oar slid from his grasp as if pulled by some invisible force, and he jumped back in alarm as the oar disappeared straight down into the muddy waters. He expected to see it bob to the surface again but it didn't. It was nowhere to be seen.

Someone having a lark, he told himself unconvincingly. Someone in one of them underwater outfits. But then, where were the air bubbles?

He stared down at his feet as he felt a bump underneath the boat, his heart pumping madly, his hands clenched tightly on to the plank seat, the knuckles white from his grip. The bump came again and he spread his feet towards the curved sides, frightened to touch the wooden planking below. Then the boat began to rock, gently at first, building up to a more violent motion. He cried out: 'Stop it. Stop it!' The pipe fell from his mouth, as the rocking continued, the side edges of the boat almost touching the water, threatening to topple him into the murky depths. Just as he thought the boat was bound to capsize, the tossing stopped and it settled back into the water. He began to moan with relief and tears of fright blurred his vision. He felt an icy chill around him, though, a coldness which seemed to sting his flesh.

Suddenly, the boat began to shudder. A fresh cry broke from his lips as this, too, became more violent, and his hands tightened on the seat again. The shaking appeared to be reaching a crescendo, and his vision was even more blurred through his tears and the vibration. Then he thought he heard more chuckling, low, animal-like chuckling with a malicious undertone. But the trembling was running right through him, through his whole gross body, through his brain, until he wanted to scream, to cry out in order to release the terror swelling up inside him. And then, he saw the dreadful thing that nearly stopped his heart, that almost made it burst with the blood rushing through it.

Long, pointed fingers were wrapping themselves over the edge of the boat, near the stern. Through his blurred sight, they looked like long, white worms, crawling over the sides, moving independently, each with a life of its own. The boat tilted and he saw the rest of the hand appear, slithering down towards the bottom of the rowing-boat, followed by its arm, followed by – nothing. There was nothing beyond the elbow, and yet it came forward, slowly reaching towards him. Then he heard the whispering again, but this time, it was right next to him, by his left shoulder, and he felt a cold – so cold – breath on his cheek, a breath that might have been released from a frozen body. He tried to jerk his head around, afraid yet wanting to see what was there, but his neck wouldn't turn, his head wouldn't move.

Finally, the scream came, bursting up from his lungs, screeching into the frozen air, and the sound helped him to move, to stumble away from that approaching monstrosity, back over the seat, scraping his shins but not caring, moving with all the speed only abject fear could muster. He scrambled over the end of the boat into the reeds, the brownish water reaching high above his waist. He thrashed through the reeds and made his way towards the river-bank, the mud at the bottom of the river sucking at his feet, trying to hold him back, to drag him down. It was like a nightmare in which his legs had turned to lead and he couldn't escape, he couldn't run away.

He splashed forward, pulling at the reeds, pulling at any-thing that would draw him forward. But he could still hear the whispering, and it sounded more frenzied and sinister. By now his lungs were gasping for air, small squealing noises came from his mouth, and tears now of self-pity rolled down his fat cheeks. He clutched wildly at an overhanging branch and, for one frightful second, it bent under his weight, his whole body going beneath the water. But it sprang up again, bringing him with it, and he used two hands to pull himself along its length, his palms bleeding with the effort.

At last he felt the river-bed rise sharply and he knew he had reached the bank. Sobbing thankfully, he let go of the branch and began to drag himself up the steep incline, grasping at roots, tufts of grass, anything he could find that would give him support. But the bank was slippery with mud, and the slime beneath his feet gave him no support for a thrust upwards. He lay full stretched against the bank, soaking wet, his whole body heaving for breath.

Suddenly, he felt cold fingers wrap themselves around his ankle below the water, and begin to tug at his body, trying to draw it back into those chilly and murky depths. He tried to resist by digging his fingers deeply into the soft earth, but they raked out deep grooves as he was slowly and surely dragged back. He screamed and kicked out with his other foot, but the grip only grew more firm, drawing him smoothly down, like an animal drawing its victim into its lair.

And then, his heart *did* burst. The pressure had been too great. The heart that had worked hard for so many years under the gross weight of the man finally gave up. He was already dead as the muddy water ran into his open mouth and through the channels of his nose, quickly obscuring the wide, sightless eyes as he sank lower ... and lower ... into the cold, welcoming river.

5

Keller woke with a start. One moment he was asleep, the next wide awake, with no intermediary stages of regaining consciousness. For an instant, his eyes stared up at the ceiling then moved swiftly towards his watch lying on the bedside cabinet. Seven o'clock exactly. What had wakened him so sharply? Had he dreamed? He'd been a heavy dreamer up until the crash, the dreams always vivid, memorable – almost tiring. But since, there had been nothing, although he knew this was impossible; everybody dreamed to some extent, whether they realized or not. For the past few weeks, though, he had just seemed to fall asleep instantly, then to wake just as quickly, with only emptiness in between, as though he had merely blinked his eyes for a half-second. Perhaps it was his mind's way of protecting him, keeping the nightmare deep within the folds of his subconscious, erasing any trace before he woke.

But last night had been different. He tried to focus his mind, but the wispy visions evaded him, mocked him. He could only remember voices. Whispers. Had Hobbs been the reason for the dreams? The strange little man had certainly disturbed him. Keller sat up in bed and reached for his cigarettes. He lit one and drew in a deep breath, then leant back against the wall that served as a headboard for his bed. He thought back to the previous night and the arrival of the spiritualist; the unease he had felt at the mere sight of him. And yet – somehow he had been expecting him, or rather he had been expecting something to happen.

'May I come in?' the spiritualist had asked, and without speaking, Keller had stepped aside to allow him.

He had closed the door and turned to face the innocuous little man who had walked to the centre of the room and now stood looking around him, not from curiosity, but with genuine interest. His eyes fell on the picture of Cathy and he studied it for a few seconds before turning towards Keller.

'I'm sorry to disturb you at this late hour, Mr Keller.' His voice was soft, but steady, as steady as his gaze. 'I tried to call you but I understand you've had your telephone disconnected. I had to speak to you so I got your address from the directory.'

The co-pilot was silent for a few moments more, not quite understanding his own sense of dread. He forced himself to speak. 'What do you want?'

'It – it's rather difficult for me to explain, Mr Keller.' For the first time, the man lowered his gaze. 'May I sit down?'

Keller nodded towards the armchair. He, himself, remained standing. Hobbs settled into the armchair and looked up at him.

'First of all, Mr Keller, I am not a crank,' he began, 'but you have to take my word for that. I was a practising medium up until a few years ago and, if I may say so, a very successful one. Too successful in fact; I was becoming too involved with the emotions of my sitters . . . and my spirits. It was draining me, you see, taking my strength. I was no longer acting as a true medium – a go-between. I sensed a danger of losing myself in the spirit world, of not being used just as an instrument of communication, but as an instrument for physical contact.' He smiled apologetically at Keller, seeing the frown of disbelief on the co-pilot's face. 'I'm sorry. I'm trying to convince you I'm not a crank, and there I go rambling on about something I'm sure you have never been familiar with. Suffice to say that, for the past few years, I have consciously tried to avoid dealings with the other world; but, to a true sensitive, it's almost impossible to close oneself off entirely, no matter how strong one's reasons are for doing so. And I had a very strong reason for giving up my connections with the other world. Nevertheless, mediums are like radio receivers that cannot be switched off; spirits still approach me and speak through me, but I allow only friendly spirits to do so. The others . . . I try to close my mind to or, at least, try to contain within myself. It isn't always easy.'

Despite his unease, Keller's incredulity was now reaching its peak. 'Look, Mr Hobbs, I don't really know what the hell you're talking about.' He didn't speak harshly, but his tone of voice implied that he believed Hobbs to be a crank. 'I don't know anything about spiritualism and, quite frankly, I don't think I even believe in it. Now, over the past few weeks, I've been bothered by the press, the authorities, relatives of the crash victims, people howling for *my* blood, well-meaning but tiresome friends, clergy who want to turn me into a walking miracle, men and women with sick minds who want to know all the grisly details, and – ' he paused, deliberately, 'idiots with messages from the grave!'

The little man started visibly. 'Someone else has tried to contact you with a message?'

'Five, so far,' said Keller, tiredly. 'I suppose you're going to be number six.'

Hobbs moved forward to the edge of his seat, excitement in his eyes. 'What messages? What did they tell you? Who were these people?'

'Two said they were Satanists, two said they were

messengers of God – and the fifth claimed to be God Himself. Which one are you? Don't tell me you're the Devil?'

Hobbs sat back in the armchair, a look of disappointment on his face, yet heedless of Keller's scathing words. He looked reflective for a few moments, then said quietly, 'No, Mr Keller. I'm none of those things. I told you – I'm a spiritualist. Please be patient for five minutes, then if you still want me to, I'll leave.'

Keller wearily slumped on to the sofa, first retrieving his bottle of whisky and a glass. Without offering anything to Hobbs, he poured himself a stiff measure. 'Go on,' he said. 'Five minutes.'

'Do you know what spiritualism is?' Hobbs asked him.

'It's talking to ghosts, isn't it?'

'Bluntly put, and not quite accurate. It's a sensitiveness, being able to register vibrations, radiations, or frequencies that our normal senses cannot capture. A medium is an intermediary – as I said before, a sort of human radio or television set, able to tune in to another world that is invisible and inaudible to the rest of mankind; but, like the radio or television set, every medium is limited in their range of reception. However, by development of their powers, they can increase their capacity for reception, whereas machines cannot. I found that my own development was becoming too ...' he looked away from Keller, '... well, let's just say, overdeveloped. Dangerously so.' He ran a hand down his cheek, towards his chin. 'Do you think I might have a drink?'

Keller almost grinned. A spiritualist with a drink problem? The thought made him feel strangely more tolerant towards the little man, so he said: 'What would you like?'

'Same as you, please.'

Keller noticed Hobbs's eyes on the Scotch as he poured. My God, he thought, he really does have a drink problem.

He handed him the glass and was only mildly surprised when half of it immediately disappeared down the little man's throat.

'Anything with it?' he asked mildly.

Hobbs smiled apologetically at him again. 'Sorry. No, it's fine.'

Well, at least it makes him more human, the co-pilot thought as he returned to the sofa. 'Can we get to the point now?'

'Of course.' Hobbs took a more moderate sip at his drink, then leant forward in his seat again. 'As I mentioned, over the past few years I've consciously tried to halt any progress in my own development of these special powers, but I cannot prevent the spirits from contacting me if their will is strong enough. I have refused to be the bearer of messages, though, and I believed they had begun to accept this.'

Keller caught himself mentally. Hell, I'm beginning to believe this. He realized it was because the little man spoke so matter-of-factly, without any hint of apology or embarrassment.

'However, two weeks ago, a new voice – or I should say, voices – began to communicate with me. They were confused, angry, and I think in great torment. There were whispers, frightened whispers, hushed voices which sounded as though, they were in a vast, dark hall, wanting to know where they were, what had happened to them. Oh, they sounded so lonely, so afraid.'

Keller felt the tension building inside him again. The atmosphere between the two men had become electric. Hobbs took another, this time longer, sip from his glass, and Keller noticed his hand was trembling sightly.

'Gradually,' he continued, 'stronger voices began to assert themselves. Their world, you see, Mr Keller, is not so different from ours; in any element, the stronger personalities will always take command. But these voices were not good; they sounded – vindictive. It was the feeling I got from them: hate and deep shock.'

Keller deliberately tried to break the atmosphere, the mesmerizing link, which the medium had created between them. He stood up and walked over to the window, taking his drink with him.

'Look, er, Mr Hobbs . . .' he began, but the medium cut him short.

'Listen, please. I know what you're going to say: you don't believe in life after death, or even if you do, you find this too far-fetched. I accept that, and when I've finished, I promise I'll leave and not bother you again if that's your wish. But I must tell you this, for my own peace of mind, because they won't leave me alone until I do. You see, after an accident of this nature, the spirits sometimes do not realize what has happened to them; they are in a state of emotional shock. They do not know they are dead! They become what *you* might call ghosts, and continue to haunt this life, trying to make contact with someone on this earth to let them know they are still alive. Or they may be tied by situations or emotions; they may feel they have to achieve something here, something they've neglected in their lives. Or they may feel they have a reason for revenge.'

Keller swung round sharply. Those last words had hit a nerve, touched something deep inside him; they had made him afraid.

'Sometimes, true sensitives can help them, can pacify these tortured souls, help them to pass on peacefully into the next world. We can do this by promising to clear up whatever is troubling them in this world, whatever is keeping them earthbound. Unfortunately, on this occasion, they're still too confused for me to communicate properly.'

'You obviously imagine they're the souls of the dead passengers from the air crash,' Keller said, his voice hard and unbelieving.

'I know they are! So many terrified souls at the same time, gathered in the same place. And there's something else, Mr Keller.'

The co-pilot felt himself stiffen. He almost knew what was coming.

'The voices – the whispers. They're calling for you.'

There was another long silence between the two men. Keller wanted to scoff at the medium's words, to shrug him off as just another crank, but for some reason he couldn't. It wasn't only the man's obvious sincerity; it had something to do with his own close brush with death. The experience had somehow left him more receptive. Nevertheless, the more down-to-earth side of his nature fought against it.

'That's ridiculous,' he said.

'I assure you it's not,' Hobbs replied. 'The voices were totally confused at first, crying out for help, calling for loved ones. I saw faces – so many wretched faces – their images kept fading then coming through again, pleading, piteous. Then, over the days, they became more concerted, more controlled. They were still in a state of panic, but it seemed as if they were being guided. That was when they began calling out your name, over and over again.'

'Why? Why should they do that?'

'I – I don't know, Mr Keller. As I said, they're confused. Their message isn't clear yet. But . . .' he lowered his gaze again, '. . . many of the voices are angry.' His eyes pierced Keller's again. 'Do you know someone called Rogan?'

The co-pilot froze for a second, then realized that Hobbs had probably remembered the name from the media. 'He was the captain of the 747, as I'm sure you read in the newspapers.'

'Ah, yes, I believe I did. I'd forgotten, although I don't expect you to believe that.'

'You're right, I don't. And now your five minutes are up. I want you to leave.' Keller walked towards the medium, who sprung to his feet.

'You had a fight with Captain Rogan, didn't you?'

Keller stopped in his tracks. 'How did you know . . .?'

'It was something to do with his wife.' Hobbs's words were a statement, not a question.

And Keller had another vivid flash of memory. Rogan was shouting at him, his face close, only inches away from his own. He couldn't hear the words, but he saw the anger there, the violence in those eyes. Where were they? It wasn't in the aircraft. No, it was in one of the hangars, there was nobody else around. It was night-time, he was sure of that. Had it been *that* night, the night of the crash? He couldn't be sure. There had been a brief struggle and he had pushed Rogan away from him. He could see the captain clearly, looking vehemently up at him from the floor. He had turned and walked away from the older pilot, leaving him lying there hurling abuse after him. And suddenly he knew what the fight had been over. Yes, it had had something to do with Beth Rogan, the skipper's wife.

'It's true, isn't it?' Hobbs's words broke through the vision.

'How did you know?'

'Captain Rogan can't forget it.'

'It's impossible.'

'Yes, Mr Keller.'

The co-pilot sat wearily on the edge of the sofa. 'How the hell could you know about that?'

'Everything I've told you is true. I don't expect you to

believe it, but at least think it over. You are the key, Mr Keller. I don't know how, and I don't know why, but you hold the answer for those poor wretches and you must help them.'

Keller raised his head from his hands. 'They want my life, don't they?' he asked, not looking at the medium.

'I – I don't know. I can't be sure,' Hobbs said.

'I can feel it. They're incomplete. I got off scot-free, and now they want to claim me. I should have died.'

'I don't think that's the answer, Mr Keller,' Hobbs said, but the uncertainty in his voice betrayed him.

Keller got to his feet and walked quickly to the sideboard. He picked up the picture of Cathy and asked, 'Did you see her face among those others?'

Hobbs stared at it, his eyes narrowed in concentration. Finally, he said, 'No, I don't think so. I saw the picture when I came in, but it struck no chord with me. I don't think she was among them.'

'Well if what you say is true, she ought to have been. She was killed in that crash!' Keller was angry now, disbelieving once again.

Hobbs held up a hand as if to calm him. 'The images, Mr Keller – sometimes they're weak, occasionally they're strong. And there are so many of them. I just can't tell at this stage whether she is with them or not, and it may be that she – as well as others – has passed over peacefully into the next world, leaving these unfortunates behind.'

Keller looked at Cathy's face longingly, then replaced it on the sideboard. His mood changed and he turned disgustedly towards the medium. 'This has gone far enough. I think you'd better go now.'

'What are you afraid of?' The question was blunt and uncompromising.

'What do you mean?'

'Are you afraid that in some way you were responsible for the crash? Perhaps because of your conflict with Captain Rogan, you made some error of judgement that led to the disaster. Are you afraid to find out?'

'Get out.' Keller's voice was low and angry.

'Yes, I will. But please think about it. Neither you nor they will find any peace until the answer is found. And I'm worried, Mr Keller, very worried. You see, there is something else involved with these spirits, something very strange. Something very evil. I'm afraid of what might happen unless they're released from their torment.'

And then, after scribbling his address on to a crumpled piece of paper, he left. Keller had suddenly felt drained of energy, and had undressed and crawled wearily into bed, falling asleep instantly, sinking into a dark world of whispers. Now he tried to remember the dream, the first he'd had for many weeks, but it was no use; his mind refused him.

He stubbed out the cigarette, then pulled back the bed covers. Walking through into the bathroom he doused his face with cold water. Still naked, unaware of the cold, he went into the kitchen and made himself some strong, black coffee. He took it into the lounge and his eyes involuntarily went to the picture of Cathy. It was this that reminded him of his nakedness. They had often gone about the flat without clothes during the summer months, both enjoying the sight of each other's body in natural, relaxed positions; his hard and firm, hers soft, slim, her legs long and tapered, her breasts small and childlike. It was the sense of freedom they had enjoyed; freedom with each other, their nakedness expressing their intimacy. He went into the bedroom and put on his robe.

As he drunk his coffee, the crumpled piece of paper containing Hobbs's address caught his eye. It was lying on the floor where it had blown from the edge of the table when the door had closed behind the medium the night before. Keller hadn't bothered to pick it up because he'd had no intention of contacting the man again. But now he did, and he straightened it out flat on the table before him. It was a Wimbledon address and Keller smiled at the idea of a little man from suburbia being in touch with spirits from the other world. And yet, it was the very ordinary appearance of the man that made his story more plausible. If he had worn a black cloak and spoken in an excited, fanatical way, the whole affair would have appeared absurd, but Hobbs's quiet and slightly humble manner had an air of authority about it. Whether he was believed or not didn't seem to matter; he was merely stating a fact. His eyes had been the only strange thing about him; they had looked beyond Keller's and deep into his inner being. Why had Hobbs appeared so puzzled when he had opened the door?

And how had he known about his fight with Rogan?

The co-pilot still couldn't remember when the argument had taken place and, because he felt it was important, he racked his brain trying to. But, as with many of his thoughts relating to the crash nowadays, the more he concentrated, the more the answers eluded him. There was, of course, one person who would probably be able to tell him: Beth Rogan. He was reluctant to see her after what had happened between them, but he felt he had no choice. He *had* to know.

He sipped at the black coffee, the image of Beth clear in his mind's eye. At thirty-six, she was still a beautiful woman, her maturity somehow making her beauty more clearly defined. How would she react on seeing him again so soon after the death of her husband? Would she, too, hold him to blame as others had done? Or was she glad he had lived? It had been quite a while since he'd seen her last so there was no way of telling what her reaction would be.

There was something else he had to do as well, and it concerned Harry Tewson's theory of the explosion on board. He knew Tewson often had wild guesses as to the cause of these kinds of accident, mental leaps he had to work back on to substantiate, and, often as not, he had been correct. So, what could be the reason for a planted bomb? And how the hell could it have been smuggled on board? He would need to get hold of the passenger flight-list and he knew just the person who could get it for him. He realized he could just sit back and wait for the AIB's report on the cause of the disaster, and that if foul play *were* suspected the police would take over the investigation as to who and why. But that would take months. And he had the notion that time was running out.

6

The Reverend A. N. Biddlestone was deeply disturbed. He trudged along the muddy footpath that skirted the field with his head down, shoulders hunched, arms folded with his hands tucked under his armpits. His breath emerged in frosty clouds into the early morning air. Although he seemed to be watching his own footsteps, his mind was focused on more important matters. His concern was for the change in the town since the awful disaster.

It was almost as if a grey veil had descended upon Eton; a veil of misery, depression. He supposed it was normal enough after a catastrophe of such major proportions, and the fact that most of the bodies had had to be buried in a mass grave nearby had helped the oppressive atmosphere to linger. Only the easily identifiable bodies had been reclaimed by relatives or friends to be laid to rest in their own private graves. It would gradually lift, he felt sure, once the town had been given a chance to forget, and everything would be right again. He knew he would never forget the night of the disaster. It had held horrors for him that the local townspeople had fortunately not been duty bound to experience. He and his opposite number from the nearby Catholic church had moved among the mutilated dead performing the Last Rites, averting their eyes from the ravaged, barely human shapes, the smell of oil and burnt flesh causing them to retch violently as they prayed. No, the memory might fade in time, but it would never dim into inconsequence; he had learnt more about the fragility of life in that one night than in all the twenty-two years he had been a practising minister.

He reached the gate leading to the back of the long, narrow garden that ran alongside his parish church and, as he went through and closed it behind him, he looked across at the field and the distant wreckage of the 747. His tall, gaunt frame shivered involuntarily at the bleak sight; the sooner these last remains – this fearful memorial – were removed, the sooner the people of his town could return to their normal lives. The wreckage still served as a macabre shrine for the morbid pilgrimages of sightseers who flocked to the town, curious only about the disaster, hardly interested in the ancient town itself. It upset the townspeople, even though it was good for business. He felt sure most of them now wanted to forget the incident; the experience had been perversely exciting to them at first – frightening even – and they had enjoyed the reporters and the investigators. However, as interest in the crash gradually waned, he had expected the spirits of the local people to lift again, and for them all to be restored to their normal selves. But for some reason, this hadn't happened. Perhaps it was still too soon. Perhaps it was purely in his own imagination, although the incident the previous night had borne testimony to just how highly strung the people had become.

It had been around ten o'clock and he had just returned from visiting a sick parishioner, an elderly woman, whose passage from this world into the next was being made as smooth as possible by the hospital in Windsor, when he'd heard the distant screams. He had stood and listened on the wide stone path that led up to the church, unsure of what he had heard. It had come again from far away, but was shrill enough to carry across the cold night air. He had hurried along the path, through the war-memorial garden with its representative grey slabs, past the tall, grey-stoned church and its grinning gargoyles, and on towards the iron gate at the rear of the garden which led into the fields beyond. His steps had quickened as the screams, still faint, had seemed to grow more urgent, more piteous. He had run into the fields and was startled to see a black shape hurrying towards him. A flashlight had been shone in his face and he had been relieved when he heard Constable Wickham's familiar voice. He was on guard duty with another policeman, protecting the wreckage of the Jumbo jet from scavenging souvenir hunters, and he, too, had been alarmed at the sudden cries from across the field.

Together, the vicar and the policeman had gone to investigate the sounds, glad of each other's company. In the land on the other side of the long field, parked close into the side of a hedge, they had found a small, dark car, and crouched on the floor inside a shaking, hysterical girl. When they had opened the car door, she had gone into paroxysms of absolute fear, struggling to get away from them, tearing at the floor of the car with bare hands. The policeman had struck her hard to calm her, almost knocking her cold, and she had fallen into a quivering heap in his arms. The only sense they could make out of her mumbled ravings was that someone had run away and left her. They would have suspected a lovers' quarrel except for the sheer terror there had been in her screams, a terror which was now very much in evidence in her voice and trembling body. Without hesitating, they had taken her to the hospital, the vicar's second trip that night, and she had been heavily sedated.

So there it was: the incident had somehow exemplified the atmosphere hovering over the town; a feeling of suppressed hysteria that was just waiting to be tipped into outward emotion. The girl had obviously been caught up in the strange feelings of the town, and the slightest shock – it may have only been an animal scurrying around in the bushes – had sent her into that demented state. And now, there was the body which had been found down by the river that very morning.

He had been out on his usual early morning walk along the river-bank when he had seen a cluster of people near the river's edge, most of them in the blue uniform of policemen, and they appeared to be dragging something from the water. He had approached them to see whether he could be of any assistance. He was told only prayer could be of any use to this poor wretch, and he saw for himself the gross body that now lay on the bank. The vicar had recognized the dead man, even though he hadn't been one of his parishioners, for he had often seen him fishing in a small boat, made to look even smaller by his huge bulk, when on his morning stroll. He had always waved and bade the man good morning and, if the boat was close to the bank, they had chatted for a few minutes. The man's name had been Bumpton, or something like that, and he had run a small shop in Windsor. A big man, but as far as Reverend Biddlestone could tell, a gentle man.

Apparently people on a passing launch had seen the empty dinghy drifting in midstream and had kept an eye out for its owner. Soon, they had spotted an arm protruding from the water, its hand still clutching on to the reeds at the river's edge. The police had thought the man had either overbalanced and fallen into the river, subsequently drowning, or that he had suffered a heart attack (and the purplish tinge to his cheeks and bluish lips seemed to support the theory) and then fallen into the river. The autopsy would tell them which.

The vicar had prayed briefly over the dead body for a few moments then sadly returned to his church, his mind greatly disturbed by the events. Had they been two unrelated incidents? First the girl, frightened out of her wits, and now the man, dead, probably from a heart attack. What had caused the heart attack? Had it been exertion – or had it been fear? Or was it all in his own imagination?

With a weary sigh, he turned away from the dreadful field and walked down the path towards the front of his church. He could have used the side door, but he liked to enter the church first thing in the morning from the front, so that its full splendour – and its humbling solitude – would hit him instantly. Somehow, the approach to the altar, the long walk towards that sacred place, prepared him, gave him time to cleanse his mind for his converse with the Almighty.

He was fumbling in his trouser pocket for the long key that opened the heavy wooden doors to the church when he heard the sound. It was as though someone had bumped against the door from the other side. Startled, he took a step back and looked up at the entrance. It was much too early for Mrs Squires, the woman who cleaned the church and made sure the flowers were always fresh, and she wouldn't have been able to get in without his key anyway. In fact, nobody would have been able to get in unless he unlocked the door. He pointed the key at the lock and stepped forward again, curious and a little irritated. He wouldn't put it past one of those boys from the College to have locked himself in overnight as a prank, or perhaps as a bet with some of his school chums. It wouldn't have been the first time they'd been into mischief in and around the church. Well, this time he would teach them a lesson. This time he would take the matter further instead of letting them off with a reprimand.

Before he could turn the key, two loud bangs rattled the door on its hinges, causing him to step back again in surprise. It was the strength of the blows that shocked him.

'Who's in there?' he called out, then leaning his face towards the centre crack he repeated his question. 'Come on, who is it in there? If it's some of you boys from the College, you'd better answer up now!'

But he knew mere boys would never have had the strength to shake the doors in that fashion. He reached tentatively towards the protruding key, the silence beginning to unnerve him almost as much as the loud thumps had.

And then the pounding started again, but this time it did not stop at two blows but continued in a steady tattoo, becoming louder and louder, filling his head with the sound so that he was forced to put his hands to his ears. The door shook, the wood seemed to swell and move out towards him under the force. He felt sure it would splinter and break. The pounding sounded as if it were going on inside his head and he staggered back away from the entrance. He looked up at the building and even the ugly grey gargoyles appeared to be grinning down at him. He looked back in horror at the door; it was bound to break, he couldn't understand how the old lock had withstood the terrible strain for so long. The noise increased even more in volume, it seemed to be reaching a crescendo.

He opened his mouth and screamed: 'Stop! In the name of God – stop!'

He wasn't sure, and later, he was even less sure, but at that moment he thought he heard a laugh. No, it was more like a low chuckle, not loud, but somehow audible above the noise of the pounding. It was just as he was about to run from the churchyard, no longer able to suffer the terrible noise, that the knocking stopped. The quiet was almost as great a shock as the noise had been. The door was still, as solid as ever, unmarked by strain. For an instant, he almost doubted if anything had happened, so peaceful was the silence. He approached the door warily, and put an ear to it, ready to spring away at the slightest sound. Was he mistaken again, or did he hear whispers?

Reverend Biddlestone was not a particularly brave man but he *was* a rational man. He could hardly go along to the police and complain there was someone trying to get *out* of his church. They would probably smile and inquire why he wouldn't let them out? And that banging: it had been heavy and loud, but somehow muffled – not caused by a sharp object. And human strength couldn't have bent those solid oak doors in that way. As a sensible, well-adjusted man, he found explanation difficult; and if he couldn't explain it to himself, how could he explain it to the police? But whoever – *whatever* – was in there, it was inside God's house, the house he, as a member of the clergy, had been ordained to keep. He turned the key.

The vicar waited a few moments before pushing the door inwards. There was a small, dark entrance hall, shut off from the church itself by two separate doors. It was empty.

The vicar swung both sides of the double door wide to allow as much light as possible to flood in, then took a cautious step into the opening. He listened for a few seconds before moving towards one of the smaller doors that led directly into the church. He pushed the door open and peered through.

Sunlight shone through a high stained-glass window in brilliant shafts, the small swirling particles of dust defining them clearly, but various parts of the interior were in deep, impenetrable shadows. The small door swung shut as he went through, creating another area of blackness behind him.

He looked around from wall to wall but everything appeared to be in order. He walked towards the altar, his footsteps echoing hollowly around the huge, cold building. He had only gone a few yards when he saw the black shape ahead, kneeling in the pew close to the altar at the front of the church. It was barely visible, for a shaft of sunlight shone down strongly between the figure and himself, making the shape vague through the rising dust. The figure seemed to be wearing a cloak or heavy coat, but at this distance it was hard to be sure. Without speaking, he moved forward towards it, expecting the figure to turn at the sound of his footsteps. But it didn't.

He drew nearer, but it was still hazy on the other side of the bright beam of light, and now he wasn't certain if it were a figure at all. It seemed too dark all over. He passed through the glare from the high windows and, dazzled by the brilliance, had to blink his eyes to accustom them to the sudden gloom. Slightly blinded by the change in light, he stopped behind the kneeling figure, reaching out a hand to touch its shoulder. As he did so, the head slowly began to turn towards him.

The vicar was suddenly aware of the chill, much more intense than the usual early morning church coldness, a chill that penetrated his bones, froze his eyes in their sockets. And he was aware, too, of the low growling sound, a barely recognizable chuckle, as the head came round, and the black charred holes that should have been eyes met his.

Mercifully, all awareness left him as he fainted and collapsed in a heap on to the hard, stone floor.

7

Keller steered his car into the secluded driveway, the crunching noise of tyres on gravel announcing his arrival. In the glove compartment he had a complete passenger list of the fatal 747 flight, obtained from the young Despatch Officer who had been on duty that particular night. The man had been reluctant to hand the list over at first, but after a little persuasion (using the argument that Keller could easily obtain it from the newspapers anyway), he had succumbed and given him some extra information about the passengers as well, which was, of course, what the co-pilot had been hoping for. Keller intended to go through the list carefully later on in the day; exactly what he hoped to find he was not quite sure – but he had to start somewhere.

His immediate intention, though, was to see Beth Rogan, the dead pilot's wife. It was a task he didn't relish: bringing up the past, opening old wounds.

The house was in Shepperton, quite near the yachting lake, a recreation he knew Captain Rogan had enjoyed immensely. It wasn't a particularly large house nor was it small, but it had the air of casual and unpretentious elegance. As he brought the Stag to a halt, he saw the front door open and Beth Rogan appear.

The last time he'd seen her, at the mass burial of the passengers and crew, she had looked pale and, somehow, crushed. He'd found her looking at him several times during the long service, but her face was expressionless, and he had still been too dazed with events himself to reach out for any mutual sympathy. Now she looked as beautiful and alive as she'd ever been, the whiteness of her blouse and trousers contrasting with the black funeral garb he'd last seen her in. Her long brown hair was clipped to one side, giving her a young, almost schoolgirl appearance. She raised her hand in a small gesture of hello, and he noticed the glass of dark liquid in her other hand.

As he got out of the car he said, 'Hello, Beth.'

'Dave,' she replied.

They looked at one another in silence for a few moments and, now he was close, he noticed the tiny tell-tale lines beginning to appear around her eyes, the faint creases in her neck that hadn't been there before. But she was still a beautiful woman. Her dark brown eyes, deep – worldly – fixed his with a fierce intensity.

'Why haven't you been to see me?' she asked.

'Sorry, Beth. I thought it better not to,' he replied.

There was a flicker of anger in her eyes now, a tiny reflection at the bottom of a deep well. She moved away from him, back into the house. She led him through into the lounge and walked over to the drinks' cabinet. 'Would you like a drink, Dave?' she asked, as she refilled her own with sherry.

'Not just yet, Beth. A coffee, maybe?'

She disappeared briefly into the kitchen, giving him the chance to settle into the flower-patterned settee and look around the room. The last time he'd seen this room, it had been filled with people, alive with talk, grey with smoke. He remembered sitting in this very place, bleary-eyed, drunk, alone. He remembered Beth looking at him through the crowd, a meaningful and not too devious smile on her face. It was a look just meant for him; for him to interpret as he pleased. And there she was again, coming towards him, her arm outstretched proffering the coffee, an almost identical smile on her face.

He took the cup from her gratefully and placed it on the floor beside his feet. She sat in an armchair opposite, one finger constantly running up and down the thin stem of her sherry glass, studying him closely, waiting for him to speak.

'How've you been, Beth?' he said finally.

'Okay.' The amusement left her eyes.

'It must have been a terrible shock . . .'

'You know we were about to split up?' she interrupted sharply.

He looked at her in surprise. 'I knew there were problems, but . . .'

This time, she interrupted him with a short, scoffing laugh.

'Problems! Well, you should know, Dave. You were one of them!'

'Beth, that was months ago. And there was nothing to it.'

'Five months to be exact. And Peter didn't believe there was nothing to it.'

'How did he find out?'

'I told him, of course.'

'Why? Why did you tell him?' His voice had a hard edge to it now. 'It was a casual thing. I was just . . .' He broke off and averted his eyes from hers.

'One of many. Is that what you were going to say, Dave?'

He remained silent.

'Yes, you were one of . . . a few.' She took a swift, angry sip of her sherry. She sat stiffly for a few moments, then the anger seemed to leave her and her shoulders sagged. She stared at the floor between them. When she spoke, her voice was weary. 'I gave him a list of my lovers a few nights before the flight.'

'Oh God. Why, Beth?'

She straightened up and her eyes focused on his. There was bitterness in her voice now. 'To get back at him. Our marriage has – had – been unsteady for years. You know me, Dave. I'm not the sort of woman to sit around waiting while her husband flies off all round the world.' She stood up and walked over to the window, her arms folded, but one hand still clutching the glass in delicate fingers. Her back to him, she gazed out on to the lawn, and said, 'Everybody knew about me except him. I think you realized it the first time you met me.'

It was true. He remembered when he'd first set eyes on her two years before: her cool appraisal of him, the almost mocking smile, her hand holding on to his for just that second too long. She'd laid down the challenge at their introduction. At the airline, there had been a few insinuations about her from people that knew Rogan and his wife, a few snide remarks, but other pilots' wives were a subject generally avoided by him and his colleagues – the married ones knew they were all open to the same danger because of their constant absence from home. Besides, Rogan was highly respected by his colleagues, and held slightly in awe by the younger pilots. Never popular, for he had a hard, brusque manner, he was known to be a man one could rely on in a crisis. He'd survived two crashes that could have easily resulted in major disasters had it not been for his skill and iron cool nerve. The first, eight years before, had been when the undercarriage of his Viscount had refused to descend, and he had brought the plane down to an almost perfect landing on its belly. Not one person had been injured. The second, only a year later, had been when two engines of his

Argonaut failed within twenty seconds of each other due to a faulty cross-feed lever causing an inadvertent fuel transfer at flight. Again, he'd managed to bring the aircraft down safely on his two remaining engines.

As a senior captain with Consul, he'd proved to be an excellent, if critical, teacher, and Keller had benefited greatly from his experience and technical knowledge. Their relationship had been something more personal than just student and mentor: Captain Rogan had recognized a natural ability in Keller, an instinct for flying that no amount of flying experience could ever instil in a trainee. It was an instinct many of the most veteran captains did not possess; they compensated for it by sheer technical skill. At just thirty years of age, Keller was in his last year as co-pilot; Rogan had already recommended that he be promoted to captain, and his last few tests towards that goal had been successful. The captain had, in fact, recognized a younger – perhaps better – facsimile of himself and had taken a special interest in the co-pilot's career because of it, often treating him a little harsher than he would the younger man's contemporaries, driving him to his limits, but always ready to back off easily at breaking point. Fortunately, Keller understood his skipper's intentions and, although sometimes open hostility seemed to exist between the two men, both respected and liked one another.

Until Beth had told the captain of their indiscretion.

The Rogans had arranged one of their rare parties – the captain had never been a socialite – but the airline had assigned Rogan to take a flight out to Washington Dulles in place of a colleague who had fallen sick. The skipper had been secretly relieved at the request because of his dislike of social gatherings – especially his own – and had accepted the flight, much to Beth's displeasure. Cathy had also been booked on to the flight as stewardess, leaving Keller to go to the party on his own. A combination of circumstances had led to his going to bed with Beth: a heated argument with Rogan that same day over some vague technical point to do with aerodynamics (Rogan's argument had later been proved to be correct); a resentment towards Cathy for having to be away that night; and an excess of alcohol (unusual for him). And, of course, Beth Rogan's determination to seduce him.

She had made advances towards him all evening, subtle at first, and as the evening wore on, more blatant. He had managed to keep her at arm's length for most of the party, but the more he had to drink, the more forced his rejections became. Maybe he had been drinking purposely to allow himself the excuse for dropping his guard, for becoming irresponsible; maybe it was his former self, having been kept willingly on a leash for so long, who was now rebelling. Or maybe it was just sheer lust.

Whatever excuses he had made for himself after the event, the damage had been done and he'd known eventually the price would have to be paid. What he needed to know now was just how high had that price been?

Keller remembered how, at the party, he had suddenly felt unsteady on his feet. He'd made his way upstairs, not quite sure whether he was going to be sick or was just going to urinate. He'd doused his face with cold water and, as he'd opened the bathroom door, he'd found her waiting for him. Beth had led him to one of the spare bedrooms and told him to lie there until his head had cleared. She'd left him, closing the door quietly behind her, and he had fallen into a semi-drunken slumber, the noise of the party below filtering through as though from a long way off. When he'd woken, the room was in complete darkness and there were no more sounds from below. He was beneath a bedcover, his shoes were off, and cool hands were touching his body. He turned with a start towards the figure lying next to him, his hand finding a smooth, naked body. He knew instantly who it was. She had pulled herself close to him, her leg going between his, her thigh pressed tight against his body. He hadn't even tried to resist – what normal man would have? – and he had made love to her with an angry passion which, rather than subduing her, had sent her into a rage of excitement that equalled, then overtook, his own.

After, he had fallen into a deep, exhausted sleep, and when he awoke the following morning, he found himself naked beneath the bedclothes with Beth lying snug against him. That had been the moment of truth for him: he was sober, he was satiated. He had no excuse. He could have got up without disturbing her, left the house, and tried to pretend it had never happened. Instead, he had woken her gently with soft kisses and a probing tongue, and they had made long, leisurely love again, she enjoying his young, hard body, he relishing her undoubted experience.

And it was only after their second lovemaking that the truth of his betrayal had hit him: betrayal of the girl he loved and betrayal of a man he admired. He had dressed and told Beth it would never happen again; he had not been unkind to her – he wasn't that sort of man – but she had smiled bitterly, and a little scornfully at him. She had watched him dress without saying a word, sitting up in bed, not bothering to cover herself, and that had been his last memory of her: her cynical smile, her beautiful body. And, as he regarded her now, that last sight of her was etched sharply in his memory. The smile was the same, but she was just a little older.

'You could have got in touch with me, Dave,' she said. 'If not before, at least after the crash.'

He stared guiltily at her. 'I'm sorry, Beth. I really am. Things have been difficult for me. The shock, the publicity.

My mind's been in a daze, and it's only now beginning to clear a little.'

She was back at the drinks' cabinet now, this time pouring herself a Scotch. 'Will you join me now?'

He shook his head. 'No.' He reached for the coffee at his feet and sipped at it.

'Beth, I'm trying to find out what caused the crash.'

She turned sharply towards him. 'That's a job for the AIB, isn't it? Why should you concern yourself?'

'I – I don't know exactly. It's just, somehow, I feel guilty. I don't know why, but I believe the cause of the crash may have something to do with me.'

'That's ridiculous. Why blame yourself?'

'Peter and I had a fight before the flight. It was over you. I couldn't remember exactly when that fight took place, but if, as you said, you told him about us a few days before the crash, then we must have fought some time during those few days before.'

'But why is that so important?'

'I keep seeing a picture of the captain. It's in the cockpit of the Jumbo, we're in flight, and he's looking up at me, shouting. Don't you see? If that fight continued as we took off – the most crucial time in any flight – and it caused some negligence on our part, some error of judgement, then your husband and I are responsible for the deaths of all those people.'

There was sympathy in her eyes now as she came over and sat beside him. 'Dave, I know you, and I knew my husband – at least one part of him. You were both too professional to allow emotion to get in the way of your jobs. Peter would never let his temper get the better of his logical mind. He was much too experienced for that.'

'But you didn't see him before the flight when we had the

argument. I'd never seen him lose control before, but he was like a madman that night.'

'I was to blame for that; I was so cruel to him. He hit me, you know. Not when I told him about the others, but when I told him about you. He was a proud man – and he was proud of you.'

Keller placed his coffee cup back on its saucer and pushed it away from him. He turned to face her, his eyes not angry, but uncomprehending.

'Why did you do it, Beth?'

'To hurt him, to get through that hard, cold exterior. To make him feel something, even if it were only hate.'

Yes, Keller remembered the hate in those eyes. The angry, seething hate. It wasn't just the hurt pride: it was the betrayal by his protégé, someone he'd coached, someone he'd taught all he knew. Someone he regarded as an extension of himself. And with the memory came another glimpse of their confrontation.

Keller remembered the angry words, the vehemence behind them, echoing after him as he'd walked away from Rogan in the empty hangar. 'Does Cathy know about it, Keller? Does she? She will now, you bastard! She'll find out from me!' And then he had begun to hate the captain, the man he'd looked up to, tried to emulate, the man he had wanted to be. A man who had now lost his dignity. A man who lay sprawled on the concrete floor, hurling abuse. A god who had become mortal.

How far had that hate between them continued? Could that cool professional mind have finally cracked beneath the emotional stress? Could his own younger, less experienced mind have succumbed to intolerant rage? The whole picture was slowly drawing together. But was it the true picture?

'Dave, are you all right? You look so strange.' Beth's voice brought him back to the present.

He took a deep breath. 'Maybe a Scotch would help,' he said.

She poured him a large measure and sat next to him again, handing him the glass. He took a long swallow and allowed the whisky to make its fiery passage down his throat to his stomach before he spoke again. 'Beth, what happened before that flight? Did he say anything when he left you that night?'

Her voice was soft but even. 'He said he wouldn't be back.'

Keller stiffened, and the hand holding the glass trembled slightly. 'What did he mean?'

She was staring at him now. 'No,' she said, 'not what you think. I'm sure he didn't . . .' Her voice trailed off. 'No,' she said again. 'He was upset, but not *that* upset. We'd spoken of divorce before and I think he was resigned to it. My telling him about you tipped the balance, I know, but I'm positive that he only meant he wouldn't come back to me. He wasn't crazy, Dave!'

Keller shook his head, but it was in agreement with her. And yet . . . Pilots were under constant pressure and he knew of many good men who had suddenly cracked under the strain. That's why both physical and mental check-ups were essential: once a year for regular flyers, twice for those over forty.

Keller felt a greater sense of dread than ever now. So much seemed to be pointing in one direction and he felt the responsibility resting even more heavily upon his shoulders. If only he could break through this barrier that clouded his mind, allowing him only tiny, occasional glimpses, tormenting him with elusory visions. Psychiatric treatment, he had been told, could possibly help, but it would take time. Anyway, psychiatrists could only help the mind to cure itself, could not effect that cure themselves.

He needed to know more about the air crash. Perhaps some detail – technical or human – had been discovered by the AIB by now, something that would trigger off his memory. Perhaps Harry Tewson had more proof of his theory. Anything – whether it absolved him from blame or incriminated him further – would be better than having his mind stay in this limbo. The compulsion was there again. He had to return to Eton.

He left the remains of the Scotch in the glass and stood up. 'I've got to go, Beth.'

She was startled and disappointment showed clearly in those deep eyes.

'Stay a little longer, Dave. Please, I need someone.' She reached up for his hand and clasped it tightly. 'Just to talk, Dave, nothing else. Please.'

He shook his hand free and said, not unkindly, 'I can't stay now, Beth. Maybe I'll come back later, but now I've got to go.'

'Will you? Promise me, Dave.'

'Yes.' Perhaps. Probably not.

He left her sitting there, a different memory of her imprinted on his mind this time: the white blouse, the hands clutching the glass, the face that had suddenly begun to show its approaching age. And strangely, the same bitter, scornful smile.

The car threw up gravel as it lunged away from the house, the tiny stones rattling against the wall. He drew cautiously out of the drive and headed in the direction of Windsor and Eton, a new nervousness beginning to rise in him.

8

Emily Platt was slowly poisoning her husband to death. She was taking her time deliberately, not just to allay suspicion when his death finally came, but because she wanted him to suffer for as long as possible.

Over the past three weeks she had kept the doses of Gramoxone small so that his health would break down gradually and undramatically, but she had been surprised at how soon he had become bedridden. The paraquat contained in the weedkiller was much more potent than she had imagined, and the first dose Emily had administered to his morning coffee had frightened her with its suddenness of attack. Allowing him a couple of days to recover his strength, she had cut down on the doses drastically so that his suffering had become less acute, and more protracted. Naturally their doctor had had to be called in at the first, most violent, attack, but he was totally mystified by the illness; he was an unimaginative man. He had told Emily if her husband got any worse within the next few days he would have to be admitted into hospital for proper care and tests to discover the nature of the illness. However, as she had eased up on the doses of the poison and her husband's condition had appeared to improve, the doctor had seen no cause for alarm. He had merely left instructions to be called in promptly if the illness did not disappear completely within the next few days. Of course,

Emily had not bothered to get in touch with him again and her unfortunate husband had been too weak to do so himself.

It was not until she had made absolutely sure there was no chance of his recovery that she would call in the doctor again. She would say the attack had come suddenly, that her husband had been fine over the past couple of weeks although a little more tired than usual, and that he had just collapsed without any warning. She wouldn't mind his being taken to hospital for she knew that even if they discovered the cause of his malady, there was no known antidote for paraquat. Whether there would be grounds for a post-mortem or not after his death, she wasn't too sure. But then, she didn't really care; she just wanted him to die. Painfully.

Cyril Platt was younger than her – he thirty-six, she forty-three – but when they had married only five years before they had agreed that the difference in age did not matter at all to their relationship. And it hadn't. It had been Cyril's strange demands that had made the difference.

She had seen Cyril for the first time gazing at a tiny and delicate figurine displayed in the window of her antique shop in Eton's High Street. She had continued to look through a stack of various local newspapers she had sent to her each week, making a list of the various bazaars, jumble sales or village fêtes that were to take place during the following week. She knew, as did other antique dealers, that it was at events such as these that rare and valuable collectors' items could be found and she spent a large part of her time travelling around the country to such functions. Competition in the trade was fierce and, since antiques had become fashionably popular, it was becoming even more so, especially in Eton where there were many similar shops. Since her father had died, leaving her to carry on the business, she had had time for little else but work.

Occasionally, she glanced up from her task to see if the young man was still there and, for some reason other than business, hoped he would come into the shop. Too often people stared through the window, their eyes lovingly examining the objects displayed, and too often they wandered on to the next shop along without bothering to come in. Even if they did, there was never any guarantee they would buy: antique shops were similar to bookshops – there for browsing but not necessarily for buying. It had infuriated her when she was younger that people could spend so much time examining – even worshipping – these treasures, asking questions, fondling them, and then walk out of the shop as though they had been merely passing the time of day. But her father had taught her never to harass or even try to influence a potential customer, and never, under any circumstances, to bargain over an object. Their profession was too dignified for that sort of thing: they could leave *that* to the street traders.

Her father had been a man to fear and respect. Even to this day she was not sure if she had ever loved him. Her two elder sisters had left home because of his tyrannical strictness. A deeply religious man, he had ruled their home with a rod of iron, a rod that had never tempered or softened even after their mother had died. He was from the Victorian era, an age he had loved because of its moral codes, its revulsion at the abnormal, its firmness of character, the dominance of the man as head of the household. It had driven her sisters away, one to Scotland, the other abroad somewhere (there had been no contact since), but she herself had relished his rule over them. She needed to be dominated just as he needed to dominate and, in that respect, they fulfilled each other's needs admirably. His death had left her alone and afraid – yet strangely relieved.

Perhaps it was because after the years of welcomed

oppression she now felt her penance was done. Penance for what? She did not know, but her father had taught her every human was born with guilt, of a need for atonement, and this shaped their lives in some form or other. The true Christian repaid most of his debt during his own lifetime; the *others* repaid it after their deaths. She felt that she had repaid most of her debt during *his* lifetime. And now that he was gone, now that the arrogant, vigorously masculine dominance had been lifted from her life, she was acutely susceptible to the gentleness of someone like Cyril.

Emily looked up sharply as the little bell above the door tinkled and he stepped into the shop. She smiled politely at him and he smiled politely back. She returned to her search through the local journals but her brain was busy collating the material it had gathered on his appearance. He looked to be in his late twenties or early thirties. Tall, but slightly built. Not very handsome, but pleasing to look at. His clothes looked a size too large for him, though comfortable because of it. His hands were tucked deeply into his jacket pockets. Married? (Why should she wonder?) She wasn't experienced enough to judge.

A shadow was cast over the newspapers, she heard him clear his throat, and, when she looked up, she found him smiling apologetically down at her. He asked her about the figurine and whether she had its matching statuette. Much to her embarrassment she replied she hadn't known it was one of a set and asked if he himself could tell her more about the statuette. He could, and did, and very soon they were engaged in a lively and interesting conversation about antiques and their sources. Their association – for it was just an association at first – soon blossomed into a shy romance; she found in him the tenderness that had been lacking in her father, and he found in her the inner fortitude that was lacking in himself.

Within three months they were married and their first three years were mildly happy with no extremes of either joy or misery.

Lovemaking was a new experience to Emily and, disappointingly, an unwelcome one; she endured, but rarely enjoyed because the whole act somehow seemed to be a betrayal of her father's teachings. No, not just that. A betrayal of her father.

Unfortunately, as her passion had simmered passively and finally waned and died, Cyril's appetite had intensified, almost as if her very passivity increased his excitement. As a stranger to sex, she could only guess that his demands were not quite normal but, after three years, when he seemed not to care so much whether she considered it normal or not, Emily knew there was something positively wrong. In the past, he had never seemed eager to consummate their lovemaking inside her, indeed, had seemed reluctant to do so. This had not unduly worried her for she felt no strong desire to have his sticky fluid filling her body, but the alternative was equally unpleasant and definitely more unsightly. He had pleaded with her to use her hands on him, almost crying when she wouldn't, demanding she fulfil her duties as a wife. It was the word duty that always made her acquiesce to his wishes; obligation had been a familiar word to her throughout her life.

And then he had wanted to use orifices other than the obvious for his climaxes. This had horrified and revolted her more than she could say, but strangely, his weakness had made him strong – if stubbornness could be called strength. She began to feel frightened of him: her father's rages had been quiet but no less forbidding; Cyril's were wild, emotional, and terrifying. Although he had never actually beaten her, the threat of violence was always there, his tantrums carrying him to the very edge of physical aggression. Emily had no alternative but to succumb. Raised in a devoutly religious atmosphere she now found it impossible to visit the church; how could she now she was a party to such perversion?

And then, after three years of such torture, Cyril's aberration took on an even worse aspect: he demanded that she beat him. Reluctantly, she had conformed but he had screamed that she was not *trying* – she was not *hurting* him. In fear, she had renewed her efforts and this time he had cried out in pain. And, oddly, his cry brought her pleasure. She had used the flat of her hand at first, but this was not enough – for her. Her eyes cast around for something that would give more pain, and they fixed upon a leather belt he had left (purposely?) by the side of the bed. She grabbed it and flayed him, rejoicing in his screams, venting the oppression of a lifetime on the thin, naked body that cowered away from her. The pity was that for all the agony – or perhaps because of it – he had enjoyed it, too, and when her anger had been spent, he begged for more. Disgust for herself, disgust for him, disgust for their life together, had swept through her, a sinking, grey misery enveloping and smothering her spirit. But now she was caught up in the inextricable downward spiral of degradation. She lived the next two years in a state of abject wretchedness as his perversion inevitably grew worse. He developed a liking for being bound and locked up and then, perhaps worst of all, a penchant for wearing her clothes. Emily discovered this last trait of his when she went upstairs one day to the flat above the antique shop to make some tea for her afternoon break. She found Cyril in their bedroom admiring himself in the fulllength wardrobe mirror. He was wearing her underwear, even her tights, and an obscene bulge pushed out against the thin material of her panties. He laughed at her shock (had he wanted her to discover him like this?) and she saw lipstick covered his ugly mocking lips.

It would all have been very funny had it not been so pathetic. And real.

Emily's one small consolation throughout was that it had all been kept within the bounds of their marriage; but now, even that was changing. He had begun to go out on his own in the evenings, something he'd rarely done in the past. She soon found out, through the suspicious and secretly delighted reports of some of the few friends she still had, he was keeping the company of some very dubious young men in Windsor. As a slight relief, his demands on her became less frequent although his desire for anal sex increased. It was perfectly obvious, even to one of her sheltered upbringing, that he had finally formed homosexual relationships with other men. She now understood that this is what their own sexual relationship had been about: he had tried to hide the stigma of his weakness from himself, but had tried to achieve the results of it through their marriage. It was inevitable that the path he had chosen would eventually lead to the one he had tried to avoid. And most perverse of all, the fact she tried to keep from herself but finally had to admit, was that she now felt cheated, cuckolded.

Had it really all been against her will? Perhaps so at the start – but later? Why hadn't she left him or thrown him out when his deviations had become extreme? They were questions she found impossible to answer and the guilt weighed heavy on her conscience. The fact of her own normality, the fact she had desperately clung to through all those years, was now gone. Her soul had been bared and she found it as unclean as his. So not only did she have to contend with his unfaithfulness, but she had also to deal with the consequent self-revelations.

It was too much for her.

The breaking point came when Cyril brought his lover home, into *her* house. Emily had returned late from a trip to one of the market towns that she frequently visited in search of rare antique bargains – bargains that were becoming increasingly more difficult to find for everybody seemed to know the value of these old pieces nowadays. She had parked the van in the yard at the rear of the shop and let herself in through the back door. Climbing wearily the stairs to their flat, she heard laughter coming from the lounge. When she'd opened the door she had been confronted by the two of them, their mocking, unashamed faces grinning up at her as she stood in the doorway. Cyril's arm was draped around the shoulders of the younger man next to him and, as she watched, he slowly turned to him and kissed his cheek. Revulsion welled up inside Emily, and she fled downstairs to the darkness of the shop. She sank to the floor and wept, praying to her father, asking his forgiveness for her five-year revolt against his teaching, her revolt against his authority.

That had been four weeks ago, and that had been when she'd decided to kill Cyril.

Strangely enough, the tragic air crash the following week had made it easier. If life was so valueless that it could be taken on such a grand scale, what did the taking of one sick and perverted life matter? It somehow made the murder a small thing.

Emily already knew about the weedkiller and the lethal paraquat it contained, for her father had been a keen gardener and she knew it was relatively easy to obtain, even though it had a restricted sale. It was usually sold only to farmers and agriculturists who were obliged to sign a 'poisons book' at any store they bought it from. However, it was easy for Emily to convince the shop staff when she next visited a market town she was a genuine buyer, and she falsified her name and address in their special book. She walked out of the store with a quart bottle of the poison, enough to kill hundreds of people.

She watched Cyril slowly die over the next few weeks with grim satisfaction, keeping the doses as small as possible in an attempt to keep the deadly process going for as long as possible. He had given her five years of torment, culminating in the terrible realization of her own guilt; she would give him as many weeks of physical torture as she could.

The poison attacked his throat and stomach first, damaging his kidneys and liver, causing his lungs to fill with fluid, making breathing almost impossible. His hair began to fall out and gradually he began to lose his sight and the power of speech. Emily had a brief moment of anxiety when Cyril's boyfriend had called in at the shop asking for him. She had told the young man that Cyril had gone away on a tour of the country in search of collectors' curios, a normal enough venture. He had shrugged his shoulders in a petulant way; he wasn't *that* interested anyway, and if Cyril couldn't be bothered to let him know, well ... He had flounced from the shop. Another time, she had heard a clatter from upstairs and had rushed up to find Cyril lying on the floor of the lounge beside the telephone. Fortunately, he had been too weak to make the call, but it indicated he knew full well what was happening, a fact that pleased her enormously.

And today, she knew she would administer the final dose.

The consequences of her action didn't really matter too much to her; if she could get away with his murder, fine, if not – at least she had made him suffer for the humiliation he had caused her, and she herself was prepared to pay for her own sins over the last few years.

Emily stirred the hot soup containing the Gramoxone; even though they both knew her intentions, the pretence had to be kept up. He would try to resist her feeding him, but she would force the soup down his throat with tiny spoonfuls that would not spill too much. He was too weak to fight her. Emily poured the soup from the saucepan into a bowl and placed the bowl on a tray. She added a cruet of salt and pepper to the tray and, as an afterthought, she broke up a bread roll and put it on a small plate beside the soup. She smiled at her own slyness, then lifted the tray and made for the bedroom. She had given up sleeping in the same room now and taken to spending the night on the sofa in the lounge; the smell in the bedroom had become unendurable for any length of time.

She paused at the bedroom door and placed the tray on the floor before it; she had forgotten the tea-cloth and she would need it to wipe away the soup that would run down his cheeks and chin as he tried to avoid drinking. Returning from the kitchen with the cloth over her arm, she stooped down to pick up the tray again. It was then that Emily thought she heard whispering coming from the bedroom.

She pressed her ear closer to the door. There was silence for a few moments then the voices started up again, low, indistinct. It couldn't be: no one could have entered his room, it would have been impossible without her seeing them. But his voice had become barely audible over this past week. Then she heard a shuffling noise, like something, some object, being dragged towards the door. Had he somehow found the strength to move from the bed, a last desperate attempt to save himself? She reached for the door-handle and pushed the door inward with a rush.

Cyril stood facing her, his pale, emaciated body grotesque in its nakedness. His eyes were enlarged, bulging from their sunken sockets, his cheekbones protruding through the tautly stretched skin, and the hollow cavities that once were cheeks emphasized the wide, grinning mouth. Yet it wasn't a grin; his mouth only took on that shape because the tightened skin had drawn back the flesh to reveal the bared yellow teeth. The sparse tufts of hair remaining on his scalp completed the skull-like appearance. He had the face of the dead.

Emily screamed as he raised a trembling arm towards her. Fear, hate – it was both, but hate dominated – welled up inside her. She ran forward, her arms flailing at the obscene thing that was her husband. They went down in a heap on the floor, Emily still beating and screaming at him. Would she never find an escape from this creature, this perverted monster who had ruined her life? Would even his death be a punishment to her? Now she was sobbing as she beat down on his still form and her blows began to slow, had less force behind them, until finally, they stopped altogether.

She crouched over him, her knees straddling his body, her arms on either side of his head supporting her weight, hair hanging down, lightly brushing against his face. She could see only the whites of his half-closed eyes and no breath came from his gaping, grinning mouth. Emily threw herself away from the stiffened body, its cold touch suddenly filling her with revulsion. She lay with her back against the wardrobe, the huge mirrored wardrobe he had so often paraded himself disgustingly in front of. Her breath came in heavy gasps, and faint sobs escaped from her lips. She looked at the body with utter loathing. He was dead. Thank God he was finally dead.

He lay with his arms by his sides, his legs obscenely sprawled, and his half-closed sightless eyes looking up at the ceiling. She couldn't understand how his skin had become so cold to the touch, nor how his limbs had stiffened so quickly. Perhaps the poison had caused their reactions prematurely, before the life had even left his body. But it didn't matter; he was gone now – gone from her life for ever. And even if she was found out and had to pay the lawful penalty, prison was a purer punishment than the one she had been suffering all these years.

Emily drew up her legs away from the corpse and lay there waiting for her heart to slow its beat, her breathing to return to its normal pace. She would have to find the strength – and the courage – to lift him back into the bed. Then she would have to dress him in pyjamas, clean him, give the appearance of having looked after him in his illness. After that, she would have to call in the doctor, act grief-stricken, pretend she hadn't realized how ill he had been. Secretly, she knew how ridiculous her story would sound, and that the doctor would only have to see Cyril's withered condition to know it had been a deterioration of weeks and not just days. But she refused to consciously admit this fact to herself.

She suddenly shivered. She hadn't had time to notice how cold the room was before. Wondering if he had somehow managed to open the window in a bid to call for help from the High Street below, she looked over towards the light source. No, it was still locked for she could see the latch in its socket, and the curtains remained half-drawn. Curiously, it wasn't the natural coldness of a winter's day; it was a deep, clammy sort of coldness. Perhaps it was just the coldness that accompanied death.

But the chill became much more than just an uncomfortable feeling when she heard the low chuckle. It became an icy cold hand that clutched her heart in its fist, causing the blood circulating through her body to freeze and her body to go rigid. She slowly forced her head to turn towards the prostrated body, her eyes unwilling to confirm what her ears had heard. Cyril hadn't moved. She watched his form for a few moments, waiting for the sound again, watching to see if it had come from his dead body. She'd heard that even after death corpses sometimes moved or made sounds; it was something to do with the build up of gases within the body. It came again: a strange, almost whispered, laughter. And it hadn't come from the corpse.

It appeared to originate from the other side of the room, from the darkened corner behind the open door, yet somehow it filled the whole bedroom. She stared into the gloomy corner and her eyes could find no hidden shapes lurking there. But she felt its presence; and it was more loathsome than the creature that lay on the floor before her. Then the door began to slowly swing shut, the room growing dimmer as it did so, the poor winter light from the half-closed curtains providing only a soft grey hue to combat the gloom. The door closed with a soft click and the shadows around the bedroom deepened.

She heard a whisper and it sounded like her name. It came again, but this time from a different corner of the room, then from behind her, then from the foot of the bed. Then from Cyril.

She looked at him in horror.

His head still faced the ceiling and his lips barely moved as he spoke – as he whispered – her name. The head turned towards her and she saw that the eyes were now fully open, but somehow still not registering. They reminded her of the eyes of the dead fish she had seen laid out on a fishmonger's slab – sightless and flat.

Emily watched with paralysing fascination as he – it – raised itself on one elbow and stretched a hand towards her. She tried to scream but only a sharp, rasping sound came from her throat. The corpse was on its hands and knees and began to crawl in her direction, the stiffness in its limbs making its progress slow and deliberate. The grin on its face had suddenly become real and full of malevolence. The thing that had been Cyril whispered her name again.

Emily pushed herself back against the wardrobe in a vain attempt to get away from this terror, her head turning, but her eyes refusing to look away from the approaching horror. She fell sideways, twisting her body, her hands scrabbling at the carpet in an effort to drag herself clear. But it had crawled over her lower limbs now and its face was against her back, parodying the sexual position he had forced her into so many times in the past.

This time she did scream as his lips drew level with her ear and he whispered an obscenity to her. And now there seemed to be others around her; dark shapes, faces that somehow wouldn't focus, figures that appeared then faded before taking form. She could hear the laughter but it came from inside her own head.

Cold, cold hands clasped at her breasts and she felt herself being lifted backwards and up. Other unseen hands clutched at her body, lifting her by her arms and her legs. Emily rose towards the ceiling and found herself looking down at the upturned face of her dead husband. One hand was gripped around her throat and the other was between her legs, supporting her weight. The hand around her throat began to tighten, forcing the life from her, making her as he was. Her eyes began to force themselves from their sockets and her tongue protruded like a living creature trying to escape from a collapsed cave. Saliva ran from her mouth on to his up-turned face in a smooth, sticky stream.

The other figures below her began to take on a more definite shape and, just in that moment before her own sight dimmed as a red mist passed over them, she saw their forms clearly. But there was something wrong with them. Her mind barely had time to realize what that wrong was before it succumbed to unconsciousness but, in a last moment of clarity, she saw that the faces, the hands, the limbs that were not missing – all were blackened and charred. It was as if they were bodies risen from a fiery hell.

The gurgling noise that was meant to be a scream faded on her lips as she fell unconscious. Still holding her aloft, the thing that had been her husband walked towards the window, the eyeballs now beginning to roll inwards in their sockets, so that only white showed through the closing lids, the grin once again becoming a grimace of death.

It reached the window and stood poised, waiting. The voices told it what to do.

9

Keller's reflexes, thanks to his excellent training and his own natural instincts, were still way above average despite the traumas he had so recently been through. He jammed on the brakes just as he caught sight of the glass from the first-floor window breaking outwards in the periphery of his vision, and the car had screeched to a halt by the time the two bodies had spattered against the unyielding concrete of the road. For a moment, the High Street had become as a still photograph, with the people standing transfixed, staring at the bloody, misshapen bodies lying in the road. Then, faces began to appear in doorways and at windows, hesitating before crowding into the street. Somebody screamed. A woman fainted. A man vomited against the side of a building. Nobody approached the procumbent bodies.

Keller sat there stunned. His car had stopped about five yards from the twisted tangle of flesh and he had an unobstructed view of the grotesque tableau they presented. Although they had not fallen far, he knew from the angle of their fall – headfirst – they would have stood little chance of surviving; their necks must have snapped on impact. It was all the more startling when he saw the fingers belonging to the outstretched hand of the figure lying beneath the other slowly begin to curl inwards then out again.

He jerked open the car door and ran towards them. He

went down on one knee, trying to ignore the pool of blood forming beneath the bodies and seeping outwards. For the first time, Keller realized that the figures were those of a man and woman, and, strangely, the man was completely naked. As the co-pilot examined the figure on top more closely he noticed, even more strangely, that the stiffened limbs, the greyish-white, emaciated flesh and the tightened, almost bald scalp, indicated that the man had been dead for some time.

The gurgling sound abruptly disturbed him from his observation of the man and he quickly turned his attention to the woman beneath. The noise was coming from deep in her throat, as though she were trying to speak, but the blood trickling from her lungs was distorting the sounds she made. He noticed the fingers of her left hand were still moving, grasping the thin body of the man beneath the shoulders, and fighting down the feeling of revulsion at the touch of cold flesh, he pulled him easily aside. Then he gently slid his fingers under the woman's head, between her face and the road, ignoring the sticky blood that flowed on to his hand. He shifted the angle of the head very slightly so that she might be able to draw in air through her mouth – if she was still capable. He had to close his eyes for a second or two at the sight of her flattened, bloody face.

Keller leant closer to try and catch her words but they were feeble and unintelligible. For an instant, the eye that was turned towards him fluttered, then opened. It looked straight into his and suddenly it widened as though in fear. Abruptly, life left it and he realized she was dead.

He stood up, feeling a deep remorse for the poor woman whose very last moments had been clouded with fear. Oddly enough, he felt nothing for the naked man who also lay at his feet; maybe it was because the frail body hardly seemed human – it was more like a frozen carcass. Or perhaps it was because somehow he knew the man had been responsible for both their deaths. He must have pushed her from the window and, because of his obviously weakened state, fallen through after her.

The co-pilot looked down at the blood on his hands then noticed the pool had spread so that he was standing in it. The blood. Cathy's face. A sudden flashback!

But the memory was interrupted by a voice at his side and the picture of Cathy's terrified face, covered in blood, those wide eyes filled with alarm, the mouth opened as if screaming or shouting something – it vanished instantly into those hidden caverns of his mind.

Tewson spoke again: 'Come on, Dave. Let's get you cleaned up.'

Keller looked up from his hands and stared blankly into the face of the AIB investigator.

'Harry?'

Tewson took the dazed co-pilot by the arm and led him away from the crowd that had now gathered around the two bodies lying in the road. He leant Keller against the bonnet of the Stag and gave him a few moments to get over the shock.

'Did you see what happened?' he asked eventually.

Keller breathed out and his body seemed to lose some of its tension. 'I saw the window break and then the man and woman falling,' he replied. 'I didn't see anything before that.'

Tewson shook his head. 'My God,' he said sympathetically, 'as if you hadn't been through enough recently. Get in your car, Dave, and we'll put it out of the way somewhere. Then I'll take you over the bridge into Windsor where the AIB's got rooms in a hotel. It'll be quicker than driving all the way round by the main road and you look as if you could do with a good stiff drink.'

Just as they climbed into the car, Tewson in the driver's seat, Keller in the passenger's, a blue-uniformed figure broke away from the crowd gathered around the corpses and came hurrying over to them.

'Excuse me, sir,' the police constable said, just before Keller had closed the door on his side, 'but did you see how it happened?'

The co-pilot repeated what he'd told Tewson. The investigator leant across Keller and flashed an identity card before the policeman's face. 'I'm with the team investigating the air crash. We're booked in at the Castle Hotel just over the bridge and I'm taking Mr Keller there to get him cleaned up. If you need a statement of any kind, could you contact us there?'

The policeman nodded. 'That's all right, sir, there were plenty of people about who saw the accident. But I was told that Mr – er, Keller? – Mr Keller here got to the bodies first and I was just wondering if they were still alive, and if they were, did they say anything?'

Keller shook his head. 'No, the man was already dead and the woman died almost immediately. She didn't manage to say anything.'

'Very good, sir. We may need a statement later and if we do, we'll get in touch with you at the hotel. I must say, I don't know what's bloody goin' on here today – strangest day Eton's had since I've been here.'

Keller looked up sharply but, before he could say anything, Tewson was reversing the car carefully back down the road. He reached a turn-off on his right and drove forward into it, parking the Stag in the small car park at the rear of the local council offices. As he fed a coin into the ticket machine, Keller, still sitting in the vehicle, began to wipe as much of the blood from his hands as possible with a handkerchief. He noticed there was some blood on his trousers where he had knelt beside the bodies and the toe of one of his brown shoes was stained a darker colour. He felt he wanted to scrub himself all over, not to rid himself of the bloodstains, but to cleanse himself from the touch of that naked dead body. There had been something abhorrent about it.

As the two men walked back towards the bridge, purposely taking the road that ran behind, and parallel to, the High Street to avoid the distressing scene, the co-pilot pondered over the constable's parting remark. Tewson was looking over towards the fields where the remains of the wreck lay when Keller asked him what the policeman had meant.

'Oh, there's been a series of incidents this morning and last night,' the investigator replied. 'None of them connected in any way, of course, but I'm afraid the people of Eton are a bit jumpy nowadays what with the crash and all, and they're lumping everything together. Must say, I've sensed a feeling of gloom around the place for weeks now. Not to worry, though – it'll all clear itself once we and the last of that wreckage are away from here.'

'What do you mean – incidents? What kind of incidents?'

Tewson turned and regarded Keller, slowing his pace slightly. 'Dave, you've got enough on your mind without bothering yourself with unrelated events exaggerated by morbid townspeople with nothing better to do.'

'I want to know, Harry.'

'There you go again,' Tewson said, and then resignedly: 'All right, at least this isn't classified information. Last night, a couple of policemen on duty around the wreck heard screams coming from the other side of a field. One of them ran across to investigate and was joined by the vicar of the local church here. They found a girl alone in a car, terrified out of her mind. She was so hysterical she couldn't tell them what had happened to her but, obviously, she'd had a bad fright. She still can't, according to the police guarding over the wreck; she's in hospital under sedation.'

'Why would she go to the field by herself at night?' Keller asked.

'Well, apparently she *didn't* go there alone. The police have traced the car to some young man – her boyfriend probably – but he hasn't returned home yet. I reckon he let his courting get out of hand and when the girl got hysterical, he ran off. Now he's too frightened to show up again.'

Keller was silent as they turned the corner leading to the blocked-off bridge. Finally, he said, 'What else?'

'A man was dragged out of the river this morning on the *other* side of the field. He'd had a heart attack while fishing.'

'Fishing's hardly the sport to give you a heart attack.'

'He was a big man, too much weight; it could have happened at any time.'

'Go on.'

'Er – the vicar – the same vicar who'd gone to help the girl – well, he was found in a collapsed state inside his church this morning. He hasn't recovered properly yet, so God knows what happened to him! Maybe it was mental exhaustion. He's had to cope with all these distraught people lately and he also gave the Last Rites to the dead man this morning; not to mention what he went through on the night of the crash, of course. I mean, it went down just behind his own church. He was bound to crack up sooner or later.'

They were crossing the old iron bridge now. 'What do you mean when you say he hasn't recovered properly yet?' Keller asked. 'Is he unconscious?'

'No!' Tewson paused. 'Apparently he's still gibbering like a madman.'

Keller stopped to gaze down at the water. 'And now, those

two people falling – or jumping – from the window. And you don't think there's anything odd happening?'

'Of course there's something odd happening! Christ, I'd be a fool to say there wasn't! But I put it down to a sort of mass hysteria.' Tewson leant back against the bridge rail and looked sideways at Keller. 'Look, nothing catastrophic has happened in this town for years – probably centuries – and then one night, bingo, the biggest air disaster ever to hit Britain happens right on their doorstep. It's bound to have a strange effect on them. I mean, they're just not geared up to cope with a disaster of this magnitude. It's brought all their hidden neuroses, all their pent-up emotions, to a head! It's like a chain reaction; and the crash started it off.'

Keller took his eyes from the water and regarded the investigator coolly. He smiled thinly. 'You're terrific,' he said.

'Oh, come on, Dave! What's the alternative? The field's haunted? Is that what you believe?'

'I don't know what I believe any more, Harry.' He began walking again.

Tewson slapped his raised hand down at his side with dismay and followed the co-pilot.

They reached the hotel and, as they passed through the lobby, Tewson ordered a large brandy to be sent up to the AIB rooms, then changed his mind and made it two. They entered the lift and rode up to the fourth floor, the investigator still trying to convince Keller that all the events were unrelated except for the general hysteria that hung over the town.

Keller stopped him by asking if he knew for sure that all the people involved were from the town of Eton. They stepped out of the lift in silence and walked down the corridor until they reached the spacious double room which the AIB had taken over as an on-the-spot operational headquarters. Here, all the information could be assimilated and sent back to their normal London offices. Gerald Slater looked up from his makeshift desk as the two men entered the room. He raised his eyebrows when he recognized Keller as the young co-pilot who had survived the crash. The other two investigating officers who were also working in the room exchanged surprised glances.

Tewson smiled at Slater uncertainly. 'Er, sorry to disturb you, Chief,' he said, 'but there's been rather a nasty accident down in Eton and Keller here was a witness. I thought, er, he could clean himself up a bit, and perhaps get a chance to recover from the shock. That all right with you?'

'Of course it is,' Slater told him gruffly, then added to Keller, more kindly: 'Please go next door, Mr Keller. There's an adjoining bathroom and a bed if you feel you want to lie down for a while. If not, rest up in one of the armchairs in there. You probably need a good stiff drink – or some tea if that's your preference. I'll ring down for some.'

'Oh, not to worry, Chief. I've already fixed that.' Tewson smiled bleakly at his superior who merely frowned back.

'If you should need anything else, Mr Keller, please let me know,' he said to the co-pilot.

Keller nodded gratefully and walked through into the next room. As Tewson was about to follow, Slater held up a restraining hand and said quietly so that the co-pilot could not hear: 'I know Keller is a personal friend of yours, Tewson, but I think it would be as well if you kept away from him until the investigation is complete.'

Tewson paused at the doorway. 'Right,' he said, and disappeared into the room, closing the door behind him.

He heard running water coming from the bathroom and

found Keller inside washing blood from his hands. He waited patiently while the co-pilot scrubbed vigorously with a nail-brush even after his hands appeared to be perfectly clean.

'Dave,' Tewson said, 'you know I shouldn't really be associating with you while the inquiry is still going on.'

Keller returned the nailbrush to the small glass shelf above the sink. He reached for some toilet tissues, dampened them, and began to rub away at the blood on his shoe.

'I don't want to get you into trouble, Harry,' he said, 'but I can't just sit around doing nothing. I was involved in the crash: I want to be involved in the investigation.'

'You are involved . . .'

'Only as a victim! I want to help find out what caused the crash.'

'But you can't. You can't even remember what happened that night.'

Keller had no answer. He dabbed away with more tissues at his bloodstained trousers. Just as Tewson was about to say more, there was a polite tapping on the door that led into the hallway. Tewson opened it and was confronted by a waiter bearing two large brandies on a tray. He signed for them and took them from the waiter who didn't wait for a tip. These Air Ministry people were tight bastards. Tewson placed the drinks on a small coffee table and as he settled into an easy chair he called for Keller to join him. The co-pilot came out of the bathroom, his jacket draped over his arm. He sat opposite the investigating officer and reached for the brandy. In two swallows it was gone.

Tewson sipped at his more leisurely. 'Would you like some lunch, Dave?' he asked. 'We could use the restaurant here. I've just remembered I was halfway through lunch down at Eton when that couple fell from the window.' He wondered briefly what had happened to the journalist with whom he'd been lunching. Perhaps it was just as well they'd been interrupted for the reporter's probing questions had been difficult to evade and he had a guilty feeling of having said a bit too much. 'No? Well, I guess I'm not so hungry myself now.'

Keller drew out the folded passenger list from his inside jacket pocket and handed it to Tewson. 'Do you think your bomb theory could have anything to do with anybody on this list?' he asked.

Tewson pushed his glasses more firmly on to the bridge of his nose and quickly scanned through the long list of names. After a few concentrated minutes he slowly shook his head. 'No, I don't think so,' he said. 'There's a few names I recognize, no political figures, though. There's Sir James Barrett, one of the directors of your own airline; Susie Colbert, the novelist – her young daughter was travelling with her; Philippe Laforgue, the pianist. Then there's a couple of oil men – both American – Howard Reed and Eugene Moyniham, who you've probably heard of. Let's see, er . . . yes, Ivor Russell, the photographer, and his girlfriend; a small party of Japanese businessmen on a world tour, drumming up business for their country; a couple more names that are familiar but I wouldn't have said important; and, oh yes – Leonard Goswell.' He tapped thoughtfully at the name with his finger. 'Now that's interesting,' he said.

'Who's – who *was* – Goswell?'

'Well, he was a man who had plenty of enemies. Yes, there might be something there, you know.' He sipped at the brandy, ignoring Keller's impatience. 'Of course, the bomb idea hasn't been proved yet, but when it is, this bloke's a likely candidate for it.'

'Why, Harry?'

'Goswell? You must have heard of him, Dave. He was one of Sir Oswald Mosley's henchmen during the last World War.

You remember the stories of Mosley and his Blackshirts during the War, don't you? He was branded a traitor here because he preached Nazism to the masses; had a lot of supporters, too, until they broke up his nasty gang of thugs and threw him into prison. He agreed with Hitler and wanted to welcome him into the country with open arms. It's said his greatest delight would have been to help the Nazis put away all the Jews in this country. Well, Goswell was even more evil: he actually began to do the job!'

It struck a chord in Keller's memory. Yes, he had heard of Goswell, but not for many, many years. He'd assumed the English ex-Nazi had died in exile long ago.

Tewson continued: 'Mysterious fires spread in and around London's East End – fires that had nothing to do with the bombings that were going on at the time – and whole families of Jews were wiped out at a stroke. Even Mosley got scared at that and threw Goswell out of the Party; then Goswell formed his own, but their activities were so outrageous, so brutal, he was slung out of the country. They had no proof, of course, otherwise they'd have hung him.'

'Didn't he come back years ago and stir up trouble over coloured immigrants?'

'That's right. And from what I hear, he was involved in worse things than that. But for the last ten or fifteen years he's been fairly quiet; people have forgotten about him. I thought he'd retired from troublemaking, but I wonder what he was doing back here? And why was he flying off to the States? Anyway, as I said, he seems to be the most likely candidate for assassination.'

'Have you any idea how a bomb could have been smuggled on board?'

Tewson's shoulders slumped visibly. 'That's the problem. That's where my theory falls down. Security is so stringent nowadays; it's difficult enough for a gun to be taken on board, let alone a bomb. Wires, timers, explosives – it's practically impossible.'

'But it happens, doesn't it? Bombs are still found planted on aircraft.'

'Yes, but as you say – *found*. There hasn't been a case of a bomb explosion on an aeroplane for some time.'

'What if it were amongst luggage?'

'Luggage on Consul flights is checked, X-rayed; you know that.'

'It could have been stowed away in the holds before that.'

'Both front and rear holds are searched beforehand.'

'Could a passenger have carried it on board?'

'Everyone is frisked, hand baggage, too. Any wiring on the body would show up on the metal detector.'

'Then your idea must be wrong!'

'Christ, you're beginning to sound like Slater! All I know – and sheer bloody gut-feel tells me – is that everything points towards an explosion and not a malfunction. *There must have been a bomb on board!*'

Both men stared glumly down at the floor. Keller because the theory he'd hoped to be proved correct was not plausible any more and Tewson because he could not resolve the weakest point in his own notion.

Finally, Keller asked: 'Any other names you recognize?'

'No, I'm afraid not. There were other first-class passengers, of course, but nobody of any real significance. As for the second class – well, they were mostly tourists and business-men.' He glanced sharply up at Keller. 'Dave, you don't still think that somehow you're responsible?'

'I don't know, Harry. If only I could remember.'

'But even if my theory is proved wrong, there are hundreds of things that could have caused the crash.'

'Like pilot error.'

'Rogan was one of the best flyers around. He never made mistakes.'

'What if he wasn't his normal self? What if his concentration had gone? What if, after all those years, something had happened that had caused him to crack?'

'You were his back-up man. That's the whole point of having a co-pilot. If the captain is taken ill, or is unable to function for any reason, the co-pilot takes over.'

'And what if the pilot and the co-pilot are not working in unison? What if they've had a dispute and it erupts again during the flight?'

'You were both much too professional for that sort of thing.'

'Were we?'

Tewson stared at Keller. 'Don't tell me any more, Dave. Let's wait until my theory – and others – have been disproved before we go into pilot error.'

The co-pilot stood up. He needed to think. What was it Hobbs had said? *The spirits might be bound to this earth to fulfil a desire for revenge.* It was something like that. Was Captain Rogan seeking revenge? Were the other victims? It was impossible. Ridiculous. The beliefs, or more accurately, the non-beliefs, of a lifetime were being shattered so easily. How could he bring himself to believe in ghosts? Was it out of sheer desperation for an answer, for relief from his guilt? Or had the crash shaken the very foundation of reason within him? After all, even the papers had voiced his own feeling: it was a miracle that he had survived.

He reached for his jacket lying over the arm of the chair and slipped it on. Tewson watched him with surprise as he walked to the door. The co-pilot heard the investigator call out to him but he didn't reply. He closed the door and walked towards the lift. Maybe *he* could help find the answer. Maybe *he* would find the answer from Captain Rogan himself. He had to return to his apartment and find that crumpled piece of paper. He needed to know Hobbs's address.

10

Colin Thatcher, like most fat boys, hated school. When your body is round and your limbs merely shapeless extensions of flesh, life in a boys' school can be a torment. If he'd had the brains or the wit to distract attention from his obesity perhaps life wouldn't have been so bad. But he hadn't; he wasn't clever and he wasn't funny. In fact, it was hard even for *him* to think of some saving quality he might have. He wasn't tough and he wasn't brave; he wasn't generous and he wasn't affable. He *was* lonely.

And, also like most fat boys, he detested games. PT, cricket, football, rowing, rugby, badminton, basketball, swimming – exercise of any sort – he loathed. Which was why he was walking away from the College playing fields instead of towards them. Which was why that cold, November afternoon would be his last.

He made his way across Colenorton Brook, hands thrust deep into the pockets of his striped dark trousers, and left the path for the wide, open fields that lay to the right. He often did this when it was time for sports and he knew, as usual, he would be missed and have to face disciplinary action from the captain of the house. How he hated the system at Eton College whereby punishment was meted out by other, more senior boys. Apart from the captain of the house, there were five other seniors who collaborated with the house master, spying and prying into the activities of the younger pupils. The Library, as they were known, had caught him dodging games four times this term and he knew if he were caught or missed this time, he could expect a call from a Praeposter summoning him to the headmaster or lower master to answer for his offences in the 'Bill', the daily court of justice.

But Thatcher didn't care very much. He despised their silly systems, their Collegers and Oppidans, their Praeposters, their Eton society known as 'Pop', their drab black tail-coated uniform, their stupid traditional Field Game and Wall Game, racquets, fencing, boxing, squash, athletics and beagling. He resented their societies – music, drawing, mechanics, essay, archaeological, aeronautical, railway and many others just as silly – resented them because he had neither the interest nor inclination to join them. His disinterest lay not in the subjects themselves, but in the unpleasantness of mingling with the other boys. If there had been an eating society, he probably would not have joined. He felt safer, more secure, during lessons when the others had no chance to taunt him, to torment him because of his physique, and he actually dreaded the sound of the bell for break, for it signified victimization time.

Apart from the physical exertion, he hated games more than anything else because he was forced to reveal his grossness to the other boys in all its nakedness. They would poke him, laughing as their fingers disappeared into mounds of flesh. They would tweak his breasts painfully for they hung down like a woman's (some of the boys touched him with a more serious intent than mere mischievousness). The showers were a special torture chamber of their own.

He kicked at an ant hill and watched the ants swarm out in terror. He squatted and contemplated their panic-stricken scurrying over the exposed earth, then he stood up and aimed his shoe at the undulating mass. He kicked at them several more times before resuming his brooding journey. He didn't care if he was expelled: he *wanted* to be expelled. Father would be thunderous – he was afraid of *that* – but Mother would forgive him. He knew she missed him for she had never wanted him to be sent away to school anyway. No, it had been Father who had insisted. Get some discipline into the boy, he had said, some backbone. Too much molly-coddling, that's his trouble. Needs to be among other boys of his own age. Needs some tradition behind him. Well, at fourteen he'd had all the tradition he could take. Tradition, as far as he could see, was that fat boys were to be regarded as freaks, to be chastised, tormented and scorned by the mob. He had to blink as his eyes filmed over with self-pity.

Lying down on the grass, not caring about its cold damp-ness, he looked up at the grey sky, his stomach rising like a distant hillock before him. 'I don't care if I'm sent home,' he said aloud. 'Sod them all!' He pushed his hands deeper into his trouser pockets and lay there, flat on his back, ankles crossed, mind drifting from thought to thought.

He suddenly shivered at the cold. He had a whole after-noon to kill. Perhaps he would sneak off to the cinema in Windsor. Call in at the bank in the High Street first, draw out a couple of quid, buy some tuck, then sneak off to the flicks. Trouble was, it was so difficult to sneak off anywhere in this godawful conspicuous uniform. Still, he would catch a chill if he hung around here too long, so the cinema it would have to be.

He wasn't sure if he'd heard or imagined the weeping at first, for it seemed to originate from inside his own head. He lay there for a few moments, eyes still staring blankly at the sky, then he raised himself on one elbow and looked around. He could see nothing but grass, trees and the distant railway embankment. The sound came again just as he was about to dismiss it as a figment of his own imagination; tiny, childlike sobs coming from somewhere behind him. He swung over on to his stomach so that he was facing in the direction of the noise and he saw the small figure about a hundred yards away.

She wore a pale blue dress and clutched something tightly in her arms. Her long, blonde hair hung loosely about her shoulders and partially covered her face which was bowed towards her chest. The girl's small frame shook gently with each quiet sob.

The boy raised himself to his knees and called out to her. 'What's the matter? Are you lost?'

The girl's weeping stopped momentarily, as she looked up at him, but then she buried her face in her hands again and continued.

He couldn't tell how old she was from this distance, but she appeared to be somewhere between five and ten. Colin stood up and began to walk towards her: stopping midway to ask again: 'What's wrong?' He saw now that the object she was clutching was a doll; he could see its tiny pink legs protruding from beneath the girl's arms.

This time she did not look up but her sobs became more anguished. He approached her slowly, not wanting to frighten or upset her any more, and stopped again when he was only two yards from her. The boy felt embarrassed: he didn't know how to handle girls, especially ones of this age.

'Can't you tell me what's wrong?' he asked awkwardly.

The girl looked up and he saw that she could only have been seven or eight. Her weeping stopped briefly but she sniffed as she regarded him with large, brown eyes, clutching the doll more tightly than ever to her chest.

'What's up?' he asked again. 'Have you lost your mother – your mummy?'

She did not reply at first, then she slowly nodded her head and said in a barely audible voice: 'Mummy.'

Silly little thing, he thought to himself, wandering off on her own like this. Goodness, she must be freezing in just that thin dress. He looked around in the hope that he would find an anxious mother approaching, but the field was deserted except for the girl and himself.

'Where – where did you lose your mummy?' he asked desperately, and when she continued to cry he moved in closer. 'Hello, what's your dolly's name?' he asked, feeling foolish as he waggled the doll's exposed foot with his fingers.

She pulled it tighter in to her, but the boy thought he saw a blemish on its plastic cheek.

'Have you hurt dolly's head? Let me have a look.'

She suddenly backed away from him, taking the doll out of his reach. 'I want Mummy,' she finally blurted out and began to cry more loudly.

'All right, all right,' he said nervously, 'we'll find her. Now, where did you see her last?'

The girl looked around her, undecided at first. Then she pointed a trembling finger in the direction of the Eton Wick main road. His eyes followed her outstretched hand. 'Come on, then, you take me to the spot where you saw her last.'

She hesitated and he thought he saw the barest flicker of a smile on her sad little face. Then, with a skip, she set off in the direction in which she had been pointing. He followed at a more leisurely pace. The child scooted ahead of him, occasionally stopping to look back, as if making sure he was still following her. She would wait until he had almost reached her then bound off again ahead of him. They reached a small path and he began to puff at the exertion of keeping up with her skipping figure. The girl disappeared through a narrow gateway and he followed without realizing where it led. He halted abruptly when he saw the gravestones.

The cemetery. The girl must have been visiting it with her mother when she'd wandered off. She must have a dead relative – her father, perhaps? – buried here. Now where's she got to? There doesn't seem to be anyone else around; her mother's probably gone off looking for her. Then he saw a flash of pale blue and he caught sight of her dashing between old, grey headstones. She stopped and looked back at him, standing perfectly still as though waiting for him to move. When he didn't, she raised an arm in a beckoning motion. With a resigned sigh, he walked up the gravelly path between the graves towards her.

'Wait a minute,' he called out, 'I don't think your mother's here!' But she ran on again.

He saw the vast, freshly dug area and wondered at it. There appeared to be over a couple of hundred mounds of dark earth, obviously outlining fairly new graves, and then he realized what they signified. This was the mass grave for the victims of the air crash! Ugh, how horrible, he thought. The poor little thing must have lost someone in the disaster. He noticed the clear centre area where the large tombstone bearing all the names of the dead would be eventually placed. The boys in his house had frightened each other with their macabre stories of how all the bodies were mixed up and nobody could be sure that the right limbs and heads were buried with the right torsos. He shuddered violently and felt goose pimples rise on his flesh.

He was about to call out to her, wanting to get away from there, back on to the road, away from the quietness, when he caught sight of her again. She stood in the middle of the

mounds of churned earth – a tiny, remote little figure, clinging to her doll and looking down at one particular grave. It
seemed somehow disrespectful to shout out in a cemetery, as
if the sounds of his voice would disturb the peaceful rest of
the dead, so he made his way carefully through the soft
mounds to reach her.

She had her back to him as he approached and she didn't
seem to hear him coming. He saw that she stood between
two graves that were slightly separated from the rest; one
was normal size, the other was smaller, much smaller. About
the size of a child's.

Still she kept her back to him and he wondered if she
were weeping again for a greater loss, not just the temporary
parting from her mother. Then a thought struck him: could
this be the grave of her mother? Had her mother been one of
the victims of the air crash? His heart reached out to her. He
understood loneliness.

Slowly, he stretched out a hand to touch the child's
shoulder, feeling compassion for the first time in his young
life. For some reason, he stopped with his arm half raised.
His fingers felt as if they had touched something cold, as if
they had suddenly dipped into an icy substance. He withdrew
his fingers in shock but strangely he drew the coldness back
with them as though pulling on an invisible thread, drawing a
more overwhelming mass of coldness to him. It seemed to
envelop him, touching his face first then drifting round and
down on to his shoulders, holding him close in its cold grip,
slowly wrapping itself around his obese body.

A movement on the ground drew his eyes away from the
girl's bowed head. He looked down past her and suddenly felt
the iciness around him clamp down and hold him paralys-
ingly. His eyes widened in horror.

The earth at the little girl's feet was beginning to move as though – *as though someone underneath was pushing it upwards*. Tiny rivulets of soil broke away and ran down the sides of the thrusting earth. He knew that something would break through at any moment but he couldn't move! His own flesh weighted him down.

The doll the girl had been holding suddenly dropped to the ground and the movement distracted his eyes from the rising soil. A low, wailing moan escaped from his lips as he saw the doll's face. Half of it was buckled and scarred, blackened, melted as if it had been exposed to extreme heat. And its eyes were alive! They stared into his, dark and searching. Its lips seemed to be smiling.

He stumbled back and fell heavily, his fatness saving him from any real harm, the action breaking the icy grip he had been held in. The earth was still rising and he saw something white emerging, as though a worm were surfacing, to be joined by another, then another! He suddenly understood that he was watching a hand breaking through the earth. The girl moved and obscured his vision, then slowly turned towards him. Her hair hung down over her face. She began to lift her head, and he heard the low, growling chuckle that came from her – a sound that didn't belong to a child. An old man's chuckle, rough, obscene.

She faced him but he couldn't look. He didn't want to see her face because he knew, instinct told him, he could never stand the horror of it. He began to crawl away, slowly at first, whimpering and keeping his eyes on the stony, gravel path. The further he moved away, the more he seemed to gather strength. He was on his knees now, still moving, a ridiculous figure of stunted fatness, but moving, moving away. He half glanced back and fresh fear quickened his pace. He thought he had seen a figure standing behind the girl; a figure that had risen from the ground at her feet.

He screamed and gained his feet but staggered forward, betrayed by his own weight again. He grazed his knees painfully against the sharp gravel but the hurt meant little to him. As he sprawled there gasping for air, he became aware of more movement all around him. The earth over other graves was being disturbed.

He lurched forward, this time successfully gaining his feet, and he began to run. But his movements seemed slow, as though he were wading through water, as though some power was holding him back. He struggled against it, and only sheer terror helped him to defeat the feeling of helplessness. He staggered between the other gravestones towards the narrow gateway. He reached it and in his panic turned and ran in the direction from which he'd come, towards the fields. He felt stronger now and his heavy legs pounded against the path and then against the softer grass of the fields. He collapsed in a heap and lay there panting, gasping huge lungfuls of air into his body, thinking for one brief moment he had escaped, but then he heard the whispers – the whispers that seemed to come from inside his own head. He looked back over his shoulder and he saw the tiny figure standing there alone on the edge of the field. He scrambled to his feet and started to run again and he heard the laughter, the low chuckling sound that could only be right behind him.

He screamed again, a high-pitched, almost girlish scream.

The field sloped upwards and he grasped at tufts of grass to pull himself forward. He slid back down once but his scrambling legs found a hold before he reached the bottom. His body soaked with perspiration, the front of his trousers stained with something worse, he reached the top of the incline and rolled over on to it.

He crawled over the gleaming silver tracks making for the other side, something inside telling him if he could reach it, he would find safety. But as he reached the edge and looked down, he saw the tiny figure standing there, her head upturned towards him, waiting. Her dress was no longer pale blue; it hung in scorched tatters around her body and her white ankle socks were now blackened and torn. She wore no shoes.

He screamed in a greater anguish when he saw that she had no face, that what should have been a mouth, nose and eyes was just a burnt, open wound.

He tripped on the gleaming silver track and fell back awkwardly, striking his head against the parallel rail and for a moment everything went black. He was dimly aware of the vibration running through the rails as he lay there powerless to move, and his senses tried to tell him that the rumbling noise that grew louder and louder was the sound of approaching death. But a small part of him *was* aware, and accepted it almost gratefully. What was so wonderful about living anyway?

The train driver saw the figure slumped across the tracks too late. He reacted fast but by the time he'd cut off his power and applied his brakes, the train had already passed over the boy's plump body.

11

It was a small, terraced house, inconspicuous from the others it stood amongst in the long, narrow street. The brown paint on the door was cracked and peeling, revealing speckles of dark green, the colour it had been many years before. Keller pressed the doorbell impatiently, the third time he had done so, then rattled the letterbox for extra, summoning noise. He was about to give up, deciding that Hobbs must be out, the house empty, when he heard faint noises from inside. A door closed and shuffling footsteps approached along the corridor. A muffled voice asked: 'Who is it?'

'Keller,' he replied, leaning closer to the door.

There was a brief pause and then he heard the door being unlocked from the inside. It opened a few inches and he saw those pale grey eyes observing him through the crack. The door swung wide and Hobbs stood in the opening, his face expressionless.

'I knew you'd come sooner or later,' he said. He stood aside and gestured for the co-pilot to enter. Hobbs closed the door behind them and the hallway was in semi-darkness. 'In here,' he said, opening a door to their left.

Keller entered the room and found the slightly musty smell unpleasant, reminiscent of age and loneliness. It was obviously a room unused to lightness. Hobbs pushed past him and parted the heavy curtains, the lace behind them still diffusing the sudden sunlight.

The medium told him to wait and disappeared through the door, returning seconds later with a half-emptied bottle of gin and two glasses.

'You'll join me?' he asked, pouring a large measure into one of the glasses.

Keller shook his head curtly. 'No thanks.'

'I have whisky, if you'd prefer.'

Keller shook his head again.

Hobbs shrugged his shoulders and took a hurried gulp from his glass. It was obvious to the co-pilot it hadn't been his first that day.

'Sit down, please, Mr Keller.'

Keller sank into the faded, but comfortable, armchair which occupied a corner of the room and the medium pulled out a chair from the round, heavily draped table that stood in the centre. He placed it so he was facing Keller.

'So you believe me now,' he said. 'What's happened to change your mind?'

'I'm not sure it has been changed.'

Hobbs was silent, waiting for the co-pilot to continue.

'It's – it's the town itself,' Keller said uncertainly. 'Strange things are beginning to happen in Eton. It's that more than anything else.'

'Strange things?'

'Three people have died there today and another two, it seems, have been frightened into incoherence.'

Hobbs finished his gin, his grey, penetrating eyes never leaving Keller's. 'Are these . . . incidents . . . connected in any way?'

'Well, they all happened around the area of the air crash. It seems too much of a coincidence for them all to happen within hours of one and other, and all fairly close by.'

'How did these three people die?'

'One had a heart attack down by the river; the other two fell from a window.'

'And there's something else, Mr Keller? Something more specifically to do with you?'

'It's just a feeling.'

'Yes?'

'It's too vague – I don't know what it is. Unease? Maybe guilt.'

'Why guilt?'

Keller took a deep breath and let it out slowly. 'You know Captain Rogan and I had an argument before the flight; it may have carried on after we'd taken off. It could have affected his or my judgement.'

'I see. The argument *was* over his wife, wasn't it?'

'Yes.'

A pause. 'And you can't remember if it broke out again on the plane?'

Keller shook his head. 'I keep getting fragments, but the minute I concentrate on them and try to remember, they just fade.'

'It could be your own subconscious protecting you from the blame.'

'I realize that. But I'd rather know for sure than go on like this.'

'You think I can help you?'

'You said you heard voices. You heard Captain Rogan's.'

'Then you do believe me.'

'I don't know! So much has happened, I'm not sure of anything any more! If you really did hear the skipper's voice, maybe you can try again. You can ask *him*.'

Hobbs smiled without humour. 'It's strange how much easier it is to believe when you need help. Like the dying agnostic who suddenly finds faith in God.'

'I didn't say I believed. You came to me, remember?'

'I'm sorry, Mr Keller, that was wrong of me. I can understand that you must be feeling quite desperate to resort to this. We're used to the cynical in this field, and sometimes we weary of it; but that's no excuse for my behaviour.'

'I don't blame you. I was pretty rude to you last night.'

'You're under a great deal of stress. More, I think, than you really know.'

Keller wondered at the words, but found no clue in Hobbs's expression.

'Can you help me?' he asked delicately.

'I'm not sure. I'm not sure that I want to.'

Keller looked at him in surprise. 'But last night . . .'

'Last night I was thinking of *them*. I've had a chance to reflect since I saw you. You might not like the answers we may find.'

'I'm prepared to risk that!'

'There are other factors, also.'

Keller's puzzled look asked the question.

'I told you last night,' Hobbs said, 'that I'd given up this sort of work; that certain forces were becoming too powerful. Let me try to explain what happens to me sometimes when I go into a trance. My spiritual body leaves the physical and I talk to entities on the other side that are in some way connected with the sitter. Meanwhile, other, often unknown, spirits may speak through my body. This began to happen to me more and more frequently, and eventually, certain spirits not only spoke through me, but began to control my body. It left me too susceptible to evil influences. I've resisted the spirits of the air crash victims because of this.'

'You said before you felt there was something strange about the voices.'

'Yes, something wicked is beginning to dominate them.

That's why I'm reluctant to give in to them, to allow myself to go into a state of trance. I may not have any choice though; my resistance is being broken down.'

'I don't understand.'

Hobbs's hands were trembling slightly now and he turned his attention towards the bottle of gin. He reached for it then changed his mind. He looked directly at Keller.

'There are two kinds of medium: mental and physical. The physical medium produces manifestations: moving objects, ectoplasmic materializations, sounds – that sort of thing. I am a mental medium: I see and hear physically. When I am clairaudient, I just hear the voices and sometimes the sitter hears them with me; when I am clairvoyant, I see the spirit forms. That is when I'm more vulnerable to trances. I'm subdued, I feel a blockage at the top of my spine, and everything goes hazy. I lose the control of my own body. I'm – I'm a little afraid of it happening with these spirits.' He reached for the gin bottle and this time he poured himself a drink.

'Will they ever leave you in peace if you don't help me?' Keller's question momentarily stopped the glass from reaching Hobbs's lips. He studied Keller for a few moments before he swallowed the contents.

'Possibly not, Mr Keller. That is my other fear,' he said finally.

'Then let's try, for God's sake.'

'You don't know what you're asking.'

'I know time is running out! Don't ask me how I know – call it instinct if you like – but I've got to find the answer soon!'

Hobbs's body seemed to straighten. Indecision visibly left him.

'Come and sit opposite me,' he said.

Keller quickly pulled out another chair from the table and sat facing the medium, a nervous tingle running through his body.

'What do I do?' he asked.

'You do nothing,' said Hobbs, putting the gin bottle and glass to one side, 'except clear your mind completely then begin to think of the people you knew on the flight. Think of Captain Rogan.'

The senior pilot's image flooded immediately into Keller's head: Rogan at the seat of the aircraft's controls, his face contorted in – was it fear or anger? The mental picture was vivid but the exact mood indefinable.

'Just concentrate, Mr Keller, and keep silent for the moment. You may or may not hear his voice. I will tell you when you can ask questions, but you must do so through me. I'll try to keep this on a fairly low level to prevent the others from coming through. Please help me by remaining calm whatever happens.'

Hobbs closed his eyes and began breathing evenly through his nose. Almost at once, his breathing became deeper. 'They're strong,' he said anxiously, 'they're so strong. They've been waiting. I can see so many of them . . . pulling me down . . . it's happening so fast . . .'

Keller was astonished and a little scared of the rapidity of it all. He had always imagined it was a gradual process, the medium purposely building up the drama of the situation for the sake of his sitters. It was all wrong somehow: the commonplace suburban house, the dull but conventional lounge, the unimpressive little man himself. He had expected something more theatrical. But it was the very ordinariness that made it so much more credible.

'Concentrate, please, Mr Keller! Think only of Captain Rogan. Form a picture of him in your mind.' Hobbs's voice sounded strained and lines of tension had formed on his face. 'So many ... so many ...' His hands that had been resting on his lap suddenly appeared on the table, fingers outstretched and quivering, indicative of the mental anguish he was going through. 'Rogan ... only Rogan ...' He spoke the words as though he were asserting his will on others.

Suddenly, his body relaxed and he leant forward slightly. 'I ... have ... him ... Mr Keller ... I ... have ...' His body grew stiff again and the tension returned to his features. 'No ... it's Rogan ... I seek ... only Rogan ...'

Keller stared at the distressed medium anxiously. The man was going through mental torment. He remembered to fix his concentration on the deceased senior pilot again and did his best to hold the image there in his mind.

Hobbs's breathing became even deeper and more urgent. He arched his body backwards and raised his face towards the ceiling. Suddenly, his head snapped forward, his chin almost resting on his chest. His body slumped in the chair.

His eyes slowly opened and looked up at Keller.

Keller felt a cold sensation on the back of his neck, icy fingers brushing his spine. It wasn't Hobbs sitting there any longer; his whole personality had changed. It was something loathsome there. Something abhorrent.

The room itself seemed darker – the shadows had deepened – and it had grown so much colder.

'Kell ... er ...' Its voice was low, raspy, just a whisper. He stared in horror at the figure that was Hobbs and yet, not Hobbs. The eyes bored back into his and the wet lips took on a sneer. 'Kill ... him ... Keller ... he ... did ... this.'

The co-pilot could not speak. His mouth was dry and his throat almost painfully constricted. Kill who?

Wetness seeped from Hobbs's mouth and began to run down his chin. 'Kill ... Keller ... you ... Dave ... Dave ...

don't . . .' The voice had changed to a different voice. Hobbs's eyes had closed again but the agony continued to show in his face. 'Dave, the crash . . . was . . .' Keller recognized the voice. Rogan. He leant across the table, his heart pounding. 'Don't . . . blame . . . away !' The voice changed again, became a snarl. 'Leave the cunt to us!'

Hobbs's eyes snapped open and glared at Keller malevolently. The words had become sharp and forceful, no longer hesitant.

'Keller, Keller, Keller! You're ours, you bastard, ours!' It was low, almost whispered, filled with malice. 'He killed us, Keller, you will kill him!'

The co-pilot found it difficult to breathe. It was as though cold hands were clasped around his throat, squeezing slowly. The air seemed stale, then fetid with the smell of excrement. He pulled at the invisible hands and inexplicably it helped.

'Kill who?' he managed to gasp. 'Who is this speaking?'

The thing opposite laughed. Coarse, obscene laughter. It grinned evilly at Keller. 'He. Must. Die! You think *you've* escaped, bastard? You think *you're* free? Think again! Go to him, and *you* come to us! Escape from death? No escape – for him! None for you!'

The stench made Keller retch. The invisible hands had moved to his wrists now and held them firmly against the tabletop.

'Dave!' The voice was Rogan's now. The grip on his wrists slackened and he wrenched them from the table. 'Help . . . us . . . Dave . . . help . . . us!' 'The bastard can't help!' The other voice. 'He can kill though.' Laughter. 'You will, won't you, Keller?' It took on a whining, simpering tone. But it was false. 'Answer, cunt! You answer! No peace for you, Keller, ever. Die with us. Why don't you? Why don't you? We won't let you live!'

Suddenly, the voices were not just coming from the medium: they came from different corners of the room, while Hobbs just sat there grinning. Whispers, only whispers; but pleading. Afraid. Hobbs laughed aloud.

'Listen to them, Keller. I rule. I have the power.' The figure spat out the words viciously.

'Who are you? Where is Rogan?' Keller leant forward across the table, anger mixed with fear.

'Rogan is with us, Keller. As you should be. Join us, Keller.'

'Who are you?' the co-pilot asked again, his words determined.

'The one they said hated. Don't you know?' Hobbs sniggered.

'Who?' Keller repeated.

'Keller, he killed me.' The co-pilot turned his head sharply. The voice had come from behind him. 'It was in the case. Remember? He . . . put . . .' The voice began to fade. 'It . . .'

'Find him, Dave.'

'Find him!'

'You must.'

'Help us!'

The whispers came from the walls, confused and overlapping, despairing. And all the while, the thing in Hobbs laughed.

'You see, Keller, they want to be free. You see how afraid they are? Afraid of me. You know me, don't you? Don't you?'

A hand suddenly snaked forward and grabbed the gin bottle at its base. He held it up then brought it crashing down, its neck breaking off against the side of the table. Keller watched in fearful fascination as Hobbs slowly raised the broken bottle to his lips, and he shouted 'No!' as the medium jammed the jagged glass against his own mouth and began to drink. Blood mixed with gin ran down his chin.

Then, with a scream, Hobbs was on his feet, his mouth a bloody mess, his eyes wide and terrifying. His shoulders heaving, he glared down at Keller, a gurgling, growling noise coming from his throat. His words were unintelligible, but as he moved around the table, advancing on the co-pilot, holding the jagged glass before him like a weapon, his intentions became clear.

For a moment, Keller sat rooted to the spot, a desert mouse waiting in paralytic fear for the snake to strike; but then he moved fast. As he jumped up and away from the approaching figure, he pulled the table up with him and pushed it violently towards the medium. Hobbs stumbled against it then sent it crashing to one side, an animal snarl of rage breaking down his disfigured lips. He lunged forward.

Keller picked up the chair and held it between them, using it as a shield. It was wrenched from his grasp with a force that wasn't human and thrown across the room to be shattered against the wall. The whispers seemed louder, filling his head, confusing him, forcing him to stay where he was. He stumbled and fell heavily, bruising his knees, but managing to take some of the force with his hands. He tried to pull himself away from the being that was no longer Hobbs, but the man was over him now. He felt his hair being pulled and his head was dragged backwards, forcing him to look into the inverted face of evil. His neck was arched and exposed. The bottle, now held upside down like a grotesque dagger, was poised above him, its contents spilling on to his upturned face. The voices inside his head were laughing.

He screamed as the broken glass began its descent, but it never reached his throat. It stopped midway and hung there, the hand that grasped it shaking, the fingers around it white with strain. Suddenly, the glass shattered completely, shards falling into Keller's vulnerable face, Hobbs's hand becoming a red, mutilated, clenched fist. He heard the scream of pain and his head sprung forward as he was released. Hobbs's figure dropped to its knees beside him, the little man holding his injured hand at the wrist, tears of pain running down his face and mingling with the blood around his mouth.

Keller lay on his side, shock preventing him from moving further.

'Keller!' The words were distorted, but the voice belonged to Hobbs. 'What's happened to me? My face! My hand!'

The co-pilot realized whatever had been inside the medium had gone now – gone back to the hell it had come from. The voices, too, were drifting away, sinking piteously into oblivion. And just as his own senses began to reel, as soft, wispy patterns began to float across his vision, he heard another voice. And as he sank and the patterns formed themselves into dark clouds that joined and swallowed up the light, he recognized the voice.

It belonged to Cathy.

<u>12</u>

Tewson peered closer at the thin score in the soil. He traced his fingers along the winter-hardened groove until they reached a point where the scarred earth became a tiny trench and finally disappeared under the surface. There were many such marks all around the field, some deep as though furrowed by a plough, others, like this, small and seemingly insignificant. But often even the tiniest track held a vital clue at its extremity: fragments of wreckage flung wide and forcefully on the aircraft's impact with the ground.

He pushed a finger into the thimble-sized hole and felt something solid embedded there. Digging at the hardened surface, he cleared an area around the object and sighed dejectedly on finding the cause of the scar. He had been hoping for some mechanical element – anything that could be part of an explosive device. Instead he found a ring, its cluster of diamonds caked with mud. He placed it in a brown envelope where it clinked against several other small but valuable objects he had found that morning; lost possessions of the dead. Even after this time, the investigators were still finding such trinkets, although Tewson knew many of the valuables not destroyed in the crash but scattered around the proximate area would never be recovered. Anything that was found was returned to Consul Airlines and checked against a valuables' list made up as accurately as possible with claims from the dead victims' next of kin or associates.

Tewson looked up sharply as he heard his name being hailed from across the field. One of his colleagues was striding towards him waving an arm in a 'come here' gesture. He got to his feet and trudged over the frosted ruts of earth, his eyes still searching for any glint of metal, any concealed clue that might help affirm his suspicions.

'What's up?' he called out, as he drew near to his duffle-coated colleague.

'What's up? Have you seen today's *Express*?' came the breathless reply. 'Slater's just sent me down from the hotel. He wants to see you.'

'Oh Christ! What have I done to upset him now?'

'You'll find out soon enough, mate. If I were you I'd get up there sharpish.'

'Well, what's in the paper then?' asked Tewson, a nagging suspicion waving a tiny red flag from the back of his mind.

'He'll tell you,' said the other investigating officer, 'if you don't already know.' He looked meaningfully at Tewson.

Tewson hurried anxiously across the field and towards the old bridge that joined Eton to Windsor. He had been lunching with an old acquaintance yesterday just before the terrible crash of glass and the screams had interrupted them. When he had rushed out to find Dave Keller crouched over the dead bodies of a woman and a naked man, he had immediately forgotten about his lunch companion. The thought now nagging at his apprehensive brain had to do with the fact that his old chum was a freelance journalist and they had been discussing the cause of the air crash! Tewson was very much aware that he had a tendency for over-enthusiasm where his personal theories were concerned; a tendency that caused him to talk too much. Discretion, unfortunately, had never been part of his make-up.

When he entered the hotel room and saw the look on Slater's face he knew his fears had been well founded.

'I want to know the meaning of this,' the investigator-in-charge demanded angrily, as he threw the newspaper across his makeshift desk towards Tewson.

Tewson swallowed hard as he picked it up with nervous fingers. A knot tied itself in the pit of his stomach and tightened its string sharply and almost painfully as he read the bold serif headline: 'BOMB CLAIMED TO BE CAUSE OF ETON AIR CRASH'. His bowels loosened slightly as he realized the implications of the headline: it had been *his* theory, nobody else's. The story – and it was confirmed in the first few lead-in lines – could only have evolved from somebody on the investigating team and, although the source of the information was not revealed, it would be obvious to anyone in the department who the culprit was. He barely registered the minor adjacent story, concerning the mysterious death-plunge from a window of a married couple living in Eton. His freelance friend had had a financially rewarding day.

'Well?' The demand for an explanation was icily gruff.

'I . . . er . . .' Tewson found it difficult to take his eyes from the headline.

'You leaked the information, didn't you?'

He nodded numbly as he saw the story had been credited to his old friend. There was no doubt at all now.

'I didn't tell him this much,' he stated weakly, scanning the story as he spoke. 'Most of it's pure conjecture on the reporter's part.'

'Is it really?' And since when has a newspaper needed proven facts to print a story?' Slater leant heavily on the desk. 'I've warned you before, Tewson, about opening your mouth in the wrong places and at the wrong time. We're going to have hell from the Ministry *and* the airline because of this! I know you've often been right in the past with your half-baked theories, but you've never before gone to the absurd lengths of announcing them to the press before they've been substantiated! It's intolerable.'

'But I told him it was just an idea – that there was no real proof!'

Slater was on his feet now, his knuckles white against the desk top. 'You had no right to tell him anything!' he stormed. 'We're bound by secrecy in this organization. You're well aware of that! What the hell makes you think you're so right, anyway?'

'Everything we've learnt so far supports my theory of an explosion! It's only a matter of time before it's proved!'

'Did it ever occur to you I might have an idea of my own?' Slater glared across at him. 'An idea that has much more substance than your sensationalized conclusion!'

Tewson could only stare back blankly at his superior. 'You've never mentioned anything to me,' he said.

'Some of us gather the facts first then search for proof before we expound on our suppositions and announce them to the world!' Slater made a visible effort to calm himself, then sat down sharply, indicating that Tewson should do the same.

When the bespectacled investigator had settled in a chair opposite him, Slater tried to keep his anger suppressed, speaking in a low and even voice: 'To a certain extent, I agree with your notion of a bomb on board because many of the circumstances point in that direction. But they are also indicative of another cause.'

Tewson was grudgingly attentive.

'In March of 1974,' the senior officer went on, 'a Turkish

Airlines DC10 crashed just outside Paris. The evidence uncovered by America's Federal Aviation Administration as to the cause bears a distinct resemblance to the evidence we have uncovered so far. I remember at the time there was speculation that a bomb might have been planted, but it was eventually found that in fact, due to a design defect, a rear cargo door fell off in flight and produced an *explosive* decompression. The passengers' cabin floor collapsed and passengers still strapped in their seats were sucked out. The pilot's control cables which run through the floor from the cockpit to the tail were severed, and it was this that caused the aircraft to plunge down, completely out of control.' He lifted a wearily patient hand to quiet the protests that were about to burst forth from the young investigator. 'Think about it, Tewson. The blue and yellow marks along one of the wings were made by the aircraft's door which bears part of the company's logo, and the sudden loss in communications – caused by the severing of control cables which itself probably caused the malfunctioning of other electrical circuits. All suggestive of an explosion, I grant you, but a decompression explosion *not a manufactured explosion!*'

Tewson was silent again, his mind racing from one thought to another. It was possible! It even sounded *more* likely. But sheer gut-feelings told him otherwise.

'Now I'm not ruling out your theory, Tewson,' Slater continued gravely, 'and we'll know the answer very soon. But the one salient fact that discredits it is this: *It is virtually impossible to plant a bomb on board an aircraft with all the mechanical checking devices the airlines have in operation nowadays!* Every major airline was sick of hijacks and bomb scares up until '75 when they finally got together and brought in the highly sophisticated machinery that ruled out such risks. And you have the gumption to announce that all their efforts have been in vain!' His voice was rising now, his anger building up again. 'We are supposed to be a responsible organization and we cannot afford the criticism that will now be laid at our feet because of your thoughtless outburst of egotism!'

He looked hard and long into Tewson's reddening face. 'As from today, you are suspended from duty while this particular investigation is in progress. We may find a use for you elsewhere soon on another case. If we do, I'll be in touch.'

It was Tewson's turn to be angry now. He leapt to his feet and leant belligerently forward over the desk. 'You haven't proved that I'm wrong yet!'

'And *you* haven't proved you're right!' Slater retorted, glaring up into the fierce eyes of the younger man. 'That's beside the point anyway. It doesn't matter who's right and who's wrong. It's your indiscretion we're talking about and your responsibility towards the AIB! Now get your things together and get out until you're called for again.'

As Tewson whirled around and stormed towards the adjoining room where he had a few personal items stored, Slater completed his tirade by shouting: 'And if you want to resign, that's your affair!'

Tewson slammed the door shut behind him and leant his back against it for a few moments to regain his composure. 'Bastard!' he said aloud, as he angrily snatched off his glasses and began to polish them furiously with the end of his tie. He strode to the centre of the room and kicked out at the leg of a small coffee table. 'I'll prove I'm right,' he told himself. 'I'll show that dimwitted old sod! How's it going to look for him when they find out the truth and the man whose suspicions had been correct was under suspension. He'll pay for it then, the bloody old fool!'

He stuffed his few odd pieces into a well-worn briefcase and left the room by the door leading directly into the hall.

Downstairs, he stomped into the hotel bar, flung the briefcase against the counter bottom, and ordered a large whisky.

The whisky burnt his throat and he reached for the soda, glaring at the barely concealed smirk of the barman. Pulling a high stool towards him, he sat with his elbows fixed firmly and aggressively on the bar top, daring the barman to smile again. The white-jacketed barman picked up a clean glass and began to polish it vigorously with a cloth. He turned his back on Tewson. Gradually, he sipped more easily at the whisky, his breathing still short and sharp but slowing down with the calming effect of the alcohol. His mind was still racing, still angry with misguided grievance, but it, too, began to calm itself and think more constructively.

If only he could find a way in which a bomb could have been planted. That was the key factor in his theory: the fact that it *was* so bloody difficult these days. The ground staff? No, there was always a check after maintenance and cleaning operations had been carried out. The luggage? Impossible; all baggage was screened first. The crew themselves? Now that was a possibility. But why should any of the crew take a bomb on board only to blow themselves up? The medical checks were too thorough to allow any nutcase to continue flying and, anyway, even they now and again went through baggage searches. So who the hell – ?

Suddenly he had it!

It was just a germ of an idea but it grew in his mind, formed a complete picture. Yes, it was possible! It could have been done that way! He stood up excitedly. Should he go back upstairs and tell Slater? No, sod him! Prove it first – that was the only way. He might be wrong, but somehow . . . it . . . all . . . seemed . . . to . . . add . . . up. He was thoughtfully silent as he ran over the possibilities in his mind. There was one man who might be able to tell him more.

With a grin of satisfaction on his face, he marched out of the bar and through the swing doors of the hotel, forgetting the briefcase he had left lying on the floor by the side of the bar.

13

The people of the town were nervous. They gathered together in small groups, their apprehension growing with each new hushed conversation. Only in the public houses did their voices rise above normal conversation level when a drink or two helped quell their rising trepidation. The women met in shops and in the High Street, infecting each other with their own personal fear; the men discussed the peculiar happenings at their desks or work benches, many scornful of the suggestion that some evil was afoot in the town, but admittedly perplexed by the sequence of events. Yesterday, a young boy from the College had been struck down by a train, his head and feet sliced from his body. On the same day a couple had fallen from a window into the High Street, the man's naked body curiously emaciated, as though he had been through a long illness. The couple, husband and wife, had kept very much to themselves, but the woman had been a life-long resident of Eton and had run the antique shop for many years. They had always appeared to be a pleasant, if conservative, pair, their lives quiet and orderly. For them to die in such a bizarre manner was disturbing to say the least.

Then there was the Reverend Biddlestone, found unconscious on the floor of his church and kept under heavy sedation since. There was the girl who had been found in a car on the other side of the field, still unable to give an account of what had happened to her. Her boyfriend had been traced and questioned by the police; his story was that a face had appeared at their car window and that the car itself had been lifted completely off the ground. He had run away in terror but the girl had refused to go with him. Naturally, the police were holding him for further questioning. A man had been found dead by the river the following morning. They said the cause was a heart attack, but it was rumoured, because of the frozen look of fright on his face, that the heart attack had been induced by fear. He had literally died of fright.

Constable Wickham sensed the growing unease, and he shared the apprehesnion. He'd had the feeling for several days now: a building-up of tension that was fast reaching a peak. There was a pregnant stillness in the air that would eventually break and somehow he knew the consequences would be dreadful when it did. The guarding of the field had been an uneasy duty for him: he sensed its brooding sullenness, its indescribable coldness – not the physical chill of winter, but a deeper, forbidding coldness that tormented the imagination. As he looked across at the twisted, torn fragments of the wreck and at the silver shell that had been a burning tomb, he could almost hear the shrill screams of panic, the terror of imminent death. His mind's eye saw those hundreds of frightened faces; he heard the crying, the praying, the pleading, the wailing. He heard the dying. He felt their pain. He suffered their grief.

Even the animals would not go near the field. The dogs stood at its edge, their bodies stiff with terror, their eyes wide and pathetic, their fur prickly and their necks contracted and rigid. The riders who used the lanes running around the fields had to fight to keep control of their mounts as the horses shied away and tried to bolt.

The field had become a shrine for the dead and Constable Wickham sensed – *knew* – that death had not yet left that shrine.

The old man rarely left the house now. Since the night of the crash and the terrible scenes he had witnessed, a part of him had become subdued, a weariness had descended upon his ageing frame. His doctor had told him it was because of the shock and the exertion he had forced upon himself in his fearful run to the field in which the Jumbo had crashed. The effort had worn him out and the carnage he had then witnessed had shocked, then sapped, his spirit. In time, the oppression would lift and his energy would return, but it would take a strong effort of will on his part to lift himself above his melancholia.

Curiously though, he remembered little about that night. He could remember sitting on the bridge and gazing up into the sky; then the drone of the aeroplane, loud and low, the brief flash as it had split open. After that there were only blurred images of fire, bodies and chunks of scattered, torn metal. He'd had a recurring nightmare since: a black shape coming towards him from out of the flames, growing larger and larger until it stood before him. A hand reached down and he saw that the flesh had been burnt away, and only blackened, skeletal fingers were stretching towards him. Then, in the dream, he looked up into the dark figure's face and he saw the two large staring eyes set in the plastic head of a doll, its pink painted lips set in a cruel, mocking grin. He would wake suddenly, his body drenched in perspiration, and he'd still see those terrible, lifeless eyes staring out at him from the shadows of his bedroom.

And sometimes, just as he woke, he thought he heard whispers.

He only left his tiny house in Eton Square two or three times a week nowadays, and that was only during the daytime and only when it was essential to buy food. The streets made him nervous. It was as if there were something out there waiting for him; the thought of venturing out during the dark hours filled him with dread, even though he missed his nightly jaunt to the old bridge. They had told him that he had collapsed at the scene of the disaster and that it had been the co-pilot of the 747, the only survivor of the crash, who had found him and carried him away from the burning wreck. He had never met the young man to thank him, but for some inexplicable reason, he felt a great sympathy towards this unknown survivor. Had he been unfortunate to escape when over three hundred others had perished? Was it something that could easily be lived with?

The old man sighed with despair at his own unanswerable question; only the co-pilot himself could know. He leant forward and stirred the glowing fire with a poker, then settled back in the wooden-armed armchair, his eyes half closed, his hands nervously clasped in his lap. It was still early in the day, but already his heart beat a little faster at the thought of the night to come.

The boys at the College were delightedly scared and did their very best to heighten their fear with fantasized stories of the more macabre genre. They had enjoyed the air disaster, the most spectacular occurrence in Eton's history, the younger pupils hardly moved at all by the appalling loss of life, but intensely excited by the publicity the town had received in consequence. The boys had poured from their separate houses, dressed in a combination of night attire and black long-tailed coats on the night of the crash, their various house masters unable to prevent their eager rush to the scene of the disaster. They had gawped open-mouthed at the burning wreck, their shocked young faces hued red by the flames, their eyes wide and bright with excitement. It had taken the full force of the headmaster's fury, and the house masters' bullying, to get them to return to their beds where, those who could watched the spectacle from their houses' windows whilst the others, intoxicated with the drama, talked ceaselessly into the grey hours of the dawn.

The headmaster, with some of his house masters and the more senior boys, returned to the scene to offer assistance, but they were asked politely and firmly by the police to return to the College so that the emergency services could cope with the unenviable task of collecting the dead bodies and searching for their missing limbs without more hindrance than was necessary.

For the pupils (except those who were unwillingly dragged back to their homes by parents who looked on the disaster with distaste and did not want their offspring to witness the publicity circus that would inevitably follow) the next few days were filled with excitement and speculation as to how and why the 747 had crashed. The novelty had eventually worn off at the College over the weeks and was replaced by a strange sulkiness, a moodiness that concerned Anthony Griggs-Meade, the headmaster, more than the morbid fascination the boys had shown previously. Many – and not just the younger ones – had begun to suffer from nightmares, natural enough after such a devastating event, but the headmaster had noticed that even his own staff members were showing signs of irritability and edginess.

And now the peculiar death of the Thatcher boy. He hadn't been popular among the other boys and the headmaster knew they had tormented him mercilessly over his grossness. But it had been up to the boy to stand up for himself, to show he could be a man. The cruelties of life had to be faced and conquered at some time in one's existence, and one was never too young to taste and overcome its bitterness. How had the boy come to be on the railway line? He should have been on the playing-fields with the other boys, not wandering about the countryside alone. His house master would certainly have to be disciplined – Thatcher had been *his* responsibility. Griggs-Meade tried unsuccessfully to push a disturbing thought from his mind, a returning thought that caused the foundations of his 'let-them-help-themselves' philosophy to wobble uncomfortably. Had the unfortunate boy's life been made so wretched that he had been driven to suicide?

The notion distressed him and caused him to wonder if his principles had become too rigid. How responsible was *he* for the boy's death? He would speak to the school in the chapel tomorrow about cruelty towards each other, that love for your fellow man was more important than life itself. He walked over to his study window and looked out, trying to shake off the curious sensation which flowed through his body in waves. He had a feeling of impending – what? Doom? No, that was nonsense.

But there was *something* in the air.

Ernest Goodwin patiently waited for the black and white image to appear, occasionally dabbing a finger into the developing liquid to push the bromide paper back beneath the surface. The first shapes began to emerge slowly, then the process quickened and the picture rushed into being, completing itself with a flourish, and unable to stop, eager to destroy itself with blackness. He whipped the photograph out of the developer, holding the shiny paper at one corner, allowing the liquid to drain off back into its tray, then he plunged the curling paper into the fix, halting the developing process. He studied the completed picture for a while as it lay on the bottom of the white metal tray beneath the rectangular pool of chemical liquid, and for the hundredth time shook his head at the tragedy revealed there.

The photograph showed the burning 747, its flames silhouetting the figures of the firemen, desperately striving to control the inferno with their impotent hoses, wretched in the knowledge that all hope of saving lives was lost. Ernest again felt the surge of guilt flush through him. He and his partner, Martin, had made a lot of money from this photograph and the many others like it they had taken on that terrible night. Even now, weeks after the event, they were receiving offers from magazines all over the world for their pictures and to date, the world's press had snapped up nearly every exposure they had taken. The thought of making money from the catastrophe had worried him at first, but Martin had convinced him it was their duty as professional pictorial recorders of life (and death) to syndicate their pictures, and if they made a bit of money while doing so, then what else were they in business for? Martin had always been the shrewd partner of 'Goodwin and Samuels, Photographers for All Occasions', and it was mostly due to his skill that their business in Eton had managed to sustain itself through so many hard years. Babies, weddings, engagements, social functions of any kind, school sports teams, industrial sites – they had tackled anything and everything, maintaining a steady but healthy income for seventeen years now.

And then, the air disaster had plunged them into a different league entirely. Both men had been working late in their small darkroom, endeavouring to meet a deadline for publicity shots of a new industrial site just springing up on the outskirts of Slough, when the terrifying roar of the Jumbo jet slamming over the High Street rooftops had almost deafened them. As the subsequent explosion made the very building shudder, they had instantly realized its cause, and Martin had rushed from the darkroom, not caring that the light flooding in would ruin their film, shouting back at him to bring as many rolls of unused film as he could carry, together with a couple of cameras.

The partners had photographed the wreck from every possible angle, recording the devastation in its most dramatic moments before even the rescue squads had arrived. They had both been too numbed to feel sickened by the destruction of human life they were witnessing, and had continued to take shots automatically throughout the night, every so often one of them returning to their studio for extra supplies of film. That night had certainly changed their lives, for they had recorded scenes that few photographers had captured before: the dramatic seconds after a major calamity.

But, although Martin had been elated in the weeks that followed, holding out for the best possible deals from the news media, exhibiting their best shots in a tasteless display in their double-fronted shop window, Ernest had felt distinctly uneasy. He had come to dread working alone in the darkroom, whether it was daytime or night-time, the darkness and the quietness adding a vivid dimension to the macabre photographs he developed. And the unease had been steadily building up over the past few weeks until his nerves had reached a barely repressed breaking point. It was as though he were being watched all the time. More than once, while alone in the darkroom, bathed in its eerie red light, he had turned suddenly at the feeling of a presence behind him. Of course, there had never been anything there and he had chided himself for his overimaginativeness. Of late, though, the feeling had become too strong to ignore completely.

When he had mentioned it to Martin, his partner had laughed and said it was hardly surprising working alone in the dark like that, surrounded by images of death, but not to worry, for very soon they would have sold everything they had taken of the wreck and would be able to relax and enjoy the financial rewards. Ernest wasn't sure he could carry on for much longer, though. It had been left to him to make all the prints while Martin carried on with the flourishing business arrangements (for which he was obviously better suited). But today, after the sudden and inexplicable deaths of certain people, there was a new tenseness in the air. It was far less subtle than the broodiness that had hung over Eton like a dark grey shroud since the crash; there was an expectant air of fresh disaster.

Ernest retrieved the photograph and dropped it into the bigger water tank to remove the chemicals from the surface. It swirled gracefully as the container automatically purified itself with fresh water then gently floated face up to the surface. Once again, fascinated by its appalling contents, Ernest examined the lazily drifting photograph, wiping the chemicals from his fingers on his white smock-coat as he did so. It showed row upon row of white draped forms, the sheets soiled and bloodied, their general shapes giving sharp evidence of the mutilated bodies they covered. The shot had been taken in the early hours of dawn and its clarity caused Ernest to shudder inwardly. To one side lay a bulkier, more durable sheet, under which large plastic sacks had been placed, tucked out of sight lest their grisly contents became too unbearable for the rescue squads. He knew they contained the missing parts of bodies; parts that would be cremated, for it would have been useless to attempt identification and return them to their rightful bodies.

And as he stared down into the floating photograph, he imagined he could see the corpses beneath the sheets; their blackened bodies, their faces twisted in hideous grimaces of death. He clutched the edges of the water tank to steady himself, his chest muscles tightening. He could almost hear them calling, their souls moaning in their anguish, their voices rising in a crescendo of misery. Their souls were still here; they had not gone. And he knew them.

It was as though, through his photography, because of the days alone in the dark with their images, he had created a link with them. Somehow, he *knew* they were waiting for something. Someone. That the tragedy was not yet over.

The Reverend Biddlestone walked weakly along the stone path, his eyes careful to avoid looking directly ahead at the tall greystone church at the end of the war-memorial garden. His companion held his arm to steady him as he swayed slightly. They went through a small gate to their right which led to the vicarage where the vicar's housekeeper anxiously waited at the door.

He entered the house, smiling at the woman's words of sympathy, assuring her of his well-being, and was relieved to sink into a comfortable chair in his drawing room.

'I do wish you had stayed, Andrew,' his companion said.

'No, no, I'm fine now, Ian. Thank you for collecting me, but I'm sure you have to get back to your office now.'

Ian Filbury, who was Eton's clerk of the council, as well as being the local choirmaster and church organist, grunted with displeasure.

'Just another day wouldn't have hurt, Andrew. I mean, you

don't suddenly go under like that for no reason. The doctor should have insisted that you stay for another day's observation.

'He did, Ian. It was I who insisted otherwise. I'm fine now. Really.'

'Have you remembered what happened yet? Why you sparked out like that?'

The vicar shook his head.

'All right, Andrew,' Filbury said, 'I'll leave you to rest now. But I'm coming back this evening mind, and if I think you're any worse, I'll have the doctor around like a shot.'

The vicar smiled up at him, a thin, wan smile, a distant look in his eyes. Yes, he remembered, but it was *his* burden.

When Filbury had left the house and the clergyman's housekeeper had disappeared into the kitchen to prepare him a light dinner, he was able to concentrate his mind. He'd been told by Ian of the two bizarre deaths the day before, and he felt sure there was a connection between them and the death of the man down by the river. He closed his eyes but snapped them open instantly. The image of what he had seen in the church was too sharp, too vivid! It frightened him beyond belief, and yet he knew he had to be there this day, this coming night. He asked that God would give him courage, uncertain of what he would have to do, only knowing he would be needed.

Slowly, he knelt down beside the chair, resting his clasped hands on one of its arms, and he prayed more earnestly than he had ever prayed in his life.

But he kept his eyes open. And occasionally he looked over his shoulder.

14

Keller eased the car into the speeding fly-over traffic, accelerating fiercely to match their pace. Once he had settled into the flow, he relaxed and glanced across at Hobbs in the passenger seat. Gauze affixed with large plaster strips covered his mouth and chin; more stretched in a narrow band across his nose. Although both men had rested for most of that day, the evening traffic, as it poured out of London, was already beginning to weary Keller.

'How do you feel?' he asked Hobbs.

The medium winced as his lips tried to form the words. 'It hurts,' he managed to say wryly.

'I'm sorry I wasn't fast enough to stop you,' Keller apologized.

'It wasn't your fault.' The words were barely discernible.

'I'm sorry you became involved.'

The medium shrugged his shoulders. 'There's little control over situations like this.'

Keller knew it caused Hobbs considerable pain to talk, but there was so much he needed to know. There was so much he still did not understand.

The violence of yesterday had disturbed him deeply and he suddenly recalled the much-publicized consequences of an exorcism conducted by two Yorkshire clergymen of a few years back. The two men – a Church of England vicar and a

Methodist minister – had cast out at least forty evil spirits (it had been reported) from a man, but had been unable to remove the final three, insanity, murder and violence. The man had been allowed to return home where he had then murdered his wife, tearing out her eyes and her tongue, ripping off half her face with his bare hands. The case had shocked the world, but Keller and, he assumed, the rest of normal society had ultimately dismissed the murder as the work of an uncontrolled lunatic, blaming the two clergymen for their part in encouraging the man's delusions. Now yesterday's incident had caused Keller to view the matter in a new light. He looked anxiously at Hobbs.

'Who were they? Why did they do this to you?'

The medium studied the co-pilot's profile in silence for a few moments, then answered: 'You know who they were, Mr Keller. But if I had realized he was amongst them, I think I would have kept as far away from you as possible.'

'You mean Goswell?'

'Yes, Goswell. An evil man when he was alive, and now it seems just as evil after death.'

'I don't understand . . .'

'You don't understand, but you believe in life after death now.'

Keller nodded. 'I've never actually disbelieved. I suppose I've just never really thought about it too much.'

'I'm afraid you've had the worst possible example of its power. Most people generally turn to spiritualism when they need comforting after they've lost someone close; others dabble in it out of curiosity or because they're after excitement, looking for the unusual. Unfortunately, you've had its reality thrust upon you.'

Keller smiled without humour. 'With a vengeance, you might say.' He found a gap in the middle lane of cars, indicated and moved into it. The Stag began to pick up speed. Suddenly, he asked: 'What happened to them? Why have they become like this?'

Hobbs shook his head sadly. He winced audibly as he spoke and put his fingers to his mutilated lips so that his words were even more muffled. Keller leant towards him to hear. 'When we first met, I told you that after an accident of this kind the departed spirits are often in a state of shock; they become what we call "crisis" spirits. We don't know just how long this condition may last: it could be hours, days, years – or even centuries. Sometimes something has to be achieved in this world before they can go on, before they are released. In this case, it seems you are the only one who can release them.'

Keller remembered Cathy's voice from the previous night. There had been so many voices – he had recognized Captain Rogan's – but when they had faded, when Hobbs had actually returned from his trance and Keller had felt as though he were sinking, his senses weakened by the spirits' onslaught, she had come to him, her voice soft with pity. She had warned him of something, but now it was all too hazy; he couldn't remember her words. He had felt her warmth though, and it was a comfort to him. He understood now why so many sought loved ones after death had separated them from each other, for their closeness, their mutual devotion, did not die with their bodies but continued, their compassion becoming a bridge between the two worlds. He had felt this and the warmth had flooded through him so that his sudden oblivion had become sweet. He knew Cathy was not among the others, that she had passed on to something more peaceful, and he knew that she had not been alone. He could not remember the words – had there actually been words or had the knowledge been conveyed only by thought? – but she had let him know that she and many of the victims had found their peace. Theirs was not the tranquillity most mortals assumed was waiting for them, for there was even more to accomplish in the next world, but rather an inner knowledge that led finally to the ultimate truth. It was as if death were only the opening of the first door; there were many, many more doors to be reached then passed through. Those that had remained earthbound had been too confused to go on and they had fallen under the control of others more powerful, others seeking revenge for their deaths and one who sought only to perpetuate his own malignity.

She had gone then, her being – for there was no physical image, only an overwhelming sense of her presence – fading rapidly and he felt, unwillingly, leaving him alone and vulnerable. His plunge into unconsciousness had continued and it had taken the injured Hobbs some time to arouse him again. When he had regained consciousness, he was immediately aware that the overbearing oppression had been lifted from the room and, somehow, he knew it was due to Cathy's intervention.

He had cleaned Hobbs's wounded face and hand as best he could and removed most of the shards of glass buried in the skin. He found his own face was covered in tiny cuts and scratches, although none were deep enough to worry about. His throat was strangely bruised as though strong fingers had dug into his flesh and squeezed, and his scalp was tender where invisible hands had pulled at his hair. After a much-needed drink, he had driven Hobbs to a hospital to have his cuts treated properly. Neither of them had felt inclined to explain to the concerned doctor in casualty just how the injuries had come about, but the story of Hobbs having tripped and fallen whilst carrying a gin bottle across the room had satisfied the medic's curiosity.

They returned to the medium's house and Hobbs had insisted that Keller stay the night. He had refused to discuss the previous events, and had assured the co-pilot that the spirits would not return that night; he sensed a protective barrier around the house. Keller had been too exhausted to argue and had fallen into a heavy slumber almost as soon as he lay back on Hobbs's old, but comfortable, settee.

The following day Keller had plied Hobbs with questions but the medium had become strangely uncommunicative, a fact the co-pilot put down to his painful injuries, and several times he found the little man regarding him with a strange look in his eye. He couldn't tell whether it was fear or curiosity contained in the look. Perhaps it was both.

Hobbs had taken on the air of someone who had resigned himself to fate; as if he were a swimmer who had given up fighting against the current because he knew it was useless to do so – he hadn't the strength – and was allowing himself to be carried along into the whirlpool. It was late afternoon when Hobbs had seemed to reach some inner decision. He announced they were going to Eton, back to the scene of the crash. Only there could the answer be found.

Keller hadn't questioned the reason for his arriving at this conclusion, for he felt the need to return to the town himself, the impulse becoming more irresistible as the day went on. But now, as the car sped along the M4, passing the turn-off to Heathrow, drawing nearer to the little town whose peace had been shattered so abruptly, fear welled up inside him. He knew the night would provide many answers. He knew after this night, nothing would ever be the same again.

He became aware that Hobbs was speaking again, his words slightly slurred as he endeavoured to control his lip movements to allow only the minimum of pain. 'I thought Goswell had died years ago,' he was saying.

'You hadn't realized he was on the 747?' Keller asked.

'No, Mr Keller. I didn't read the newspaper reports of the air crash. I long ago lost interest in mankind's self-inflicted tragedies.'

'But you knew of him?'

'Goswell? He was a most corrupt man. Hardly in the class of The Beast, Aleister Crowley, but there were many similarities between them. You no doubt know of his wartime exploits in this country, his association with Mosley, and the investigation of some of his more hideous exploits which eventually led to his having to flee from the country.'

'I'd heard about him, and a friend told me a few more facts yesterday. But I didn't believe anyone took him seriously.'

'Oh yes, he was taken very seriously by people who knew of the mysteries he dabbled in.'

'You mean Devil worship, black magic – all that nonsense?'

'After all you've been through, you still don't understand that much?' Even though muffled, Hobbs's tone was incredulous.

'Life after death? Yes, I believe in that now. But Satanism?' Keller shook his head for an answer.

'It exists as a religion, Mr Keller, just as much as any other religion. The difference is, its devotees worship Satan rather than God. There are at least four hundred known covens in England today, so whether you actually believe in it or not is immaterial. It *exists*.'

'But magic?'

'It has been called by some the science of the mind. Crowley gave many examples of the power of *his* mind, most of which was turned towards evil purposes. You witnessed, yourself, the power Goswell is exerting over these unfortunate spirits, the power he had over me! How can you deny it? And then there is the question of your survival.'

Keller forced his eyes to remain on the road ahead, but he was startled by the last remark. 'What do you mean?'

'How do you imagine you survived such a crash when every other person on board perished? Can't you believe some strange power saved you?'

'Why me? Why should I be the one?'

'I don't know. Perhaps you were the only one who could accomplish whatever it is they want.' Hobbs fell into a brooding silence. Keller continued driving, his mind confused and shocked.

Hobbs began to speak again, slowly, thoughtfully. 'You said the voices spoke of a bomb last night. Goswell hasn't been heard of for years – the last I heard of him was at least fifteen years ago and the word was he'd started a new religious order in the United States. You can imagine what sort. Now, he still has many enemies in this country, particularly among the Jews, who, even after thirty-odd years since the end of the Second World War, are still claiming retribution for atrocities against them. Suppose they discovered he had sneaked back into the country, perhaps to spread more evil as in the old days; then they'd do their utmost to even the score.'

'You mean plant a bomb? Kill all those innocent people as well?'

'We've seen what the fanatics of this world will do, Mr Keller. The innocent, no matter how many, do not deter these fanatics' plans for vengeance.'

'So?'

Hobbs took a deep breath. 'What if you were saved to avenge Goswell's death?'

'That's crazy!' The car swerved dangerously and Keller fought to control it. When he had, and the horns of other angry motorists had died down, he said: 'If he had that kind of power, why didn't he save himself?'

'Because he was an old man. Too old to seek out his murderers and claim his revenge; he needed a younger man.'

'It's preposterous! Even if I found the person responsible, why should I do anything about it? If Goswell is as evil as you say, he'd want me to kill, and I certainly wouldn't do that.'

'You may not have any choice. You saw what happened to me.'

'But you contacted the spirits. You opened yourself to them.'

'Yes, last night I did. But there was another time when I didn't, and yet a spirit managed to control me. A woman came to me because her husband had committed suicide when he had discovered her infidelity with another man. She pleaded with me to contact her husband so she could beg forgiveness; she really loved him, you see. I was a powerful sensitive at that time – too powerful – and contact with the dead man's spirit proved to be no great problem. He seemed distressed at first, but readily forgave his wife. There was one condition though: she had to visit him regularly through me.

'I was prepared to carry on with the sittings for a while, even though I discouraged too many such visits – the living become too dependent on them – but in this case, I saw it was for a worthwhile cause. It went well for a while; the dead man seemed a kindly sort of chap, gentle – trusting. I didn't realize he was merely using the time to develop his powers on the other side, to make a firmer bond of contact between us personally.

'Then, one night, he took over my physical body, and I went for his wife. You see, all he wanted was revenge. He wanted to commit the act he had never had the courage for when he was alive! And I was his instrument! Fortunately, as

I was choking the poor woman, my own inner spirit rose up and cast out the man's evil spirit. I was lucky the woman never pressed charges against me, but she seemed to understand what had happened – or in her own remorse decided the action had been just. She committed suicide three days later, so the husband had his revenge after all. After that, I gave up spiritualism; I had become *too* receptive.'

Keller risked a quick glance at the medium. My God, is he mad or am I? He wanted to stop the car and kick the little man out, but something in Hobbs's calmness prevented him from doing so. The medium looked across at him and Keller felt, rather than saw, his painful smile of sadness beneath the bandages. 'You still don't believe, do you?' Hobbs said.

'I don't know any more,' Keller replied. 'It's all too incredible. Give me time to take it in – it's all happened so fast.'

'But there isn't enough time, Mr Keller. Perhaps I'm wrong about Goswell – it's just a theory. If you really knew the man, you'd go at least halfway to believing me. You've no idea of the power of evil. Nevertheless, I understand your disbelief and sympathize; but tonight will, I hope, answer a lot of questions.'

Keller saw the sign for Colnbrook and edged over into the inside lane. He left the motorway and, at the roundabout, turned off towards Datchet. The roads were dark and the absence of other cars made him uneasy.

They drove along in silence, Keller more confused than ever, Hobbs thoughtful and becoming increasingly apprehensive about the night that lay ahead of them. It had been his decision to return to the scene of the disaster, the strongest possible place to make contact with the spirits of the dead; but was it wise? He knew there was conflict between the victims and he hoped he could help the good amongst them to overcome the evil. He hadn't told Keller yet that they would need a priest, simply because he couldn't be sure of the young co-pilot's reaction. But Hobbs knew they would need all the help they could get.

He realized his theory and subsequent story about himself had somewhat destroyed Keller's faith in him, but he'd had no choice; the young man had to know what was involved. What he tried not to admit to himself, let alone the co-pilot, was that he was afraid of him. There was a disturbing power in the young man, something indefinable, intangible. And, despite his obvious confusion, there was a great strength in him, too. A strength they would both be in need of throughout that night.

They passed through Datchet and turned off to the left, into Eton Road. Keller switched his headlights to full beam, throwing the trees on either side of the road into flat, eerie relief. The co-pilot became calmer as they drew nearer to Eton and the wreckage. The doubts, the fears, seemed to be leaving him, draining away with the passing miles. Perhaps it was because he knew he would be doing something positive that night, something meaningful at last. Or perhaps he had passed beyond the boundaries of shock, and had reached that stage where all one could do was react, where emotion or indecision played no part.

Turning the car into Windsor Road, he saw the lights of Eton College ahead of him. They had crossed the hump-backed bridge and passed between the first of the College's tall buildings when Hobbs suddenly clamped a hand on his arm.

'Stop!' the medium commanded.

The Stag screeched to a halt and Keller looked at his passenger questioningly. Hobbs pointed a wavering finger ahead of them, towards the centre of the little town. 'Look there. Don't you see it?'

Keller pulled himself forward by the steering wheel and peered through the windscreen. He looked back at Hobbs. He could see nothing, only the lights from the High Street.

'There, man, above the town!'

And it slowly became visible to Keller's eyes.

A luminescence hovered over Eton. A subtly pulsating effulgence, so faint, so tenuous, that Keller had to blink hard to make sure it was really there and not just a watery mist in his own eyes. It seemed to vary in its intensity, appearing as a thin luminous vapour in some places and almost as a star cluster in others. There was no telling its size, for there was no telling its distance: Keller could only guess it might be anything from a hundred to five hundred yards in length. Its shape seemed to be constantly changing at its ragged outer edges, like a cloud torn at its extremities by unfriendly winds.

'What is it?' he asked in awe.

For a moment, Hobbs was unable to speak. Then, his voice distorted, he said: 'They're waiting for us. The dead are waiting for us.'

15

He crouched in the darkness and tried to keep very, very still. The heavy overcoat and thick woollen scarf barely kept the chill from his bones but he daren't light a fire; *they* would be able to see him too easily.

He moved his eyes around, their lids strangely held open by vertical white strips of sticking plaster, without moving his head, and peered into each dark corner of the room; no, they hadn't come yet. They would, though. They came every night now. Sometimes during the day. He would hear them whispering to one another. Occasionally, they laughed. He knew they wanted him, but if he hid in the dark and kept very still, they'd never find him. He hugged the black-metalled shotgun between his thighs, its barrel pointing up towards the ceiling. Grinning to himself, he ran his fingers along its smooth length in a masturbatory gesture, enjoying its coldness, its strength. It would protect him from them, nothing could stand against its explosive power, not even those already dead. And they were dead, weren't they?

They had frightened him at first when they had come in the night, calling for him, taunting him. But they couldn't touch him! He had realized that after his initial fright; they could conjure up images, scream at him – even try to enter his mind – but physically they could do no harm. Because they weren't of this world; they had no substance.

He knew they wanted to drive him mad; but he was too cunning for that. *He* had said months ago that he was mad, but *he* had paid for that now, hadn't *he*? And other things! *He* was amongst them, one of the voices; *he* wanted his revenge. The man, crouching in the dark, clutching the gun, laughed aloud, then quickly stifled the sound. Mustn't let them know where I am. Mustn't let *him* know.

He had paid for his betrayal; *his* death had been the price. The others who had died with *him* were unimportant; their lives had no value. He was pleased they were still suffering: death had been no release for them! And *he* suffered with them. That was good.

Yes, they had frightened him at first, frightened him so much he hadn't dared leave the house. But he'd found the answer in locking himself away, keeping away from places where accidents could so easily happen, keeping away from people who could do him harm. He had written to the company – his company, the company he had created – and told them he would be resting for a while, that he would return as soon as he felt up to it. Well, they had probably been pleased with that; hadn't they urged him to do so before?

He smiled, and a snigger escaped from his lips. He clasped a hand to his mouth and looked around warily.

They had sent someone from the company to see him, but the person had gone away when he hadn't answered the door. The same person had been back several times, but he'd given up now. They would all give up soon; even the voices. How they had tried, those dead ones. But my will is stronger, so much stronger than theirs. Oh, how frustrated they had become! Fools. Did they think mere apparitions, words, thoughts, could harm me? It was all in the mind, and my mind is stronger than theirs. And more cunning.

The voices told him someone would come for him; *they*

would send someone. Hah! Did they really think that was enough! He had come, all right – when had it been? Today? Yesterday? All the days had merged into one now. He'd seen the man approaching from his bedroom window; ducked back behind the curtain when the man had looked up. He'd rung the doorbell for ages it seemed, and the man's persistence had irritated him. Then he'd heard his footsteps going around the side of the house, round to the back. He'd crept downstairs then, stealthily, not making a sound, along the hall, pausing outside the kitchen door to listen for sounds. The man, whoever he was – *whoever he had been* – was banging on the back door, rattling the handle.

He'd quietly, ever so quietly, opened the kitchen door and crept in. He could see the man's dark shadow against the two frosted-glass panels of the back door. The curtains of the windows were drawn, as were all the curtains in the house, so the man was unable to see him. He stood without breathing by the kitchen table as the shadow moved away from the door and suddenly appeared at the window. The shadow defined itself more clearly through the drawn curtains as the figure pressed close to the window outside, trying to peer through the tiniest chink at the curtains' centre.

With a start, he realized he'd left the gun upstairs on the bed. It would have been so easy, so satisfying, to put a shot through that window, to see the shadowy image for a brief instant become living flesh before it disappeared from view below the window-sill, torn apart by the blast. But he relaxed and smiled broadly when he saw the bread-knife lying beside the stale loaf on the table. He picked it up and moved against the wall beside the window just as a shadowy hand reached up and slid something thin into the crack between the top and bottom frames. He heard the sharp click as the catch was pushed back.

The window squealed in protest as it was pushed up and the movement stopped abruptly. It continued rising, this time more slowly, cautiously. The curtains parted and a foot appeared. He noticed the bottom of the shoe was speckled with dried mud as if its owner had spent time trudging through damp fields. He remembered how curious it had been to notice something so trivial when he was about to take the man's life away.

A leg followed the foot and his breathing became heavy; so heavy he thought the man might hear. The arm holding the knife suddenly became locked in pain and he almost dropped the weapon. It was part of his illness; the creeping paralysis that came and went, and would eventually remain. The paralysis that had already cost him the muscular control of his eyelids. He reached up with his other hand and grasped the knife, holding it with its sharpened edge upwards. His other arm immediately relaxed and the blood flowed evenly through it once more.

The man's head and shoulders appeared through the window now and he stopped, looking straight ahead, staring at the open kitchen door. The intruder suddenly seemed to become aware of his presence, but it was much, much too late. Just at the instant when the head was about to turn and look in his direction, he brought his stiffened left hand down, grabbing at the man's hair, pulling it up sharply, and, at the same time, pushed the knife past the exposed neck, drawing it back swiftly and deeply through his throat.

The blood had poured on to the kitchen floor as the man slumped forward, his body dangling limply, caught astride the window-sill. He grabbed the man's coat and pulled him all the way through.

He smothered a giggle as he thought of the body downstairs now, propped up in a chair at the kitchen table, for all the world looking as if he had just unwillingly dozed off while enjoying a snack.

'Is that the best you can do?' he asked the empty air mockingly. 'Is that your messenger? Well, he's joined you now, hasn't he?' He laughed aloud, knowing they hadn't finished with him yet, but almost enjoying the game.

The mood did not last for long, though. As the night grew more still, the silence almost a sound, and the cold began to bite into him once again, the fear pierced his madness, puncturing the barrier of his insanity with tiny holes that spread, tore, and merged into one large opening. His body succumbed to the creeping paralysis that was part of his illness, and grew rigid, unable to move. Only the eyes stirred, darting from one side to the other, their lids held open by the sticking plaster, the enlarged pupils revealing his despair. It would pass, he knew, but until it did, he was totally helpless.

He crouched in the darkened room and waited for whatever they might send next.

16

The Reverend Biddlestone stirred restlessly in his sleep and his foot kicked out at the empty cup and saucer that lay by the side of the sofa. He woke with a start at the clatter of china on china and for a moment his sluggish mind failed to orientate itself. Sitting upright, he stared at the flames before him, a continuation of his dream. He relaxed with a sigh as the light from the fire revealed the familiar objects and furniture of his own sitting room. He must have dozed off after Mrs McBride, his housekeeper, had left. The dear woman had fussed over him like a mother hen, building up the fire, bringing him tea and two of her delicious homemade scones, and fluffing up the cushions, propping him up comfortably. He must have dozed off after she'd left, the heat from the blazing fire inducing his exhaustion.

He couldn't have slept for long, for the fire was still in full flame. Yet strangely, the heat had gone from it and the room was unpleasantly cold. He could even see the vapour from his mouth as he breathed out. How strange. And the dream had been so terrible. It had been the night of the crash again and he had found himself walking amongst the victims, administering the Last Rites. This time, however, the field was burning and he had walked through the flames to the maimed and injured, blessing and comforting them. And all the victims had still been alive, suffering terribly, but crying out for compassion; for forgiveness.

He shuddered at the memory. Those poor, unfortunate souls. He was sure of one thing: many had not yet found peace. The 'thing' he had seen in his church: it had been purely the manifestation of a soul in torment. The horror of its features had only been in his own mind; the evil it had exuded was only his own fear. The dream had told him this, for the flames represented their torment, and that torment was still going on for them. They had pleaded for release from their purgatory, and he would help them find that release by prayer.

The vicar didn't know what drew his eyes to the window at that moment, but the sight of the small, white face looking through the glass did not startle him as much as it should have. It was almost as though he had been expecting it.

He rose from the sofa, the clatter of the cup and saucer he had already knocked over once causing him to look down sharply. When he raised his eyes again towards the window, the face had gone. He moved over to it swiftly and pressed close against the black window pane, shielding his eyes from the reflection of the fire. His breath on the pane momentarily blurred his vision and he quickly wiped a hand across it, then held his breath.

Out there in the dark, at the bottom of his garden, a tiny figure waited. It looked like a child, and appeared to be holding something white in its arms. He tapped on the window and beckoned for the child to come forward. The little figure remained where it was, however, unmoving.

The vicar straightened up and hastily left the room, making for the back door. By the time he had unlocked and swung it open, the child had gone. He stood there for several seconds, searching the darkness, oblivious to the coldness of the night. Stepping on to the garden path, he walked along its length, careful not to stray on to the frozen flower beds. He stopped near the hedge at the back and looked over it; he could see the wreckage of the plane in the adjacent field lit up by two small lamps, twin beacons in the night. He turned in despair and his heart jumped as he saw the pale, spectral figure near the side of the house walking away from him. He hurried after it, but the figure disappeared into the opening that led to the church. He, too, followed through the gap and stopped once again to look around for the child.

He saw her not far away, waiting for him, near enough for him to tell it was the figure of a little girl, aged about six or seven – certainly no more. There had been several children involved in the disaster, of course, but he remembered reading of a child who was accompanying her novelist mother, a little girl aged six. What had been her name? He couldn't remember. But he knew her body had never been recovered; or at least, never enough of it to be recognizable. Could this be the ghost of the poor little creature, wandering lost around the fields, a tiny soul searching for its mother? He reached a pitying hand towards her but she moved away along the path, her back towards him, never once looking round to see if he followed.

The Reverend Biddlestone did follow her, his anguish for a forgotten soul dismissing any fears he might have had. She disappeared into the porch that stood at the side of the church, the small entrance he usually used during the week. He rushed forward, knowing that the door would be locked, that she would be trapped inside the porch. But when he reached it and stopped at the entrance, breathing sharply at the sudden exertion, he saw the door to the church was open and a flickering light was shining through from within.

His footsteps became leaden as he was irresistibly drawn

towards the opening, towards the unsteady light. Now the old fear was returning. Now, when it was too late, the trepidation coursed through him.

As he climbed the few steps leading into the open doorway, he saw the light come from burning candles, their flames sending thin spirals of black smoke into the air, filling the church with acrid, waxy fumes. Their combined glow failed miserably to brighten the vast interior and shadows dominated the long nave; the chancel and small lady chapel were in total darkness. The vicar moved uncertainly into the church, wanted to turn and flee, but was unwillingly drawn forward. The girl knelt at the altar, the doll she had clasped to her chest now dangling loosely on the ground, held by a limp arm. Filled with grief he stepped forward towards her, both arms raised compassionately. 'Let me help you, child,' he said pityingly.

But something else moved from out of the shadows before he reached her. Something blackened; something that chuckled hideously.

The sickening smell of burnt flesh now filled his nostrils, and he stopped dead in his tracks, his arms still held outstretched. He looked into that same charred face, those same blackened holes that should have held eyes, that same wide grinning cavern of a mouth, containing only a thin sliver of brittle, crispy flesh – the remnants of a tongue; the burnt remains of the corpse he'd seen in the church the day before.

The Reverend Biddlestone sank to his knees in horror. Tiny sounds came from his mouth as he opened and closed it, desperately trying to scream, to call out – anything to release the dreadful tension that was building up inside him. He tore his eyes from the charred form and looked piteously at the girl. Surely she would help him; give him the strength to flee from this abhorrent thing? As she twisted her small body to look at him, he saw that the dress she wore hung loosely around her in scorched tatters. And there was no sympathy in her expression, for she had no face. But he heard her giggle and her shoulders shrugged with mirth, only the sound came from the mocking lips of the doll lying by her side. Its plastic face was buckled and burnt, but its eyes, large and round, stared at him with a magnetic intensity; the little girl's giggles made it almost a living thing.

Other black shapes were emerging from the shadows, some dragging themselves because their limbs were missing. Their voices echoed around the stone walls of the church, low murmurings, almost whispers. They advanced on him slowly, down the aisles, through the rows of pews. So many.

He drew back and, as he did so, he fell on his side. The figure on the altar, the one closest to the creature that had been a child, came nearer and leant forward, the choking smell of its burnt flesh causing the vicar to retch violently.

'Well, Man of God, have you come to save us?' The voice was low, the words hissed out, forced through scorched vocal cords. It made the laughter that followed sound even more malevolent.

The vicar tried to crawl away from the child, but his limbs would not obey. The shapes had gathered around now and stared down at him, many with sightless eyes. The small girl pushed through them, clutching the doll, its eyes seeing for her.

'Is this the one?' he heard one of them say. 'No,' another whispered, 'not this one.'

He saw details of them now, so many sickening details: sparse clumps of scorched hair clinging to their bare scalps; lips burnt away to reveal grinning, blackened teeth; hands that bore no fingers; bodies that were torn wide open, exposing innards alive with crawling things.

'Dear God in Heaven, help me!' he managed to choke. And then his voice rose to a scream: 'Help me!'

He turned on to his stomach and raised his knees so they were under him. Pushing his face down on to the cold stone floor, he covered his cheeks and ears with his arms. Whimpering, his tears leaving a damp trail on the floor, he shuffled his body forward, pushing through the legs of the surrounding obscenities, an inch at a time; he had no strength, no courage, to raise himself and walk through them. And all the time they mocked him, prodded him with their blackened finger stubs, and laughed at his craven figure. Their sounds rang through his head, filled the church, taunted him. He now clasped his hands to his ears and raised his head, his eyes pressed tightly shut. He lifted himself up and, crouched on his knees, raised his face towards the high ceiling. 'No!' he screamed. 'No!'

The voices stopped. All movement stopped. Slowly, he opened his eyes and lowered his face. They were all turned towards the door, staring at the man standing in the entrance.

'Help me,' the vicar pleaded quietly. But his friend, Ian Filbury, could only stare in horror at the scene inside the church.

It had been a long day for Constable Wickham, a day that had stretched his nerves to breaking point. He had been acutely aware of the pressure building up around him, of the general air of nervousness in the town. He knew at times like this there was nothing one could do except wait for the mounting tension to erupt, then move in fast and deal with it as best as one could. He wasn't quite sure what he was expecting, but he hoped it would break when he was off-duty.

His had been a long shift and his own anxiety had lengthened the hours agonizingly. The extra money earned came in useful, true, but he'd much prefer to be involved in an interesting case or, at least, something that would keep him active. The weeks of pacing around this field, watching over this wreckage as if it were valuable bloody property, had made him edgy. Just an hour to go, though, and he would be off home to a blazing fire, a good meal, and a few hours of telly. That would help soothe his unease.

And then, the moment he had been dreading arrived.

He jumped when he heard the cries for help coming from across the field.

'Did you hear that, Ray?' he called to his companion who was somewhere nearby in the dark, keeping a watchful eye on the field's boundaries.

'I heard it, Bob,' the other policeman replied, switching on his torch and plodding over to Constable Wickham. 'It came from over there, I think,' he said, pointing towards the northern end of the field.

'No, no, that way!' Wickham disagreed, indicating to the east. His assertion proved to be correct as the cries came again.

'It's over by the vicarage! Come on, Ray, let's get over there.'

The two policemen ran across the field, shining their torches ahead of them, their boots crunching on the hardened earth.

'Quickly, over here!' they heard someone shout.

Constable Wickham saw the figure, arm beckoning, over by the gate that led to the parish church. He shone his torch full on the man's face and was surprised at the wide-eyed look it revealed.

'It's Mr Filbury, isn't it? What's wrong, sir?' he asked,

coming to a halt in front of the gate. Ray pulled up behind him, his torch adding to the dazzle of light on the clerk of the council's face.

'Thank God! I knew there'd be someone on duty guarding the wreckage,' Filbury gasped, holding a hand up to protect his eyes from the glare. 'Is that you, Wickham?'

'Yes, sir. *Constable* Wickham. Now, what's up?'

Filbury looked back over his shoulder at the church and the two policemen flicked their eyes in that direction. They saw a dull glow shimmering from its side entrance.

'It's Reverend Biddlestone. Come and help me please.' Filbury swung the gate open and allowed Constable Wickham to walk ahead of him. 'I'm afraid it's happened again,' he said, following closely on the policeman's heel. The constable didn't bother to ask what had happened again, for they were already at the entrance and he knew he would shortly find out for himself.

He climbed the few steps then stopped in the doorway, the other two men bumping into his broad back. A look of utter dismay spread across his face.

The vicar was cowering on the floor of the church looking up at them, his eyes bulging, his face ashen. He was on his knees, one hand supporting his weight on the stone floor, the other raking his face in agitation. His whole body trembled and shook uncontrollably, his face was shiny wet from tears and drooling saliva. His silvery hair was stiffened and stood out like bristles on his scalp; a constant incomprehensible gabble came from his lips.

'Good God!' was all Constable Wickham could exclaim as he shone the torch on to the cringing figure.

Filbury's voice quivered with emotion. 'This is how I found him just a few moments ago. Alone in the church crouching there, terrified. He must have been lighting the candles when – when—' Filbury's words were choked off by his grief. 'Poor Andrew,' was all he could say.

'Another breakdown,' Constable Wickham said, more to himself than the others. 'This time, it looks as if he's gone right over the edge.'

He shook his head in pity, then wrinkled his nose at the odd smell that hung in the air. 'Smells like he's been burning something, too,' he said. It was a revolting, nauseating smell, and it reminded him of something. He'd experienced the same odour before and he had to control his stomach as he remembered where and when. It was on the night of the crash. Amid the flames.

It was the smell of roasted flesh.

17

It had taken Keller and Hobbs well over an hour to convince the priest of their sincerity – and their sanity. And, even now, Father Vincente was not so sure.

He had recognized the younger man from the night of the air disaster and seen his haunted features in the many newspaper articles that had followed. He had been the co-pilot of the Jumbo jet; the only survivor of the crash. The priest was sure he'd never met the other man before, the one whose mouth, chin and part of his nose were covered in bandages. There was something disturbing about him, though, and it wasn't just his facial injuries: it was his piercing grey eyes. So sharp, so keen, looking far beyond any super-ficial barrier one might interpose between them. The man's eyes, more than anything else, influenced the priest's judge-ment as to their integrity.

Keller had, at first, been reluctant to involve a priest, but Hobbs patiently explained it was often necessary to have a religious minister present when fighting against such mal-evolence. The power of evil could only be combated with the power of light – and most holy men held that force.

They were directed to the Catholic church and were surprised to find it tucked away behind the High Street, facing the South Meadow, the field in which the 747 had come down. As they left the car in the adjoining car park,

Keller was even more surprised to see the Protestant church standing blackly against the night sky not more than a few hundred yards away. He turned his attention to the wreckage still lying in the field, lit eerily by two lamps, the light occasionally broken by the shadowy figures of patrolling policemen. Looking up into the sky, he saw the shimmering cloud hung directly over the field.

It was a curious little church, a perfect miniature of a Roman basilica, and he wasn't prepared for the quiet beauty of its interior. It had been a long time since he'd entered a place of worship – the funeral for the victims of the crash had been held out in the open because of the vast crowds it was assumed (correctly) would gather – and he wondered at the sudden warmth that flushed through him. Religion, while not being a taboo subject with him, was one that did not hold his interest for long. Cathy, who had been a fairly religious person, although privately so, would never force the subject on him. She had always felt that people found their own beliefs eventually and, although they could be guided gently, they should never, under any circumstances, be pushed. But now he began to understand the comfort people derived from their faith because, as he entered the church, he felt an upward surge of spirit. The calmness he had felt earlier broadened and spread through his body like a sedative; the experience was curious – and quietly awesome. It meant no sudden turning point for him, no abrupt conversion to the worship of God; nothing so dramatic. Simply a new-found peace that he needed time to evaluate. He saw that Hobbs was studying him with that now familiar expression of curiosity mixed with puzzlement.

The church contained one main altar with six small chapels on either side of the nave; marble covered its main pillars and various altars. A service appeared to be in progress, although the congregation consisted of no more than seven or eight people, and the two men waited patiently at the back until it was over. They approached the priest only after the last person had left the church.

He had listened silently, never once interrupting their story, studying the two men intently as they spoke. The younger man – the co-pilot – had not said much, but there was something about him that inspired belief. Father Vincente was puzzled by his frequent glances towards the crucifixion statue on the altar; he appeared as if he were only just realizing its significance. The older, smaller man was different. He, too, inspired belief, but for a different, more penetrating reason. He spoke of unbelievable matters so factually, his strange eyes never wavering; he spoke undefiantly as if there could be no reason to disbelieve. It obviously cost him a great deal of pain to talk through his injured mouth and Father Vincente often had to lean forward to catch his words. Of one thing he was certain: the men were not lying. Nor was there any hint of exaggeration in their tone.

Although only in his late thirties, the priest had heard too many lies, too many untruths that were not even realized to be false by the person telling them, to doubt the two men. If he had one quality, it was the ability to discern fact from fiction, honesty from deceit. He was sure of them, but he wondered if they were misguided. He did not even bother to ask if either of them were of the faith; it was obvious they were not. Instead, he rose from the pew in which he had been sitting and turned round to face them as they sat in the second row, and said simply: 'Let's see what can be done.'

Keller was astonished. 'You believe us?' he asked, incredulously.

The priest smiled grimly. 'I've felt the oppression over the town for weeks now – and it's been growing worse, like a leaden weight over us all. Strange things have happened in my own church: statues smashed, seats overturned, pools of blood suddenly appearing, an altar cloth torn to shreds. I've managed to keep it to myself so far – I know the alarm incidents of this nature can cause. Until now, I had supposed it was due to vandalism; but I know it was only shallow comfort – there *is* an evil influence afoot. And I know, too, that what has already occurred is only mild compared to what may happen if this influence is allowed to gather strength. The unusual deaths yesterday were only the beginning.'

'Thank God you have the sense to appreciate just what's happening,' Hobbs breathed out through pained lips.

The priest looked at him sharply. 'I'm not sure that I do, Mr Hobbs.'

'But you will help us?'

'I said we'd see what can be done.'

'You'll come with us to the wreck?'

Father Vincente nodded. 'If there is more to find out, I agree with you – it's there we'll find it.' He turned towards Keller and added, 'There's one condition though.'

The co-pilot was puzzled.

'I want you to carry this, Mr Keller.' The priest put his hand beneath his cassock and drew something out from his trouser pocket. He pressed a sharp object into the palm of Keller's hand and held it firmly, never once taking his gaze from the co-pilot's eyes.

He seemed satisfied after a few moments had passed and released the hand. Keller looked down to see what the object was. He found he was holding a small, wooden crucifix, approximately three inches in length, two inches wide. He looked up at the priest in consternation, but his questioning eyes were met only with an enigmatic smile. Hobbs grunted to himself. He had understood the priest's intention.

'Now, if you'll allow me to change from my vestments and don something more practical, we'll proceed,' Father Vincente said, almost cheerfully.

As he disappeared into the sacristy at the side of the main altar, Keller turned to Hobbs and said: 'Why was he so willing to believe us?'

Hobbs was thoughtful. 'When we came in I saw that the church belonged to the Augustinian Canons Regular which is, to say the least, a well-travelled order. I should think the good Father has been in many primitive countries where much stranger things than this have happened.'

'Stranger than this?'

'You'd be surprised. The other point is that the priesthood is primarily concerned with the fight against evil; that's a natural part of the worship of God. They're well used to the manifestation of evil in any form. Naturally, they don't encourage the spread of stories about black magic or exorcism; they don't want their religion to be seen as mumbo-jumbo by the more sophisticated cynics of this world. But they certainly believe in evil as a physical force – a force that has to be constantly beaten back, or at least held in check. The pity is – and you'll never get one of them to admit it publicly – that the Church is losing ground. Evil – call it the Devil if you like – is gaining the upper hand.'

Keller felt reluctant to get involved in a philosophical discussion as to the reality of *that* dubious statement. 'Why did he give me the cross?' he asked to change the subject slightly.

'It was a test,' Hobbs answered.

'A test?'

'A test to see whether you would accept it or not.'

Keller turned the plain wooden cross over in his hand, examining it curiously. 'And if I hadn't?'

'Then perhaps you may not have been what you seemed.'

The co-pilot was opening his mouth to say more, but at that moment the priest rejoined them, a relaxed smile on his face. 'Shall we go, gentlemen?' he said. He wore a dark suit with the usual clerical collar. In one hand he carried a battered old briefcase. They walked from the church into the cold, black night and all three immediately missed its reassuring sanctuary.

As they walked, Hobbs said to the priest: 'Father Vincente, do you see anything in the sky?'

The priest looked up and shook his head. 'The stars. It's a very clear night.' He brought his eyes down and regarded the medium oddly. 'Is there something there I should be seeing?'

This time, Hobbs shook his head. 'It's not important.'

Keller was disturbed to see tenuous strands of the cloud breaking away from the mass in long streaks, dropping downwards but quickly fading into nothingness. He turned to ask Hobbs if he saw the same, but an imperceptible nod of the medium's head answered his unasked question. The three men continued in silence until Keller remarked: 'The police may not let us go to the wreckage.' They had crossed the narrow road and were entering the field through a wide gap in the surrounding fence.

'Perhaps I can persuade them,' Father Vincente said.

But there was no need for, apart from the broken shell of the aircraft and its remaining scattered chunks of twisted metal, the field was empty. They trudged across the uneven surface, their eyes slowly becoming accustomed to the gloom, waiting for the shout to 'Halt!' that never came.

'Where the hell are they?' Keller muttered to no one in particular as they drew near to the poorly lit wreck.

'They may have been called away to more urgent duty.

Let's be thankful for our good fortune; it'll save a lot of awkward and embarrassing questions.'

They reached the huge, cone-shaped structure of the Jumbo's fuselage; the main frames near its centre were exposed and bent. The aircraft's belly had been almost completely flattened on impact with the ground, destroying its circular shape, making it an ugly, crouching thing. There was something pathetic, and moving, about the Jumbo's disgraced majesty. The priest peered into its broken hulk and shook his head in pity. 'How much bigger will tombs become?' he said quietly.

Keller hadn't heard his remark for he was already making for the broken-off front of the 747. Most of the interior would have been destroyed and what was left of the pilot's instrument panel and the flight engineer's electronics panel would have been removed for intense laboratory examination; but he wanted to get into the cockpit. It had been Hobbs's idea: the co-pilot was to get as close as possible to his original position on that fateful night; to think back and imagine what had happened, to go through the motions. *To try and mentally resurrect the events leading up to the crash!*

'Wait for us, David,' he heard Hobbs's muffled voice from behind. He was conscious of being pleased that the spiritualist had finally dropped the 'Mr Keller'. The two men caught up with him and they gathered together in the dark beside the looming, mutilated metal shape.

'What is your intention, Mr Hobbs?' Father Vincente asked softly.

Hobbs replied just as quietly, 'David is going to enter the aircraft and turn his mind back to that night. He'll think back to the nearest point before the accident and work backwards from there.'

'But I thought all this had failed before. The newspaper

said the co-pilot's mind was a complete blank as regards the crash. You told me so yourselves this evening.'

'It's never been tried under these conditions,' Keller cut in.

'And I shall be helping him,' said Hobbs.

'May I ask how?' There was no scorn in the priest's voice.

'I'm going to call on the spirits to guide him, to re-create the atmosphere of that night.'

'My God! Isn't that terribly dangerous?'

'Yes, Father, I think it is. That's why I wanted you here with us. We may need your protection.'

'But I'm only a priest, man! There's a great malevolence here – I may not be strong enough to deal with it!'

'You're all we have,' Hobbs said evenly, 'and time's running out.' He patted Keller on the arm and produced a small torch from his pocket. The co-pilot took it and shone it into the gaping hole in the aircraft's side. He then climbed up, and found himself inside the gutted shell of the 747. The darkness, apart from the thin beam of the torch, was absolute. He pointed the light towards where he hoped the twisting staircase leading up to the first-class lounge and the cockpit would be. It was still there – scorched and buckled, but usable. He heard the two men struggling to get through the hole behind him. While he waited for them, he examined the huge rent that was providing them with a convenient entrance. It had been the forward passenger door, the one Harry Tewson said had been blown out by the explosion. Its edges were misshapen and ragged; a long jagged tear continued towards the roof of the aircraft revealing the stars outside. When the door had been blown out, whether it was before the crash or on impact with the ground, it had taken the surrounding metal with it. He shone the beam down into the interior and saw where the giant aircraft had cracked wide open close to the wing span; the whole fuselage had been as fragile as an eggshell under the tremendous impact. He could see the exposed body frames further down, the two stout main frames still erect but at an angle, like the broken ribs of a huge whale. He felt the pang of regret every pilot felt at the sight of a destroyed flying machine, be it big or small. He heard the two men stumbling in the dark and turned the torch in their direction to help them.

'Holy Mother of God!' he heard the priest exclaim softly as he looked around the interior. The heavy smell of charred metal and burnt material still hung in the air and Father Vincente knew it was an odour that would always be with him in his mind. 'What now?' he asked his two companions.

'Up there.' Keller pointed the beam towards the staircase and upwards.

'Will it still hold us?' the priest asked.

'If we go one at a time it should be all right,' the co-pilot reassured him. He moved towards the narrow staircase, the priest and the medium close on his heels. Testing each step, he made his way up, careful to avoid the gaping holes in some of the stairs. One side of the staircase was completely open to the first-class passenger compartment and he briefly shone the light down into it, then wished he hadn't. Hardly anything at all remained in there.

He soon found himself in the passenger lounge, but was careful not to step into it; the whole floor tilted precariously downwards and there was a long narrow opening at its end leading back into the main body of the aircraft. He turned his attention forward, to the cockpit. The small door leading into it was open, loose on its hinges, but still intact. Keller pushed through and surveyed the confined compartment. As he knew they would be, all the instrument panels had been ripped out and taken away for further examination. The front of the cockpit had caved in from the floor upwards and, incredibly, he could see parts of the glass-fibre radar cone, which was carried in the very nose of the Jumbo, pushed forward into the cockpit. There was hardly anything left at all of the pilots' seats and for the thousandth time he wondered how the hell he'd escaped such devastation. A mangled hole in the roof provided a possible clue: could he have been thrown through that opening after it had been made by flying metal? He felt the cold night air seeping through the gap, its icy current tightening his flesh. No, it was impossible. Any piece of metal of that size which had travelled with enough velocity to cause a hole like that would have had to pass right through him. It would have killed him instantly!

But this thought led on to another possible solution: suppose there *had* been an explosion below, and the forward passenger door had been blown off with the blast? And suppose he had been out of the cockpit for some reason at the moment of impact and thrown clear through the open doorway? It was hardly feasible. For why should he be out of the cockpit at such a point? Panic, perhaps? Or maybe he had come down to inspect the damage caused by the blast? No, there wouldn't have been time. Hardly feasible, and yet – it was a slender thread to cling to! It could at least help him keep his sanity.

'Are you all right up there, Mr Keller?' he heard the priest's voice from below.

He turned back towards the staircase. 'Yes, I'm fine.' And he was. Apart from the natural sadness at the sight of the destruction of such a fine machine, he now felt little remorse. He felt puzzlement, he felt wonder, but the melancholic depression that had been dogging him for so long had lifted. Perhaps it was the experience last night: the positive feeling of Cathy's presence, the reassurance that her death did not mean she no longer existed. To him it was a new and exciting concept, a concept that would need time to grow in his mind, to be finally accepted and appreciated. And there was more, too, because he felt close now, close to solving a mystery. What was the mystery? His survival? The cause of the crash? No, it was something much greater, but he had no idea what it was. Just a feeling.

'May we come up, Mr Keller?' The priest's voice interrupted his thoughts again. 'It's awfully dark and lonely down here.' Father Vincente was making an effort to keep his voice light.

'What? Sorry, yes, please come up. One at a time,' Keller called down to them. 'Mind the gaps in the stairs and the hole in the side panelling.' He shone the torch down into the dim stairwell.

The priest came up first and Hobbs quickly followed. 'Through there,' the co-pilot pointed as the three of them crowded in the tiny area between the cockpit and the passenger lounge. He led the way. The priest's face was grave when he saw the damage to the cockpit. 'Those poor, poor men,' he said, and looked up at the co-pilot. 'You were a very lucky man, Mr Keller.'

'Was I?' he replied, without rancour.

Hobbs spoke. 'I suggest we proceed with haste. If the police return, it could prove to be very awkward. I'm sure they'll make us leave as we've got no authority to be here.'

'Yes, I'm sure you're right,' Father Vincente said. 'They may have allowed us to be here if I'd spoken to them first, but under these circumstances . . .' He left the sentence unfinished.

'How do we begin, Mr Hobbs?' asked Keller.

'We begin by laying down a few ground rules.' The priest had spoken before the spiritualist could answer. 'We must agree to call the experiment off if it seems to be getting out of hand.' He looked searchingly at Hobbs, then added: 'By any means we deem necessary. Also, if the strain becomes too much for any one of us, the other two must stop immediately and help that person. Lastly, whatever happens here tonight will be kept to ourselves, until such a time when all three of us feel it would be right to let the facts be known. Have I your word on that, Mr Hobbs?'

'Certainly,' came the instant reply.

'Mr Keller?'

The co-pilot was more hesitant, but finally he nodded and said, 'Yes.'

'Then let us proceed.' The priest placed his briefcase on the scorched floor of the cockpit and opened it. He removed two long candles and lit them immediately. 'These will provide us with some extra light,' he said, handing them to the two men. They found suitable resting places for the candles and turned their attention back to the priest who was draping a length of dark material around his shoulders. In the brighter, but more eerie light, they saw it was a purple stole. He next took out a crucifix and placed it on the floor before them, then reached back into the bag for a vial of clear water and a darkly bound book. 'I want to consecrate the area with Holy Water before we begin,' he explained, unscrewing the lid of the glass container. He dipped his fingers into the blessed water and sprinkled it around the interior of the cockpit, intoning a barely heard prayer as he did so, and frequently making the sign of the cross. Before closing the lid, he sprinkled water over the two men, his lips moving in quiet supplication. Keller was impatient to get on, but he did not resist the priest's ritual.

At last, screwing the lid of the vial loosely back on, Father Vincente smiled at the two men. 'Not much of a preparation, gentlemen, but then I don't know how far you intend to go.

As it is, I may just be over-cautious.' He put the container close to the crucifix, within easy reach. Straightening up again, he told them: 'I intend to pray from the Litany of the Saints whilst you proceed. Just an added precaution.' He smiled and opened his book. 'I won't interrupt you.' Then he paused before adding: 'Unless I have to.'

Father Vincente again wondered briefly at his own faith in these two strangers. They had come to him in the night with their distressing story of discarnate souls bound to this world for undiscovered reasons, pleading for his help in unravelling the mystery that was in some way connected with the young co-pilot, the answer that would release those wretched souls and perhaps free the young man from his guilt. Why had he believed in them? Apart from their obvious sincerity, the answer was perfectly simple: he had been expecting them! Or at least, he had been expecting something like this to happen.

Many years ago, in his native Switzerland, a village not too far from his own had suffered a terrible tragedy. A skiing resort, full of holidaymakers, men, women and many children, perched high above the village on a mountainside, had been completely destroyed by an avalanche, the people crushed to death, none surviving. The villagers had grieved over the loss, but their mourning seemed to extend for many more months than was entirely natural. There was a feeling of strange oppression in the little hamlet and then queer things began to happen: accidents, sudden deaths, madness. A priest from his own order had been summoned – an older, much wiser man than he – and an exorcism had been carried out. Whether it had been only in the villagers' imagination, or there really had been a tangible 'haunting' in the village, he had never been quite sure, but certainly life had returned to normal soon after the priest had performed the ceremony. There had been other incidents, too, in his ordained life as a priest, incidents that were neither dramatic nor of great importance, but proved to him without a doubt there were influences around them all that were not of this world.

If what these men claimed proved to be true, it was his duty to investigate then recommend the matter to be handled by a higher authority than his. He was a mere parish priest; there were others of his order that were trained and infinitely more capable of dealing with affairs of this nature.

'David, can you get yourself into a position close to where you would have been on that flight?' Hobbs asked.

'It's not possible, I'm afraid.' The co-pilot pointed towards the shattered front of the aircraft. 'My place – and the captain's – has been completely destroyed.'

'All right then. Just get as close as you can.'

Keller scrambled over debris, aware that the weakened floor might collapse at any moment, pitching the three of them into the cabin below. And there were too many pointed spikes of mangled metal below for them to escape without injury. He reached the farthest point he could then squatted on the floor before the jumbled wreckage. It gave him an eerie sensation which he tried to ignore.

'Okay,' he called back over his shoulder. He could hear the priest's soft litany as Hobbs crawled forward to join him.

'Now, close your eyes, David, and try to think back to that night. If you can't, think beyond it. The nearest point you can remember.'

Keller concentrated, but it was no use; everything was still a blank. He shook his head.

'Try hard. Anything before the flight even,' Hobbs urged.

He thought back to the fight with Captain Rogan in the hangar. The senior pilot's angry face. His words, filled with hate. He tried to bring to mind the consequences of that fight, but it was no use. There was nothing. He raised a hand to his eyes and rubbed them roughly. Oh God, why can't I remember? His new-found confidence began to drain away from him. His resolution wavered. Cathy, can't you help me? I know you haven't gone from me. Please, please help!

Nothing.

He breathed out wearily and looked round at Hobbs and stiffened when he saw the spiritualist's expression in the gloom. His eyes were half closed, only their whites were visible; there were rigid lines on his face. Keller suddenly noticed the temperature in the confined space had dropped by several degrees and the air in Hobbs's lungs escaped in small clouds of steam. Not only had it become noticeably colder, but the atmosphere in the cockpit had changed. There was a tension, a terrible feeling of oppression, an almost physical sensation of a huge weight being pressed down on them.

Keller tried to move, but he found his limbs were locked by some unbreakable bond. He tried to speak but his throat was dry – the words would not form. The prayers of the priest behind him faltered for a few seconds, then continued, the voice sharp, hesitant, as though forced.

The co-pilot suddenly felt a pressure on his back, a cool, icy cool, sensation at the base of his spine travelling upwards. The muscles of his neck and shoulders hunched together and he struggled to move his arms. It felt – it felt as if ... something were trying ... to enter ... him! The feeling of revulsion was nauseating and bile rose in his throat. He fought against the force, a living, physical thing that struggled equally against him, which was trying to dominate him. His ears pounded with the blood that rushed through them and he felt the movement of his heart as it raced madly, then began to slow, to become leaden. He feared it might stop, but abruptly, it speeded up again, and ran fast, too fast! Where was the priest? Why wasn't he helping?

But Father Vincente did not understand the battle that was going on inside Keller. He was aware of the terrible presence in the aircraft, the loathsome, malevolent thing that had descended upon them, and he renewed the strength of his prayers. But he failed to recognize the condition of the two men in front of him. The light was bad and he could only see their figures, Hobbs kneeling beside the crouched co-pilot. There was nothing to indicate their plight. He reached for the crucifix and held it to his chest.

Keller was losing. The monstrous entity – whatever it was – was spreading through him, sapping his strength, dominating his will, devouring his soul. He heard the chuckle then – low and coarse. *Demonish!* His eyes, the only part of him that could move, looked towards the spiritualist kneeling at his side. The sound had come from him! With horror, Keller saw his eyes were fully opened now and were regarding him with a gloating, baleful pleasure. The dry chuckle escaped from his sneering lips again.

'Welcome, Keller.' The voice came from Hobbs, but it didn't belong to him. It was the same low-pitched snarl Keller had heard the night before. 'You've come to me at last, eh, bastard?'

Father Vincente heard the words. He was struck rigid as he realized what was happening. His body began to tremble with fear. 'In the name of God, no!' he screamed, lunging forward and snatching at the vial on the floor as he did so. But in his haste, and in the dark, he stumbled and the vial slipped from his grasp, rolling out of sight beneath strips of fallen metal. He dropped to his knees and desperately searched for it, but the glow from the candles, and even the torch, had dimmed considerably.

Hobbs – or the thing that now was Hobbs – turned his head slowly to regard the scrambling priest with disdain.

'Grovel, priest, you sucker of spirits, you leech of the cloth.' The low, husky chuckle. 'Do you think a few drops of piss would drive me away?'

Father Vincente stopped his searching and looked up at Hobbs. Suddenly, he thrust the cross forward and began to shout: 'Holy Lord, Almighty Father, Everlasting God and Father of our Lord Jesus Christ. Who once and for all consigned that fallen tyrant to the flames of hell. Who sent Your only begotten Son into the world to crush that roaring lion; hasten to our call for help...' The thing in Hobbs laughed aloud, horrendously, filling the priest's ears with its braying sound. It reached a high pitch, and the spiritualist's body rocked backwards and forwards, mocking the priest. Father Vincente faltered, then continued: 'Hasten to our call for help and snatch from ruination and from the clutches of the noonday Devil this human being made in Your image and likeness. Strike, terror, Lord, into...'

'Stop!' the creature screamed. 'Fool. Do you think words are enough?' He glared at the priest.

Suddenly, the crucifix in Father Vincente's hand glowed red hot. He dropped it with a cry of pain and fell back. The metal crucifix lay on the cockpit floor between the priest and Hobbs, black trails of smoke rising from it.

The creature laughed again and the priest immediately resumed his incantation: 'Into ... into the beast ... now laying waste Your vineyard. Let Your mighty hand cast him out...'

Keller felt the pressure ease slightly. The droning words of the priest came through to him and somehow filled him. He had felt himself sinking, sinking, falling into a void of blackness where only a round white object waited for him. As he fell towards it, he saw two dark, cold eyes drawing him down, rose-bud lips silently mocking. Hands constricted his throat and breathing became difficult. He saw the long, buckled blemish, the brown scorched plastic of the doll's face! The doll's face! He remembered the little girl boarding the aircraft, carrying the tiny plastic doll! He remembered that!

And then the priest's words had come droning through, as if from a great distance away, but growing louder, louder as they reached for him. He found himself saying the unknown words with the priest, words he'd never heard before. No sounds came from his lips, but inside himself, inside the cavern of his being, he spoke them: '... Of Your servant, so he may no longer hold captive this person whom it pleased You to make...' He began to emerge again, to float to the surface, towards light. '... In Your image, and to redeem through Your Son, who lives and reigns with You...' The unseen hands fell away from his throat. '... In the unity of the Holy Spirit...' He was reaching the surface, the voice was louder. '... God, for ever and ever...' With a gasp he fell forward, released from the terrible pressure that had held him in its suffocating grip.

Hobbs was staring at the priest, vile obscenities pouring from his twisted lips. Keller staggered upright and struck out at the spiritualist, knocking him back against crumbling metal. The thing lay there in the dark and glared at the co-pilot, his malicious eyes filled with hate. A leer, a twisted snarl of a smile, spread across his face. 'Think you've escaped?' he rasped.

Suddenly, the broken shell of the aircraft began to tremble. Chunks of metal were dislodged and fell with a dull clatter. The thing on the floor was laughing aloud, grotesque in its derision of them. The trembling became more violent, the broken aircraft began to vibrate with a rising intensity. A high-pitched whining howl filled the small compartment, stinging their eardrums with its sound, penetrating to a point behind their eyes, causing agonizing pain. Keller lost his balance as the shaking increased, crashing back against the framework of the removed electronics panel. The aircraft seemed to be crumbling around them, whole panels of stained metal falling inwards, sending up choking clouds of sooty dust. The two candles were knocked over, leaving them with only the dull light from the torch. The quivering world seemed to be a cauldron of sound: the clang of toppling metal; the groaning of the aircraft itself as it suffered the new onslaught on its already violated body; the shrieking that dominated every other sound, the obscene mocking laughter of the thing inside Hobbs; and, throughout, the priest's fervent incantation, rising in pitch to compete with the noise.

Keller clasped his hands to his ears and rocked his head from side to side. A cry rose from his throat as though the inner sound would act as a barrier against the external. And then, just when it seemed the aircraft must collapse under the onslaught, the floor they crouched on must fall in, tossing them into the cabin below, bringing the walls down on top of them, the whining howl began to fade. Keller wasn't aware of its decline at first, for his head rang with the after-sound. It was only when the trembling stopped, suddenly and almost jarringly, that he realized an uneasy stillness had descended upon the wreckage. He took his hands away from his ears and heard only the drone of the priest's prayers. In the faint torchlight he could distinguish the huddled figure of Hobbs.

Keller then became aware of the odour: the fetid, revolting stink of decay and worse, the sickening smell of burnt flesh. Darker shapes seemed to be swirling around the cockpit and he thought at first it was merely the unsettled ash, disturbed by the vibrations, falling once again on to the charred floor. But then, he heard the voices. Whispers. Confused and frightened. Something cold touched his hand and he drew hastily back against the wall.

An animal grunt came from the other side of the cockpit and he saw the black figure of Hobbs rising to his feet.

The whispers became harsher, strident. Clearer voices came through. 'Keller ... he's here! ... Keller ... is it him? ...'

The co-pilot whirled around as a voice came from only inches away, as though someone were crouching next to him, whispering into his ear. 'Dave ... help us ... find him for us ...'

The voice was Rogan's!

It sounded strained, husky, but there was no doubt in his mind that it belonged to Captain Rogan.

Keller's voice was weak, tremulous. 'Find who, Skipper? Who must I find?'

A different voice spoke, but the sound came from the same spot. 'Find the one who did this to me!' The tone was angry. 'To us! We can show you!'

'Fools!' Hobbs was standing in the beam of the torch, glowering down at the co-pilot. 'We have this one! He belongs with us! We'll take him!'

Keller drew his legs up, ready to spring away from the medium should he advance on him.

'No ... no ...' It was Rogan's voice again. 'Not Keller ... the other one ...' Other voices joined in. 'The other one ...'

A whimpering of a child came from a far corner. 'Mummy, I'm frightened. Where are we?' A scream split the air. 'We're crashing!' Another voice, a plea: 'Help us!' A wailing broke out, echoing around the walls, drifting out into the night through the hole in the aircraft's roof.

'Be silent!' the thing inside Hobbs screamed. And then, he chuckled. The low, menacing snigger that struck dread into Keller's heart. The co-pilot watched as the figure bent low and reached for something. He came up with a jagged object in his hand and, in the dim light, Keller saw it was a twisted bar of metal. Hobbs took a step towards the hunched co-pilot.

Father Vincente had been watching in horror, his lips still reciting the soundless prayers that had proved so inadequate. How foolish he'd been to allow this to happen! He was not worthy to deal with a perversion of this kind. He saw Hobbs moving forward towards Keller, wielding a jagged piece of metal, raising it aloft, ready to strike. But the weapon trembled in his grasp as though some internal battle were taking place within the possessed medium's mind. Hobbs's face was a mask of fury. His glaring eyes seemed as if they would burst from their retaining sockets. A large, purple vein throbbed in his temple. One side of his mouth drew back in an unnatural way, the bandage now torn from his face, revealing bloodied, mutilated lips, exposing the teeth and gums in an ugly grimace. He called out, his language foul and degenerate and, slowly, the grimace turned into a leer of triumph. The hand holding the jagged metal began its swift descent.

But Keller, a look of sheer rage on his face, was already lunging forward. His shoulder smashed forcefully into Hobbs's chest, both men falling heavily against the wall, arms and legs thrashing in a desperate struggle. Dark, shadowy shapes whisked past the priest's shocked eyes, discarnate bodies swirling in confusion. Father Vincente knew, without seeing, not just the cockpit, but the whole of the aircraft's smashed body, was filled with such shapes. Tormented, bewildered souls, many – he could sense it – vindictive, vengeful; others just frightened.

Keller's body suddenly came hurtling towards the priest, thrown with abnormal strength by the demon controlling the medium. He heard the mocking laughter as he fell to the floor, the co-pilot's body crushing the breath from him. He lay there gasping for air, inhaling the sooty dust into his lungs, retching with its clogging stench. The torch had been kicked sideways, its narrow beam cutting weakly through the darkness, past his face, reflecting back against something shiny lying against the restraining metal struts that had once held the flight engineer's seat. The object was made of glass.

Hobbs was on his feet now, lumbering towards Keller, who was slowly drawing himself to one knee, sucking in air noisily, but ready to spring again at the advancing monstrosity. He felt no fear, only a loathing disgust, a hatred for this creature using the little man's body. Hobbs held on to the side of the cockpit for support, not wanting to stumble on the treacherous floor now that the prey was almost his. The voices of the others screamed at the demon, most urging it on, a few, the ones it had not yet fully corrupted to its way, fighting against it still, as they had when it had been about to smite Keller down with the piece of metal. But it held them in abeyance. They were no match for its cunning, its power, a power already developed in the physical world by the man Goswell. Its sniggering laughter became a growling sneer as it faced the co-pilot. It saw no fear in the man's steady gaze, but then the fool was unaware of the everlasting state of his danger.

It ran forward with a screech of triumph and the co-pilot quickly crouched forward to meet it. But a dark shadow rose up between them. Liquid splashed against the medium's face and the demon screamed in fear and pain as the Holy Water burnt into the flesh, tearing, rending, driving it from the human body. Hobbs staggered back and fell to the floor, his hands clutching at his burning face. Blisters were already forming between his fingers, the skin hissing as though acid had been poured over it. The demon within struggled to keep its hold over the mortal, but the priest did not relent. More Holy Water drenched Hobbs's hands and neck. The skin on his head fell away as the blessed liquid touched it, white curls of steam rising from it, huge welts appearing instantly. The demonic soul howled with anguish. The pain was too much! It twisted within the body in agony. It was losing! Others were helping to drive it out: the sensitive, anxious to reclaim his body; spirits which still refused to bend to its will, even though they were confused and lost!

It was weakening and the torture was unbearable. It fled.

Keller, still crouching forward, stunned by Father Vincente's action and the subsequent horror, felt the rush of cold air sweep by, the incredibly fetid stench assailing his nostrils as though something foul had just breathed on him. The shock, the instinctive reaction to get out of the path of this invisible malignity, made him stagger back through the open doorway where he fell, tripped by unseen debris. He tried to save himself, but metal crumbled in his hand and he felt himself falling down the stairwell, his head striking the steps, his body turning over, pulling away chunks of panelling as he went. He landed in a heap at the bottom of the stairwell and inky blackness closed in on him.

He lay there, still, unmoving. His eyes were open, yet he saw nothing. He heard voices, but they were remembered voices, not the whispers of these dead things. Captain Rogan's, Cathy's, Alan's, their flight engineer; others – passengers – voices of excited children, nervous mothers, businessmen calling out to one another in overloud jocularity. He heard the aircraft's engines starting up, the Jumbo jet becoming a living thing, trembling with its unleashed power.

He felt the gentle movement as it was pushed clear of the passenger terminal by a tractor. And then Captain Rogan's voice came filtering through: 'Consul 2802, request taxi clearance.' And he heard the mechanical reply: '2802, you are clear to taxi for twenty-eight right, when clear of the cul-de-sac call one-one-eight decimal six-five for departure clearance . . .'

He was back on the flight deck again, Captain Rogan in the seat on his left, speaking into his headset, patiently going through the usual take-off drill.

Once again it was the night of the 747's journey into oblivion!

18

The demon fled into the night. It seethed and moaned in agony. As it gathered its forces together, those that would come, it cast itself about, seeking revenge.

The wailing of the ambulance had disturbed Ernest Goodwin from his work. He left the darkroom, checking that there was no unexposed film unshielded before he opened the door. He went over to the window which looked on to the High Street, opened it and stuck his head out, craning his neck to see where the ambulance had come to a halt.

It looked as if the vehicle was near the church again. Oh dear, don't say the vicar's had another relapse! He tutted to himself. Reverend Biddlestone had only returned from hospital that afternoon, so he'd been told. Bloody doctors nowadays! Sending patients home before they're properly fit just because their hospitals are crowded! You've got to be dying to get a hospital bed these days – and then you'd better die fast or they have you out again! He shook his head in disgust and drew back into the room, closing the window with a thump. As he walked back into the darkroom, he paused to look at the stacks of freshly glazed photographs lying on a working top waiting to be trimmed. Picking one up from a pile, he studied its contents again. This was the one that fascinated him, the one showing the rows of sheet-covered corpses. Why did he feel his peculiar affinity with it, almost as if he knew the people lying beneath the bloodstained shrouds. He shrugged. Having been on the spot the night of the crash, having spent hours alone with photographs of the ensuing holocaust, he was more familiar with the disaster than anyone. Almost as much as the victims.

He walked leisurely over to the guillotine and placed the photograph on the wooden cutting base, pushing its edge against the squared-up length of metal at one side. He raised the handle of the steel cutter about a foot, and slid the picture so it overlapped the edge by a quarter of an inch. He brought the blade down swiftly and a thin sliver of bromide paper drifted to the floor. He repeated the process on the other three sides. All the photographs he had printed that day would have to be trimmed in this fashion, but he still had more prints to develop. However, Martin had promised to come back and help him. He hoped his partner would not be too long; he was anxious to hear of the deal he'd pulled off. He returned to the darkroom, taking the picture of the rows of corpses with him, hardly aware of the deep chill that had just struck the room.

Closing the door tight behind him, Ernest placed the photograph on a workbench, and turned his attention to the enlarger. He positioned a sheet of smooth photographic paper beneath the metal retaining masks, shiny side up, and clicked on the enlarger's light, timing the seconds with an old-fashioned stopwatch. There was no need to check the focus or size of image, for he had already taken a couple of dozen prints from the same negative. Nor did he bother to look at the image projected on to the surface of the chemical paper.

At the appropriate time, he flicked off the switch, raised the mount, took out the undeveloped paper, and placed it into the developing liquid, dipping it under daintily with a finger, ensuring every corner was fully immersed. He swirled the fluid against its surface for a few seconds, then bent forward as the image began to appear. He had expected to see a shot of one of the Jumbo's jet engines, lying alone in the field, separated from the wing it had been housed under, a mangled sculpture of sophisticated metal rendered useless by the impact. A group of men, all carrying clipboards, were standing around it, examining its exposed machinery, one of them gingerly lifting the displaced thrust cone lying several feet away. That's what he had expected to see.

Instead, the image that came through, slowly at first, then with a rush, was that of a man. The strangest, most evil-looking man Ernest had ever set eyes on. He was totally naked, his thin, emaciated body twisted with disease as though the worms that welcomed corpses laid to rest beneath the ground were already devouring his living body. His gaunt face was a mask of grinning evil, the eyes burning malevolently from the darkening paper, the mouth revealing broken teeth amid glistening lips in its wicked leer. Sparse clumps of hair hung from his bare scalp, and deep lines, the black wrinkles of perversity, filled his face as though it were a rocky landscape from some far-off rain-starved land. The sparrow-like shoulders were hunched forward, the rounded abdomen and thin pelvis thrust forward in an obscene gesture. In his bony, claw-like hands he held his over-sized, swollen penis, the testicles hanging like two grotesquely stretched sacks almost to his knees. The reed-like legs that supported his skeletal frame were riddled with pockmarks, evidence of some still-lingering pestilence.

As the chemicals continued their function, the developing process unchecked, the image began to grow darker, gradually succumbing to the enveloping blackness, until only the eyes, with their darkly glowing, hypnotic pupils, glared out at him. And then, they too vanished.

He heard the snicker of laughter behind him just as his frightened mind tried to recall where he'd seen that face before. It had been years before – at least fifteen, perhaps twenty – in a newspaper or magazine. Something to do with the man's wartime activities in this country, his forced exile, and more trouble in the States. He couldn't remember the details, but the face was one that could never be forgotten. The face of a beast! He stared down at the floating black photographic paper, his own red image reflecting back at him.

Ernest froze and was afraid to turn and see what was in the room with him, to discover just *what* had laughed in that coarse, malicious way. He felt the cold pressure at the back of his neck, felt the chill, pungent breath on his cheek. The low chuckle was so close now. He could only watch his own reflection, gently rippling and swaying in the yellowish fluid, his own eyes staring back at him as if they understood his fear.

The coldness closed around his body like encircling arms.

Martin Samuels climbed the stairs to the studio, irritation surging through him, his mind jumping agitatedly from one thought to another. Cheapskates! A hundred pounds per neg indeed! Those magazines were all the same! Imagine a world-wide publication like that trying to rook him with such a miserable sum! Schmucks! Two-fifty each would be the least he'd accept. He'd asked three-fifty but they'd laughed in his face, claiming it was old news now, that the photographs had been seen by everyone, they were no longer exclusive. He'd pointed out that all his shots had not been used; there were many others, less interesting perhaps, but still dramatic, still poignant. He was offering the whole packet, sole rights! It was a bargain! Why, he knew top London photographers earned more than four hundred a day just for advertising shots! He was selling true-life tragedy, on-the-spot drama! They had no imagination these people. He'd rather accept the offer from *Paris Match* than deal with gonifs like them! They'd made quite a bit of money out of the air crash so far, but this was to have been the killing – the *coup de grâce*. With the money from this deal they'd have been set for life! They could have branched out, broadened their scope. He could have concentrated on more reportage, while Ernie could carry on with the more mundane aspects of their work: the portraits, the weddings, the industrial sites, etc. Ernie had his limits. Maybe they could move over into Slough, be more in the centre of things. Rents in London were far too high to consider even with their new-found wealth. Oh, those sodding cow-sons! Still, there were other magazines, bigger magazines, who'd be interested. Grumbling to himself he pushed open the door to the studio.

'Ernie?' he called out, flicking on the light switch. 'You in the darkroom, Ernie?'

There was no answer.

Where the hell was the schlemiel? He knows there's a lot of work to be done. He can't have done it all himself already! Martin clucked his tongue and shrugged himself out of his overcoat. He hung it up behind the door and walked over to the stacks of untrimmed photographs waiting on the bench, rubbing his hands together to warm them. My life, it's cold in here! he thought, looking towards the windows, checking they were shut. He examined the shots, squinting to make sure of the focus. Stupid bastard hasn't dusted the lens again! he cursed, when he saw the tiny white specks that dotted the prints. Well, I'm not staying up all night spotting. He can bloody well print them again!

He banged disgustedly on the darkroom door. 'Ernie, you in there?' He waited for a reply but none came.

He caught sight of the guillotine, it's blade standing upright, at right angles to its base. That was another minor source of irritation to Martin. His partner was always leaving the blade standing instead of tucked down beside the wooden base. Someone's going to chop their fingers off one of these days! He was always telling him. He walked over to the cutting instrument ready to lower the offending blade, but his attention was caught by the photograph lying on its desk. He peered down at it. Huh, such a morbid shot! All those rows of dead people! I don't know why Ernie is so fond of this one – probably because it's one of his! Such a depressing scene; no drama, just melancholic stillness, but something small and white in one corner caught his attention. He hadn't noticed that before. It looked like a tiny body lying in the mud, separated from the white-covered corpses. My God, was it a baby? He breathed a sigh of relief when he saw the little body was in fact that of a doll. Yes, I didn't think there were any babies on the plane, he told himself. Funny I hadn't spotted the doll before, though. Makes it very poignant. Maybe it's not such a bad picture after all!

He bent closer. Such a strange look on the doll's face. Almost human. No – almost *in*human!

And then, an amazing thing happened.

Wisps of white smoke began to rise from the photograph and the edges started to curl inwards. He jumped back in surprise. What the shit was happening? Tiny flames began to lick at the black and white image, creeping across the surface, eating away at the chemically treated paper, the white-covered corpses again destroyed by flames. It curled almost into a loose ball then, with a sudden burst, the fire consumed it completely, leaving only black ashes that drifted slowly upwards.

Such a thing! How had it occurred? The middle-aged photographer shook his head in wonder. He touched the remaining flakes of charred paper with a tentative finger, and they crumbled into a fine ash. He felt the movement rather than saw it, and hastily drew his hand away as the guillotine's blade came flashing down. He staggered back in fright as the three foot length razor-sharp metal thudded down with a swift, grinding-chomping noise.

His heart beat wildly with the shock. My God, it could've had my hand off! What's going on around here? And where's that *meshugana* Ernie? Martin shivered at the icy blast that suddenly swirled around the room. Goose-pimples rose on the backs of his hands and along the lengths of his arms. He heard a sound from the darkroom. A thump.

'Ernie, is that you? Are you playing games with me, Ernie?' He heard what sounded like a muffled chuckle coming from the processing room. He marched over to the door and put an ear to it.

'Are you in there, Ernie?' There was no reply, but he thought he heard movement. He banged on the wood, once, hard. 'I'm coming in, you goy! There'd better not be any film out!'

For a photographer, even if he were of the more basic variety, Martin Samuels had a distinct lack of imagination. Perhaps if he'd had more, he wouldn't have opened the door so readily. He knew the oddest things were happening in Eton, he was aware of the tension in the town's residents, but, over the past few weeks, he had been too busy to feel it himself. The burning photograph, the falling guillotine – his mind would not allow itself to dwell on the mystery. They had just happened and, of course, there was a simple explanation for the phenomenon. But he had more pertinent problems to think about – financial problems – and he had precious little time to ponder over the imponderable. He turned the handle and angrily pulled the door towards him. The foul stench that rushed out made him wrinkle his nose in disgust and the icy blast that greeted him caused his whole body to shiver involuntarily. He drew out a handkerchief and held it to his sensitive nose. He screwed up his eyes, trying to penetrate the gloom.

The red light seemed even dimmer than usual, but he thought he saw a dark figure standing at the back of the little room next to the water tank.

'Ernie, is that you?' he inquired hesitantly.

For the first time, real fear gripped him. His imagination had been finally sparked into life. It was the heavy, grunted breathing that instigated his fear more than anything. It was deep, growling, as if it came from scarred vocal cords. Unearthly!

The smell was overpowering and he swayed as its noxious fumes drugged his senses.

'Who – who's there?' he cried out, holding on to the side of the door for support.

He heard the terrible snigger.

Then the voice.

'Hello, Jew,' it said.

He felt something push him from behind. Invisible hands. Powerful. He stumbled forward and fell on his knees into the red glowing room. The figure stepped out of the darkest shadows towards him and stooped down. He found himself looking into the crimson face of his partner. And yet, it wasn't him! The features were the same but the expression was totally alien to Ernie's. It contained all the viciousness that existed in the world. All the ills of mankind somehow drawn together and given physical expression. The face of the Devil!

Martin whimpered in abject terror. Never had he experienced such total, paralysing fear. The tiny muscles surrounding his hair follicles tightened, the pupils of his eyes widened, his heart pounded like a mad thing in his chest. Blood emptied from his gut into nearby muscles causing a heavy, sick feeling in the pit of his stomach. Chemicals were released into his bloodstream causing a tingling throughout. Muscles jerked and twitched, his whole body quivered. His bowels loosened and brown fluid ran hotly down his legs. He opened his mouth to scream, but only a dry, choked gurgle emerged.

'Jew bastard,' the voice said. 'Look how you tremble. How you shit yourself.'

Martin felt iron fingers grip him under his soaking armpits. The demon face moved closer, and grinned. 'How pleased *Mastomah*, the Prince, will be to receive one like this! How *Agaliarept* will gloat! How *Glasyalabolas* will rejoice!'

The photographer felt himself lifted, the evil face still remaining only inches away from his, its fetid breath entering his open mouth, descending into his lungs, spreading through his body.

'Well, Jew, nothing to say?' A mocking snigger. 'See how your partner carries you. Do you know where? Why not call on *Yahweh* for help?' Again, the growling laugh.

His feet dragged uselessly along the floor as his plump body was dragged over to the water tank. The cruel voice whispered in his ear. 'They think they destroyed me. The priest thinks water will kill. You see how these religious morons think, Jew? It burnt me, yes, as the fire burnt my body. But I am not dead. I cannot be dead.'

Martin finally managed to scream as he was dragged off

his feet and his body bent over the tank. The scream became a gurgling roar as his head was thrust beneath the water, the black and white prints swirling around him in a frenzy. His nose was pushed flat against the round-holed grille at the bottom of the wash and he struggled to twist his neck to ease the pressure. But the hands that trapped him were too strong.

Water gushed into his screaming mouth and up his nostrils. He was forced to suck in and the water raced down his throat and filled his lungs, as had the beast's breath a few moments before. The effect was more deadly, and a greyness seeped into his mind, gradually forcing all visions from it like a descending curtain. When the grey curtain had completed its fall, life drifted away from him like a bored acquaintance.

When the body had ceased its struggles, and the short legs hung limp, exhausted from their death kicks, the demon released it, allowing the torso to lie face down in the water.

It walked from the darkroom and as it passed the stacks of dried prints on the workbench, they smouldered, then burst into flame. The demon swept the rows of hanging negatives into one arm and hurled them to the middle of the floor. Wrenching open cupboards, it pulled out hundreds of yellow packets containing rolls of film and many rectangular boxes that held sheet film, and threw them into the pile of curled negatives. Then, the demon walked over to the burning prints and lifted several stacks of them, ignoring the blisters that immediately appeared on its hands.

The pain meant nothing to the demon, but the soul it held subdued deep inside screamed and writhed in agony as it felt the flames destroying its body.

The creature carried the burning stacks to the middle of the floor and dropped them among the heap of negatives and boxes of film. With a whoosh, the dark grey negatives caught alight and quickly engulfed the yellow boxes. The figure of Ernest Goodwin stood amidst the growing inferno and the thing that possessed his body laughed aloud. Fire was an old friend now. Once flames had consumed its mortal body; now they sustained it.

It walked through the blaze and opened the studio door, bidding the others to follow. There was more, much more, to do that night.

19

'London Ground, Consul 2802 for clearance.' Captain Rogan became impatient. He hated any delay of departure time, hated the wastage of fuel, the forced retention of the throbbing power building up in the four jet engines. So far, they had only been delayed for one minute, but the senior pilot's foul mood had already been caused by other, more personal, reasons and the late take-off was a further irritant.

'Hold, 2802,' came the firm metallic reply.

'Come on,' said Rogan irritably, but to himself, not into the headset.

Keller glanced across at him, and the captain avoided his gaze, looking straight ahead, out into the night.

Christ, thought the co-pilot, that's the end of our relationship. Why hadn't Beth kept quiet? What possible good could it have done to tell her husband of her unfaithfulness with his friend and protégé? There were plenty of other names to mention, so why his? A one-night stand. Nothing serious. A lapse on his part. Unforgivable, yes; but among so many others probably a lot more serious, why even mention it? But then Beth had wanted to hurt Peter Rogan where it most hurt – his pride – and she'd succeeded. It wasn't just her unfaithfulness that wounded him so deeply; it was the humiliation of having been duped by his own subordinate! Someone he'd trusted.

The question was: would he tell Cathy?

Keller had already decided he himself would do so as soon as he got the chance. It was pointless to live under the threat of someone else revealing his duplicity. She'd be hurt terribly when he told her, but if it came from another person . . . He shut the thought from his mind. She'd get over it if her love was strong enough and providing he was honest with her. If she couldn't . . . It was another thought to be shut from his mind. Whatever happened, he made up his mind he would never lose her. She was too precious now. But Rogan was another matter. He knew he could never really make amends, and knocking him down yesterday hadn't exactly helped. I'm sorry, Skipper, he apologized mentally. Maybe I'll make it up to you too, some day.

'Consul 2802,' the metallic voice broke into both men's thoughts, 'your clearance is flight planned route for Washington Dulles. Standard instrument departure Daventry two, with flight level three-fifty for cruise. Squawk Alpha 4208 with altitude.'

With a relieved sigh, Captain Rogan read back their flight plan.

'Roger, Consul 2802, read back is correct,' came the prompt reply. 'Contact one-two-one decimal three.'

'London Ground. Consul 2802 at the holding point twenty-eight right.'

'2802, behind the landing DC8, line up and hold.'

'2802 behind the landing to line up.'

'2802 cleared to take off.'

'2802 is rolling.'

The 747 rumbled down the runway, gathering speed, the thrust from its jets pushing the passengers and crew alike gently back in their seats. In a matter of seconds, V1, the point at which the pilot is committed to flight, was reached and passed. Captain Rogan accelerated to VR and called out, 'rotate', as the Jumbo reached its climbing altitude, then he brought the Jumbo's nose smoothly up into the air and the monster began to lift, incredible in its power, pushing into the unresisting air, becoming a graceful giant in flight as it rose into the night.

Keller relaxed as the Jumbo gained height and drew a great curve in the sky, heading for its assigned airway, Amber One. It was true: when you took off in a smooth-running flying machine such as this, you left all troubles back there on the ground. Even the skipper looked more relaxed as they went through the after-take-off checklist, the tension visibly draining from his face. Keller watched him as he gave the all-clear for the removal of safety belts, the permission to smoke. For a brief second, the senior pilot looked across at him, then turned away to check his instruments, his face inscrutable.

It was at that moment Cathy came bursting through the door.

'Captain Rogan,' she said urgently.

'What is it, Cathy?' he asked stiffly, eyes never leaving the instruments.

'One of the first-class passengers has found a device in his briefcase.' She glanced quickly at Keller, a flicker of emotion passing between them. 'It looks like . . . a bomb!'

The captain's head snapped round.

'Are you sure?' he barked at her.

She flinched at his rough tone. 'It – it seems to have some sort of timing mechanism. The passenger doesn't know how it got into his briefcase.'

'Are the other passengers aware of it yet?'

'In the first-class compartment they are. Those near the front in second are wondering what the commotion is about.'

'All right.' He looked across at Keller. 'Get down there and check it out.'

'Will you change the squawk to the distress code?'

'Not until you've checked it out!' Rogan snapped.

Cathy looked at the two men curiously, her mind off the danger below for an instant. She had never heard the captain speak to Dave that way before, and they'd been through other crises in the past. Keller had already unharnessed himself and was staring down at the senior pilot as if about to speak. Rogan regarded him coldly and Cathy felt the tension between the two men.

'Well?' the captain demanded angrily, his upturned face betraying his rage, but no fear. 'Get your bloody self down there!'

Keller turned without a word, squeezing out from the confined space and confronting Cathy. He saw her face was pale, concerned not for the possible danger, but for him. He smiled reassuringly and held her arm. 'Lead the way,' he said.

As he passed the flight engineer, who had already broken out into a sweat, he clapped him on the shoulder and shouted over the noise of the engines: 'Don't get your parachute on yet, Al!' The flight engineer grinned back weakly and gave him a 'thumbs up' sign. They hurried through the narrow cockpit door and began to descend the curving stairwell. Cathy glanced back over her shoulder at him, her face now very pale, her eyes wide. Again, he reached for her, cupping her upturned face with his hand and running his fingers across her soft cheek. He smiled encouragement and they continued their descent.

The chief steward, Brody, was waiting at the bottom of the stairs and, as he saw Keller, he pointed in the direction of the first-class compartment. The co-pilot wasted no time asking questions. He swung round into the compartment, ignoring the rows of anxious, lip-biting faces behind him. He stopped dead at the scene that greeted him.

Sir James Barrett sat sideways in his seat, his feet in the aisle, a black, slimline briefcase open on his lap, a look of consternation on his face. The other passengers' attitudes varied from sheer panic to nervous curiosity. The younger man next to Sir James, his private secretary, cringed back against the porthole, as if willing himself to sink through the aircraft's fuselage away from the menacing contraption housed in the case. Four Japanese businessmen, who had occupied the next rows of seats, had moved to the nose of the Jumbo and were cowering and jabbering excitedly. A woman cradled a small, weeping girl in her arms and seemed near to tears herself. A plastic doll had fallen into the aisle and was regarding the drama with cold, unseeing eyes. A man with an American accent was bellowing angrily for him to do something, while his companion tugged at his sleeve trying to calm him.

And one man stood alone, one hand on the back of his seat, the other on the back of the seat in front, supporting himself. He was ghostly thin, his skin yellowish, his face a mass of deep-etched wrinkles. He was smiling. A smile that contained a mixture of fear and excitement. And mockery.

Sir James seemed unable to take his eyes away from the case resting on his knees but, as Keller approached, he carefully turned it around, revealing its contents to the co-pilot. Keller knew as soon as he saw the elaborate network of wires, the plastic tubes, the timing device, that it was a genuine bomb, and he also understood how it had got on board. He opened his mouth to tell Sir James not to move but, at that moment, a blinding white light erupted before him, and a searing blast lifted him off his feet and hurled him back down the cabin, his whole body wrapped in a scorching cocoon of light.

He felt his body crash against something solid and then he fell to the floor, incredibly feeling no pain, just an overall numbness. He forced his eyes to open and wondered why the world was at such an odd angle, why passengers were floundering, spilling down the incline of the floor, why flames were enveloping the cabin. Then he saw the forward passenger door, half torn from its surroundings, hanging miraculously by slender threads of metal, the black night air howling through the gap that had been created; and what had happened gradually sank through to his shocked brain.

He tried to raise himself, wondering why he felt no pain, succeeding only to get an elbow beneath him. He tried to cry out as he saw Cathy crawling towards him, her horrified face a bloody mask, her eyes wide with terror – and compassion – her mouth open, screaming. But he heard nothing, for the interior of the aircraft had become a silent world of turmoil. Just as that world began to dim and fade, as his eyes began to close out the horror, he caught one last glimpse of Cathy, her shaking, blood-covered hand reaching towards him, her body fighting against the odd angle of the aircraft, grief now implicit in her eyes.

And then, everything disintegrated into a peaceful blankness, a restful slumber.

He felt his eyelids being lifted, and was instantly awake, blinking and pulling his eyes away from the forceful thumbs. He stared up into the concerned face of Father Vincente.

'Are you all right?' the priest asked him. 'Don't move until we've made sure nothing is broken.'

Keller lay still as expert fingers probed his body for breakages and he strived to bring his senses back to the present. It all came flooding back, a vivid vision of a nightmare: the bomb, the explosion, the tilted angle of the cabin as the aircraft plunged to the earth, and the anguish on Cathy's wounded face, her reaching for him. A tear filled the corner of each eye and he rapidly blinked them away. Perhaps it would have been better not to have remembered.

But at least he was sure of the cause now! The antagonism between the captain and himself had played no part in the destruction of the 747. There had been no neglect by either himself or the senior pilot; it had all been out of their hands. And now he realized how the bomb had been taken on board without detection. He struggled to sit upright, but restraining hands held him back.

'Be patient, Mr Keller, I'm nearly through,' Father Vincente said.

'I'm okay,' Keller insisted, looking around. 'Where's Hobbs?' he asked anxiously.

'I'm here, David,' a muffled voice came from the shadows. A figure stumbled towards him, and the medium came into view clutching a red-stained handkerchief to his lips. The candles had been re-lit, and the beam from the torch was now stronger. There was a quiet stillness about the aircraft.

'Hobbs, it *was* a bomb! When I blacked out, I remembered everything that happened that night!'

'Yes, I know it was a bomb,' Hobbs said wearily.

Keller tried to discern his features in the flickering light of the candles, the torch beam aimed directly at his own body. Angry, dark red welts had appeared on the medium's forehead and cheeks; his hair had been burnt away in several places, revealing a proliferation of blisters, many forming even as he watched.

'Christ!' was all he could say.

'Nothing appears to be broken, Mr Keller,' Father Vincente announced, straightening up from his rapid, but thorough, examination.

'No, I told you, I feel okay,' said Keller, unable to look away from Hobbs's mutilated head.

'Mr Hobbs needs to get to a hospital right away,' the priest said. 'He's suffered from some severe burns. The cuts around his mouth have opened up again; they'll need to be treated. I think a strong sedative wouldn't harm any of us either.'

'No.' Hobbs took the bloody handkerchief away from his mouth so he could be understood more clearly. The priest and the co-pilot winced at the sight of his swollen, bleeding lips. 'There's more to be done this night.'

'But you can't go on in your condition,' Father Vincente protested.

'There's no choice,' came the simple reply.

'He's right. It's not over yet.' Keller pulled himself into a sitting position. He said to Hobbs, 'Why are *you* sure it was a bomb?'

Hobbs tried unsuccessfully to stem the flow of blood from his lips. He grimaced with pain as he spoke. 'While I was ... under, another voice spoke to me. It was a different voice – confused and as frightened as the others – but not the same.' He bent forward in his agony, and the two men reached out to steady him. 'No, no, I'm all right. Just let me rest for a moment.'

They waited in silence until the medium had gathered enough strength to carry on. 'The ... the voice ... managed to tell me ... what had happened ... who was responsible. We've got ... got to get to this person ... tonight ... if we're to prevent . . .' He fell forward again, groaning.

Keller held his shoulder. 'The voice. Who was it? Who spoke to you?'

Hobbs fought to control his distress. 'I . . . I don't know. It was confused . . . trying to help us, though . . . I can take you to . . . the person.'

'Who? The one who planted the bomb?'

'Yes!'

'How can you do that?' the priest broke in.

'Picture in my . . . mind. He . . . showed . . . me.'

'It's a matter for the police then,' Father Vincente said resolutely.

'No time . . . no time.'

'He's right,' Keller agreed. 'How could you explain all this to the police anyway?'

'We have . . . to hurry. Must get there . . . tonight.' Hobbs struggled to get to his feet, the priest and co-pilot helping him. He was unsteady, but able to walk.

Thoughts raced through Keller's head. The bomb. Carried aboard by Sir James. As simple as that. As well as being a director of various other companies, he played an important role as a director of Keller's own airline and it was often his privilege to dispense with the tedious customs checks and the personal baggage scrutiny by boarding the aircraft with the crew. It was all unofficial, of course, and a prerogative not always used; but this time, Keller was sure, it had been. It was all so easy.

But who had planted the bomb? What maniac would kill over three hundred people just to get one man? Or had mass murder been the true intention? And why hadn't Sir James been aware of the bomb before he boarded the Jumbo? There were still so many questions that remained to be answered. His own escape, for instance. He had heard of cases before, when a person standing directly in the path of an explosion had somehow miraculously escaped injury. It was something to do with the rushing air, pushing the person ahead of the blast, forming a protective shield around his body. It was improbable, but not impossible. His body had struck something solid and been forced round it, almost into the stairwell. It could have been that which protected him from the ensuing fire flash accompanying the explosion. Then, when the 747 had plummeted to the ground, the loosely hanging door had been wrenched free, flying back, scraping the wing as Tewson had surmised. And he, lying close to the doorway, had been thrown clear to land in the soft mud of the field.

He felt relieved: relieved at finding the explanation of his survival; relieved to know the disaster could in no way be attributed to the actions of himself or Captain Rogan. But it was an uneasy relief.

They scrambled clear of the aircraft, surprised to find it hadn't disintegrated completely, surprised not to find a reception committee of policemen waiting for them. Surely the terrific din from the wreck had attracted some attention. Then, the priest pointed towards an obvious reason for the lack of attention.

To the east, towards Eton's High Street, the night glowed red as flames licked into the sky. It looked as though one of the shops or buildings along the High Street had caught fire.

And the fire was spreading.

20

The three boys crept stealthily along the shadowy colonnade, two carrying small cans of paint, past the numerous names of Old Etonians killed in the 1914–18 War, morbidly – but proudly so – inscribed on the stone walls. One of the boys tried desperately to stifle a giggle.

'For Chrissakes, Greene, shut up will you!' the leader hissed. The offending boy did his best to smother the sound with a dirty handkerchief.

They reached the solid wooden door of the antechapel and paused, listening for any sudden shouts, any pursuing footsteps.

'Look, Spelling,' one of the boys whispered breathlessly, 'd'you think we should go back? I mean, if we're caught we'll be slung out on our ear.'

The leader turned to him and said with disgust: 'Bugger off if you're scared, Clemens. You were the one who thought of it in the first place!'

'Yes, but it was just a joke. I mean, it was just an idea. I didn't think you'd take me seriously.' He scratched nervously at a pimple on his neck.

'Well, we did! And you're in on it, so keep your sodding trap shut!'

It was an idea that had come to Clemens the night before as they lay awake in their beds, restless because of the exciting but spooky stories that had flown around the College that day. The stories were all concerned with the mysterious death of Thatcher, the dramatic deaths of the couple who had leapt from a window into the High Street, the corpse down by the river, and the other unusual happenings – not the least of which was the vicar going bonkers that very day. The stories had spread and grown, the boys revelling in their own particularly macabre versions.

The favourite so far was that the vicar was an occultist, a black magician, and the couple who had committed suicide were part of his coven. The fat boy had been their sacrifice to the Prince of Darkness and the man who had died down by the river had come across one of their secret ceremonies and had been frightened to death! But the Devil hadn't been satisfied with the sacrifice so had made the vicar potty, and the other two had killed themselves out of remorse! It didn't bother the younger boys that the time sequence was illogical, nor the fact that the next day the Reverend Biddlestone had been seen returning from the hospital, as sane as anyone. The vicar would have to be watched with a cautious eye from now on, and gold crosses would have to be worn for protection against his hypnotic evil (a Saint Christopher medal would do if you didn't own a cross). The older boys had scoffed at the juniors and the 'Pop' had reprimanded all of them for spreading such silly gossip.

But to the three fifteen-year-olds, Spelling, Greene and Clemens, who shared the same room in their particular Oppidan house, the stories were too gruesomely enjoyable to let die so soon. And they provided an excellent chance to use the keys to the chapel. They weren't the real keys, of course – just replicas skilfully cut by Greene in the manual crafts class, the originals having been 'borrowed' from Saunders, the janitor, who looked after the chapel and made sure visitors didn't carve their initials on the ancient woodwork. They'd been returned before he'd even known they were missing – after an impression had been made in Plasticine, of course. What to use them for, that had been the problem.

And then, it had all fallen nicely into place when the stories of ghosts and black magic had swept round the College. The original and fairly feeble intention had been to sneak in and carve their own initials, not amongst the hundreds of past Etonians, many of whom had become famous figures of history, but in some better, more obscure place, where nobody would find them. A secret place which only they would know about, so they could sit and gloat with each other during services, smug in the private knowledge that their names were there with the immortals! It was a practice that had been banned, but that, of course, only made it all the more desirable. The place they'd agreed on was Provost Thomas Murray's elaborate tomb which was on the left of the altar; possibly somewhere on the carved effigy below the tomb. No one would ever spot the initials if they etched them discreetly; and think of the satisfaction in years to come when one returned to the College and could point out their names to their wives, or children – or mistresses! That had been the intention, but Clemens's plan was better.

What if, one day, when all the school filed in for morning service, they found the chapel daubed with black magic signs, emblems of witchcraft, symbols of the occult! What a furore there'd be! What a commotion! The College would never get over it! And the atmosphere was exactly right. It could all be cleaned off afterwards, of course, so there'd be no *actual* damage done. It would be something to laugh over for years to come!

Spelling had purchased a book on the black arts in one of the old second-hand bookshops in the High Street that very morning, and there were lots of smashing pictures of diabolic symbols they could copy. They'd have to get rid of the book as soon as their deed had been accomplished, of course; the consequences would be disastrous if the prank were ever traced back to them! The keys would have to be destroyed, too. But the beauty of the idea was that they could lock the doors behind them so it would indeed look as if supernatural forces had been responsible for the damage!

As the evening had drawn on, Clemens had become more and more reticent about the whole adventure. It had been a stupid idea! They would be expelled without a second thought! And, anyway, it was pretty creepy around the chapel at night. Spelling had threatened to bash him if he continued whining; it was the best wheeze anyone had thought of for years at the College – possibly for centuries! What a chance to get back at old Griggs-Meade, the headmaster, the self-righteous bastard! This would make him change his tedious sermons on how evil was just inside oneself. This would make him realize evil was a real, physical, living force! Dennis Wheatley said so!

Greene sniggered again. 'Come on, you clots!' he whispered loudly. 'Let's get on with it.'

Spelling took one last furtive look around, then drew out a long, gleaming key from his trouser pocket. He inserted it quietly into its accommodating keyhole, all three boys holding their breaths and clenching their teeth. He turned his wrist and exclaimed: 'It's already unlocked!'

Still with bated breath, he gently pushed the door open, thanking God Saunders kept the hinges well oiled.

'Let's go, Spelling. I mean, there must be someone already in there if it's open,' Clemens said, nervously looking around him.

'No, look! There's no lights on inside. That silly old bugger

Saunders must have forgotten to lock it.' Spelling poked his head through the gap, then slipped inside. 'Come on,' they heard him command from the darkness.

'Go on, Clemens, you first.' Clemens was shoved roughly through the door by Greene. He was pushed again when he bumped into Spelling in the dark.

'Watch it, you bloody oaf!' Spelling hissed. 'Come on, Greene, get in and shut the bloody door. Then we can switch the torch on.'

The long gap narrowed and disappeared completely as the third boy entered the hall to the antechapel and closed the door behind him.

A thin beam of light cut through the blackness as Spelling switched on his pencil torch.

'Are you sure there's no one else here?' Clemens asked anxiously.

'Well, they could hardly have climbed the stairs in the dark, could they?' Spelling retorted. 'Now just shut up and let's get into the chapel. Follow me.' He crept silently up the wide wooden steps and the other two followed hastily, their ears acutely aware of every creak and groan of the old staircase.

They reached the door to the antechapel and to their surprise found this unlocked also.

'Bugger me, old Saunders must have been on the juice,' Greene exclaimed. Then he chuckled. 'Tell you what, we'll lock up for him when we leave.'

The others tittered in nervous appreciation. Spelling peered round the door again, shining the thin beam around the walls of the antechapel, which was a sizeable hall, as big as many a small community church. They listened intently for any noise before entering the heraldically decorated antechapel, then moved cautiously over its stone floor towards the entrance to the main chapel, Clemens half-expecting the whole place to be suddenly flooded with light and an angry voice to demand what they were up to. But there was no disturbance of any kind.

The chapel itself was infinitely brighter because of the high stained-glass windows which allowed light from outside to enter the vast hall in a muted diffusion of colour. To Clemens, though, the chapel still presented a forbidding and gloomy interior, and if Greene had not been following so closely behind him, he would have turned and fled there and then. The three boys stared down into the depths of the high-roofed fan-vaulted chapel with its rows of beautifully carved dark wooden pews facing each other across the wide aisle, those at the rear bearing the inscriptions of wealthy or famous past Etonians. The impressive marble altar, backed by its exquisite tapestries, at the end of the perpendicular architec-tured chapel, was barely visible to them and the fragmentary wall-paintings running along the first half of the chapel's length were just grey blurs of darker shapes.

All three failed to see the white-coated figure sitting in the dark at the back of a row of pews. But all three were aware of the dank coldness that seeped through to their bones.

'C-Christ, it's bloody cold!' murmured Spelling.

Clemens, shocked by the profanity in such a holy place, could only stare at the white blob of Spelling's face.

'Let's get painting,' said Greene eagerly, and he marched down the aisle of the chapel swinging his can of paint cheerfully, humming his current favourite tune. He seemed unperturbed by the coldness which clung heavily to the chapel.

'After you, spotty,' Spelling said cruelly to Clemens, sure he would make a bolt for it if he got the chance. The boy shrugged his shoulders dejectedly and followed Greene towards the altar. Spelling took one last look behind him and did likewise. He thought he'd seen a white blur against the left-hand wall but, as he began to swing the feeble torch towards it, Greene's disgusted voice distracted him.

'Smells as if a sodding cat's died in here,' Greene said, wrinkling his nose at the odour. 'I say, Spelling, where shall we do our daubs? Over the altar?'

'No,' came Spelling's reply. 'On the walls, I think, and perhaps on the floor in front of the altar.'

'Right. You do the walls, I'll do the floor.'

'We've only got one torch, idiot. We'll have to do one at a time.'

'Come on, then. Floor first.' Greene began to prise open the lid of his half-pint can of paint. 'Here, Clemens, you hold the torch while Spelling and I do the paintings.'

Spelling thrust the torch into his companion's shaking hand and began to open his can of paint. 'What have you got, Greeney? The red?' he whispered across at his friend who was gingerly holding the lid from his tin with thumb and finger, careful not to get paint on himself.

'Er . . . red,' Greene replied.

'Yes, I've got the black. Now, let's just have a look in the book. Shine the light over here, Clemens.'

As he leafed through the book, searching for an appropriate symbol, Clemens glanced around the chapel. His eyes were becoming more accustomed to the gloom now, but for a moment he wondered if they were playing tricks on him. For just a brief second, he thought he'd seen the long rows of pews filled with dark unmoving figures. He blinked his eyes vigorously, then looked again. No, it had been his imagination, there was nothing there.

'Keep the sodding light still, will you, Clemens!' Spelling said harshly. 'Ah – this one will do for a start.' He grinned at the picture he'd found, his face evil and gnome-like in the light from the torch. He screwed up his eyes to read the caption running beneath the illustration. 'The goetic or sorcerous circle used for black evocations and pacts,' he read aloud.

'Sounds all right,' commented Greene. 'Bit complicated, though.'

'We'll simplify it.' Spelling lay the book down on the floor and produced a two-inch-wide paintbrush from his jacket pocket. He dipped it into the black paint and, bending low and shuffling backwards, began to trace a rough circle on the floor in front of the altar.

'Not very round,' Greene said, when he'd completed the full circuit.

'It'll do. You paint the triangle on the inside while I draw an outer circle.'

Both boys eagerly set to work, giggling as they bumped into each other.

'Right,' said Spelling with satisfaction, straightening up and admiring their work. 'Now, what's that inside the triangle?'

'Three circles joined by a cross and . . . it looks like . . . a sort of curve with . . . flames coming out of it,' Greene told him, cocking his head to one side and concentrating hard on the symbol.

'Okay. Black circles and cross – and you can do the curve and flames in red.'

Clemens watched their bent backs with rising trepidation. Why *had* he suggested this daft idea? He thought he caught a movement in the periphery of his vision, and he shot a glance towards one of the small side chapels. It was the Lupton Chapel, screened off from the main hall by intricate and delicate stonework. A black shape had seemed to duck from view behind the screen.

'I – I say, you blokes. I think there's someone in here,' he whispered urgently to the others.

They looked up at him. 'Don't be so bloody wet, Clemens. Nobody could have got in here.'

'The doors weren't locked, were they?'

Now Spelling and Greene regarded each other.

Greene gulped noisily.

'What did you see?' Spelling asked.

'I don't know. Just a shadow over there, I think.'

'Well, shine the sodding light over there then.'

Clemens did so, but there was nothing to be seen.

'It – he might have ducked down,' Clemens insisted rather reluctantly.

'Oh, give us the torch,' snapped Spelling, and marched over to the small side chapel shining the beam ahead of him. Clemens and Greene watched his silhouette disappear behind the ornate stone screen, suddenly vanishing completely, the light with him. They froze as they heard a low moaning coming from the chapel and sucked in their breath as a ghostly face slowly rose between a gap in the stonework, its features made grotesque by deep shadows and harsh highlights.

'You silly bugger, Spelling!' cried Greene, almost in tears, though instantly relieved.

Spelling laughed helplessly as he returned from behind the stonework, taking the lighted torch from under his chin. 'That got you going!' he choked between bouts of hysterical giggling.

Greene made as if to throw the tin of paint over him and Spelling scooted down the aisle, raising his knees in comical haste.

'Silly bugger!' Greene called after him.

'Ssssh!' Clemens was worried about the noise they were making now.

Abruptly, Spelling flicked off the torch and darted up a narrow gangway between the pews, tripping on one of the steps as he went, sprawling forward on to his chest. He lay there panting, trying to smother his giggles.

'Come off it, Spelling!' Clemens hissed in the darkness. 'Turn that bloody torch on. Come on, Greene, let's go if he's going to play silly buggers!'

But Greene had joined in the game too. He was nowhere to be seen.

'Oh, for Chrissakes, you too! It's not bloody funny!' Clemens's anger, along with his fear of the dark, rose. He whirled round as he heard a bump then a muffled giggle from behind him. 'Come out, Greene. I know you're there!' He became desperate. 'I'm going if you carry on like this!'

He stepped backwards with a start as something white caught his attention at the back of the pews and his heel kicked against one of the paint tins, knocking it over, its contents spilling on to the floor, spreading darkly across the freshly drawn symbol, an expanding pool of sticky wetness.

The boy scrambled away from the spilled paint, not wanting to have his shoes ruined. The back of his knees caught the edge of the seat of the front pew on that side and he sat down with a jolt. He remained in the sitting position, his chest heaving, his eyes staring directly ahead and slightly upwards at the white blur sitting motionless at the back of the opposite pews. The pale, claw-like hand which appeared from behind went unnoticed until it clamped down on to his shoulder and Greene shouted: 'Boo!'

Clemens screamed and fell to the floor, scrabbling his body away from whatever had grabbed him.

'Shut up, you clot! Do you want everyone up here to find out what the noise is?' Greene was angry at the blubbering figure on the floor, and almost regretted his little joke. If they were found in the chapel – especially with all that paint on the floor – they'd be for the high jump. 'I think we'd better get out now. Where's Spelling? Come on, you idiot, before we're found out!' He hissed the last remark across the aisle to the pews opposite. It was then he noticed the white shape.

'Spelling? It's you, isn't it?' he asked uncertainly.

Clemens followed his gaze, the poor light restricting his vision. They both heard the low, husky chuckle.

As Clemens shrank against the edge of the front pew, he saw there were other shapes sitting there in the darkness, shapes that hardly seemed to move, yet never seemed to be still. He slowly craned his neck round to look at Greene and he saw that the pews on their side were also filled with dark, nebulous figures. A low murmuring suddenly began to fill the chapel, no more than a whispering, but somehow becoming incredibly loud, filling the boys' heads with the sound. Above the voices, they could hear the laughter – the snarling, cruel laughter – coming from the white figure opposite. The stench of something charred and burnt swilled in the air, sweeping over the boys in nauseous waves.

Spelling, who was still lying sprawled on the floor, now paralysed by the sounds he heard and the stiffened, frozen muscles of his back, reached out a hand in an attempt to push himself to his feet. It touched something brittle but flaky. His fingers crept along its length and reached what could have been an ankle. He felt crispy flesh.

The boy drew his hand away with a cry of horror and he looked up into an ugly, almost fleshless, grinning skull. He backed away on all fours, down the narrow passageway between the rows of pews, past hideously disfigured faces peering down at him, whispering; the fingerless hands pointing accusingly.

He began to whine when he reached the aisle but he continued to crawl backwards, towards the rear of the chapel, away from the altar, away from his transfixed friends, the mewling noise from his lips lost in the sound of the whispers. Back, back, so conscious of the dark shapes that filled the wooden seats on either side of the place of worship, but his mind refused to let him suffer the full realization of it, refused to let him understand.

The chapel was alive with the sound of the dead. It was full of the smell of decomposed corpses.

As Spelling scrabbled backwards along the hard stone floor, he saw a white figure rise from a rear seat and descend the narrow gangway towards his two friends. The boy's tears left a trail of glistening spots along the aisle and his knees were rubbed raw against its unyielding surface. He saw the dark puddle through the gloom, the blurred whiteness of the two paint tins, one lying on its side. He saw the dark bodies rise and converge on Clemens and Greene. He saw the figure strangely garbed in white reach for the boy who lay prostrate on the floor. He saw the other boy look around wildly for a place to run and sink to his knees when he realized he was hemmed in, only the paleness of his face visible over the back of the front pew.

Then Spelling failed to see anything but a dark mass of moving shapes, obliterating the boys and the figure in white.

And only then did he scream and scramble to his feet and run from the main chapel.

*

The headmaster's footsteps clattered along the uneven stone pavings of the cloisters and his eyes examined each lurking shadow as he passed. It had been a habit of his over the years to take a leisurely late night stroll around the College, not really to check all was well, but to indulge himself in his own solitary nostalgia of centuries long gone, to listen to the ghosts of past Etonians, to imagine himself back teaching pupils who bore names such as Walpole, Pitt, Shelley or Gladstone. Whom among his boys today would rise to the height of these famous men? Did past tutors recognize the potential of certain students? Could they possibly have guessed the important roles the *man* would play in England's future? Which one would be his Shelley? Which one his Gladstone?

Tonight, there was an urgency in his stride, a purpose to his late night walk. A feeling of building pressure had been with him all day, distracting his thoughts, nagging at his concentration. He passed through the arch of Lupton's Tower and hurried along the cobbled centre path of School Yard, the ancient buildings overlooking the wide quadrangle silent and unaware of his anxiety. On reaching the centre of the yard, a position occupied by a weather-worn statue of Henry VI, he paused and slowly revolved his body as though he could sense rather than see or hear any source of trouble. He did this twice and each time he found it necessary to tear his eyes away from the grey, looming chapel which dominated the quadrangle and the surrounding buildings.

Griggs-Meade looked up at the high stained-glass windows, seen only as huge black holes from the outside, as though they themselves would provide evidence of unrest. A faint rustling noise seemed to float across the yard towards him, and the more he strained his ears to listen, the less sure he was that it wasn't just the sound that lived within one's own eardrums. And then, a small, sharp scream gave his hearing something more tangible to relate to.

It came again; shrill, like a young girl's. The headmaster broke into a run, cutting diagonally across the yard, heading for the entrance to the antechapel, his long legs swiftly covering the ground. As he reached the large old door, wondering whether it would be open or not, he heard footsteps pounding down the wooden steps inside, a muffled tattoo of panic-hurried feet. He pushed at the door and it swung wide. And from the darkness, a smallish body threw itself at him, limbs flailing, terrified screeching noises emitting from a tightened throat.

The impact knocked Griggs-Meade back, but he clutched at the struggling figure and managed to grab an arm above the elbow. He shook the boy violently to control him and looked down into the pale face. Dragging the boy out into the yard in order to distinguish his features more clearly, he felt the body grow rigid in his arms. He thought he recognized the face – the name would come to him later – but the boy's condition was hardily conducive to questioning. His mouth was frozen open and his eyes looked past the headmaster at the door he'd just come through. His face glistened wetly as though he'd been crying, and now fitful whimpers escaped from him. Griggs-Meade realized that whatever had frightened his pupil was still back there in the chapel. He began to drag him back towards the door, furious at the breach of rules, wondering just why the boy was out of bounds and who else was in there.

Spelling understood the headmaster's intention and began struggling to free himself, his broken whining turning into screams of refusal, falling to his knees to hinder further progress. 'Stand up, boy!' Griggs-Meade thundered at him, but the pupil had become a hysterical, blubbering wreck by now. He was torn between leaving the boy in such a fearful state, and investigating the reason behind it. He looked up at the chapel and made his choice. Leaving Spelling lying rolled up in a ball on the ground, he dashed through the dark entrance and up the wooden staircase.

The coldness hit him as soon as he entered the antechapel. He felt as if he had suddenly plunged into a gigantic freezer. Hardly pausing, he rushed to the entrance of the main chapel, oblivious of the darkness, full of anger for anyone who would dare violate his beloved chapel.

And there he stopped, unable to comprehend the sight before him.

It appeared that the vast hall was filled with dark, moving forms; forms that wavered and faded, undulating in a constantly changing mass, the eerie light from the enormous coloured windows confusing rather than accentuating the shapes. When he tried to concentrate on one figure, or a particular group of them, it seemed to disappear and form again after he had shifted his gaze. An overwhelming noise hit him, a bustling, howling sound, tumultuous in its overall effect. Listened to individually, however, the sounds were only whispers. Coarse and parched. Burnt voices.

In the dimness at the front of the chapel, before the altar, he could just make out a white-coated figure through the twisting throng. It seemed to be clutching two smaller bodies in a tight embrace. Fascinated, and horrified, the headmaster walked forward into the main chapel, the fascination drawing him in, the horror urging him to run away. He resisted the latter because he realized the figure in white held two boys in his arms – undoubtedly *his* pupils. His premonition of danger earlier that day had been correct; he did not understand what was happening, but he knew the boys – the College – was in mortal danger.

Griggs-Meade was neither a brave man nor a coward. He was merely governed by an overriding sense of duty.

The noise in the chapel was reduced to a hushed silence at his approach, as the hazy shapes turned to look in his direction. They seemed to waft away before him, clearing a path down the long, wide aisle so that he could have a clear view of the white figure and the two boys locked in its tight embrace. Some inner sense told him not to look at these spectral shapes as he passed through them; the horror of their nebulous features would be too much – he would be forced to turn and flee. But the stench that assailed his nostrils could not be denied. It was the smell of rotting death.

The sniggering, cruel chuckle ahead allowed him to fix his attention on the white-coated figure. Even from this distance the man seemed vaguely familiar. Could it be? He looked very much like the photographer who had done so much work for the College over the last decade. What was his name? He had a studio along the High Street.

'What are you doing here?' Griggs-Meade demanded to know, his voice much stronger than he actually felt. 'Why are you holding those boys?'

The man's low snigger made the headmaster shudder. It wasn't human.

'Answer me! Why are you here?' Griggs-Meade tried to appear angry. He almost succeeded.

Suddenly, the snigger became a cackle and the man threw out his arms, but still held the boys by their throats. The headmaster stopped in his tracks as he saw the boys' eyes begin to bulge, their cries cut off when their tongues protruded from their mouths as vice-like fingers began to squeeze the life from them.

'Stop that! Stop that!' the headmaster shouted, but he could only watch in horror as the man slowly raised his arms with super-normal strength, still holding them out sideways, lifting the two struggling boys off their feet. He was hanging them with his own hands. The choking sounds the boys made as their faces began to flush a deep purple galvanized the headmaster into action. With a cry of rage, and fear, he launched himself forward.

But then an astounding thing happened which made him fall back with shock. The figure in the white smockcoat suddenly burst into flames.

First the head, a fiery ball that simultaneously laughed and screamed in pain, the mouth a gaping hole amid roasting popping flesh. The hair disappeared instantly in a bright flare and the eyes slowly extended down the cheeks hanging by slender threads blackened by the blaze. The fire moved along the outstretched arms and down the body, so the man became a burning cross of howling anguish and perverse, mocking laughter. The flames reached the two boys at the same time and engulfed their heads. Their screams meant nothing to the sprawling headmaster, for he was already rigid with shock, far beyond any point emotion could reach.

The interior of the vast hall was now brightly lit by the flames, patterns of red and yellow dancing on the walls, the four kneeling child-like statues on the altar apparently smiling in the flickering light. The shadowy figures filling the chapel crouched and fell away from the burning trio and, as Griggs-Meade looked slowly around in emotionless wonder, he saw the near-invisible tongues of flame lapping at the transparent bodies, saw the writhing of the tortured souls.

But he also saw the real curls of smoke rising from the rows of wooden pews as the spectres fell on them, their vaporous shapes twisting in silent agony. The wood glowed red and soon tiny flickers of flame spread along their lengths, meeting and joining, growing into bigger flames.

His attention was caught by one of the smaller shapes falling away from the central burning trio as the bones in the man's fleshless hand grew brittle and snapped. The boy fell to his knees and immediately rose, his back and arms a ball of fire. He ran towards the altar as if to save himself, but he crashed against it, falling to the ground. Rising again, Clemens staggered around the altar, twisting and turning as he went, falling again and clutching at the tapestries to save himself. The fire from his body shot upwards, spreading across the ancient material as though it were paper, greedily devouring the treasured scenes.

The two remaining figures before the headmaster, the man and the now dead boy, slowly crumbled and fell to the floor, the screams of pain dying with the body, but the harsh chuckling laughter continuing, still coming from the burning corpse.

Griggs-Meade vaguely wondered why he seemed to be sitting in a sticky red pool and, as he raised his hand, he saw it was covered in the fluid. It looked like blood and his mind was no longer able to tell him it was only red paint. Indeed, the paint had spread so that it touched against the bottom row of pews, and as the flames crept down the old wood they found an able and willing ally in the sticky substance. They kissed the paint and clung to it in rapturous welcome, spreading swiftly and eagerly towards the headmaster's outstretched legs.

Soon the whole interior of the chapel had become a furnace, a raging inferno that cared little for tradition and as much for human life. Outside, the small adjoining buildings that had always cowered under the chapel's magnificence now cowered under its burning threat.

And the boy who huddled in the yard shivered and wept.

21

'Go left. Here.' Hobbs's voice was weak and hoarse. Keller followed his instructions and turned the Stag into the lane opposite the College chapel. The medium's brooding eyes looked back at the chapel as they sped away from it. He said nothing.

Keller brought the car to a halt as they reached a fork in the road. 'Which way?' he asked.

Hobbs could only raise a weary finger and point to the right. The co-pilot gunned the engine and the car leapt forward again.

They had left the priest behind. He had tried to dissuade them from their purpose, urged them to go to the police. But all three knew there would have been little point. How could they explain? Who would believe the story they hardly believed themselves?

Father Vincente had helped Keller half carry Hobbs across the field to the car, his anxious eyes rarely leaving the red glow in the sky, the flames that leapt furiously into the black night. One of the shops in the High Street was ablaze and they could see the fire was spreading. Even as Keller yanked open the door of his car and eased the pain-racked medium into the passenger seat he heard the distant wailing sirens of fire engines.

The priest was uncertain as to whether he should go with

the two men or stay behind to help his community face whatever strange danger lay before it. He sensed the fire was only the beginning, and as it spread so would the heavy mantle of oppression that had hung over Eton for so many weeks manifest itself. A force of evil. And a priest would be needed.

He said a swift silent prayer for the two men as he ran off towards the High Street and the burning shop.

Keller watched until the black-robed figure had disappeared into a narrow alleyway squeezed between two buildings which led to the main street; then he started the car and drove out of the car park, leaning slightly towards Hobbs to catch his directions. He'd had to stop before entering the High Street as two fire engines flashed by, screeching to a halt not far down the road from them, blue-uniformed figures leaping from their interiors in their haste to quench the raging fire. The co-pilot had driven slowly away from the scene, praying that Hobbs would remain conscious long enough for them to reach their destination. For not only was the medium badly burnt, but he was also in a state of shock. His weary brain needed rest and his tired, injured body needed stillness. But Keller could see the little man was forcing his mind to concentrate, willing his body not to lapse into unconsciousness. The question was: How long could he keep it up?

Keller increased speed as he drove away from the town, slowing when he reached Eton Wick, Eton's sister town, glancing at Hobbs, waiting for fresh instructions.

'Keep ... going.' The voice was becoming weaker, less coherent.

The car gathered speed again as it left the town, the road becoming dark, night falling over them like a tossed blanket. Keller switched to full beam, increasing his speed rather than slowing. He knew the medium would not last much longer. Flat fields lay on either side of the road, frozen and colourless in the powerful beam of the headlights and, as the car swept round a long curving bend, the light rippled over the surface of a sunken pond. A small cluster of lights ahead told Keller they were approaching another town and he wondered if this would be the place, if this was where they would find their quarry.

But Hobbs's fingers clasped surprisingly strongly around his lower arm. 'Stop! Stop here!'

Keller jammed his brakes and the car slid to a halt. He automatically switched off his main beam and turned to the medium.

Hobbs's breath was coming in sharp gasps as he struggled to speak.

'The voice, David. It's fading. It's leaving me. But it says . . . it's here. The man is . . . here.'

Keller wound down his window and peered out into the darkness. He could see nothing.

'Are you sure?' he asked Hobbs. 'There's nothing out there. Just fields, trees.'

Hobbs slumped in his seat. 'It . . . says here. Somewhere here. The voice – so frightened, bitter. It's gone now.' The medium made an effort to raise his head and look out into the night. 'It's nearby, David. I can feel that.' He suddenly winced, then groaned as the sharp pain subsided. 'My head . . . can't see properly. Look around, it must be here.'

Keller pushed his door open and was about to step out when another car swept round the bend, tooting its horn angrily as it swerved around the Stag.

He saw the house for a brief instant, caught in the beam from the other car's headlights as it turned sharply to avoid hitting his car.

The light had struck diagonally across the field to his right, and there, set well back from the road, stood the isolated house. Keller's fleeting impression was one of considerable size – and loneliness. It had suggested wealth, but its solitary position had implied emptiness. He closed the door again and eased the car slowly forward, keeping his light on dipped beam, searching for the side road that would lead up to the house, never bothering to question his certainty.

He knew the answers were waiting for him there.

Keller soon found the narrow gravel road and turned off his lights as he drove into it, cautiously following the pale outline against the darker fields on either side. After about fifty yards, he stopped the car and sat in silence, waiting for his eyes to adjust themselves to the night. Hobbs's breathing had now become deeper and more even. Keller tried to stir him with a gentle shake, but the medium only groaned, his horribly disfigured head lolling to one side.

'Hobbs, can you hear me?' Keller's voice was soft. He felt tenderness towards this little man who had suffered so much because of him. There was no reply, but the co-pilot continued in the hope that his words might penetrate the medium's unconscious state. 'I'm going into the house. I know the answer's there – God knows why, but I'm sure. Don't move, just rest. You've done enough now. The rest is up to me.'

He got out of the car and closed the door quietly. Then he stood, oblivious to the cold, and stared towards the house. It was still at least a hundred yards away and the co-pilot now saw other lights on either side of it, partially hidden by high fences and dense, but naked, trees. All the dwellings were at least a couple of hundred yards apart, providing a secluded privacy for their tenants, a high-priced tranquillity. But the house he sought had an aloofness of its own.

It was difficult to define the difference separating it from its neighbours. Perhaps it was because the other houses seemed alive, the warm lights seen through chinks of curtains betraying their inner life, their hidden activity. This house seemed dead.

Keller moved away from the car and walked towards it, his shoes crunching tiny stones and his mind all too conscious of the sound. And then, the dormant structure seemed to stir itself into a strange wariness. The black windows watched his approach, questioning his presence, his intention. It became a sly thing, guarding its secret, forbidding him to enter and yet, daring him to. He paused at the gate and searched the windows for signs of life. But its stone face was inscrutable.

He pushed the gate open, heedless of the creak made by its rusted hinges, and walked along the path up to the front door. Fear was still with him, but curiosity overrode his nervousness.

He rang the doorbell, then listened.

Nothing stirred inside. There was no sound.

He rang again, hearing only its bell faintly through the door.

No one came.

He stepped off the path and pushed through the shrubbery that surrounded the house, making for a side window. The curtains were drawn and the thin crack where they joined revealed only blackness. He stepped back, away from the building, and peered up at its upper windows. Was it his imagination or had he really seen the barest flicker of a curtain? He returned to the front door and rang the bell once again.

Still no answer.

Could Hobbs have been wrong? Had the tiredness and the pain taken over his mind, tricking him with his own imagination, the new voice just his own desperate attempt to find a solution? No, he, Keller, felt it, too. The answer was here. Inside this house.

He walked round to the back.

In the darkness, Keller failed to see the other footprints in the mud of the ill-kept garden. As he rounded the corner, something struck at his determination; his resolve weakened momentarily as a curious, almost electric, sensation surged through him. His heart beat wildly and he had to steady himself with one hand against the side of the house until it had calmed itself to a reasonably steady rhythm again. Fear? Partly. But mostly – apprehension. He felt close to discovery now: the reason for the deaths of all those people, how it had been accomplished. And something more. Perhaps the reason for his survival.

New strength pushed the weakness from his body and he thrust himself away from the wall. His footsteps became more cautious. He saw the black shape of a door and then a window beside it. A movement at the window made him suddenly crouch low, frozen into immobility. With relief, Keller realized it was only the curtains moving in the cold breeze that crept through the open window.

But why was the window open?

Keller moved stealthily towards it and a faint, odious smell reached his nostrils. It was a smell he had lately become familiar with. The smell of corrupted flesh.

It wasn't very strong, but there was no mistaking the odour: not the incorporeal putrescence of the spirits, but the physical decay of human flesh. There was a corpse inside.

With the unconvincing thought that it might only be the remains of a dead animal, Keller carefully parted the curtains and tried to see into the darkness. There was only blackness.

He pushed his head through the gap, his nerves tingling, his breathing held in check. He was still unable to see anything. Pushing the curtains wider, he raised a foot over the sill and stepped halfway into the room, pausing and listening as he straddled the window-sill, giving his eyes time to accustom themselves to the decreased light. The smell was stronger, although not overpowering. He pulled the rest of his body through, then stopped with his back against the window, his head turning slowly from left to right, tensing for any sudden movement, any sudden noise. But the silence prevailed.

Almost painfully, Keller let stale air escape and breathed in again. Now the odour hit him more strongly, but it was still bearable. Whatever was dead hadn't died too long ago.

Slowly, carefully, Keller moved around the edges of the room, feeling with his hands before him, never leaving the stabilizing protection of the wall. His eyes began to recognize things in the dark: two squarish white objects to his left could have only been a cooker and refrigerator; a larger, darker object that must have been a cabinet of some kind; a round shape in the centre of the room was obviously a table. But there was something darker slumped across its surface and he knew it was a body.

Keller fought down the urge to run, to get away from the dark, forbidding house. But the sense of urgency, the sense of time running out, was too acute, holding him there, insisting he find the truth. Keeping his eyes on the table and the body it supported, he continued his journey around the room, moving faster now, but just as quietly, his night sight gradually improving. His knee hit a stool or chair and he nearly pitched forward over it, only just managing to keep his balance by pushing his hand against the wall. Once again, he stood still in the dark, wondering if the clatter had been heard – if there was anybody to hear it. After a few seconds, he proceeded and, when he'd reached the next wall, he began to feel for a door. If there was a door, there'd be a light switch next to it. His searching hand finally found the frame and he swiftly felt around for a switch. When he touched the square-shaped plastic, he flicked the switch without hesitation, keeping his eyes closed as he did so. The light flooded the room and stung through his eyelids. He waited for a few seconds then opened them, blinking at the pain, and keeping his face to the wall until his eyes could focus. Then he turned and ran his eyes quickly around the room, ascertaining that it was empty apart from himself – and the body.

The corpse was sitting in a chair, back to the window, sprawled forward across the round kitchen table. Congealed blood spread from beneath its head and arms across the table's surface, a deep red stain that was shaped like a pool with small, dried-up rivers running from it to the table's edge.

The face was half-concealed by one arm slung forward and bent at the elbow, the fingers almost touching the back of the man's head. Even in this awkward position there was something vaguely familiar about the body: the thinning gingerish-brown hair, long strands splaying over the coat collar at the back; the black arm of the glasses, half of one lens just peeping over the top of an elbow, glinting with the reflection from the overhead light.

Keller walked round the table, the anguish already begun before he'd confirmed his suspicion, anger tightening his lips into a thin line. He grasped a shoulder and pulled the body back into the chair, feeling the stickiness of drying blood on his fingers.

Harry Tewson stared up at him with wide, lifeless eyes, his mouth slack, the corners turned down. His face was totally white with the barest tinges of yellow and blue on his cheeks near his ears, the blood from it having drained through the long, deep slash in his throat. His shirt and the front of his jacket and overcoat were dyed a brownish red, his chest completely covered by the still viscid blood. His glasses were tilted across the bridge of his nose. One lens was cracked neatly into two pieces.

Keller clenched his fists and squeezed his eyes shut, sorrow and fury merging into one seething groan. Harry. He must have guessed how the bomb was planted; must have discovered the connection between Sir James Barrett and the person who owned this house. It *must* have been why he came here. Whoever caused the explosion had to live in this house – he had to be the one who killed Harry Tewson. Had the investigator confronted the man with his knowledge? Oh, the bloody conceited fool! Why hadn't he gone to the police? Why hadn't he told someone?

And where was this man now?

For the first time, Keller saw the blood on the floor by the open window. He must have stood in it as he'd entered. Was that how Tewson had been killed – climbing through the window? But how would the murderer have known the investigator had guessed the answer? And why hadn't he disposed of the body yet? Why place it in such a prominent position? Judging by the smell and the stiffness of the body, Tewson had been dead for at least a day. The coldness of the weather would have preserved the body for a while, slowing the deterioration process, but for no more than twenty-four hours. With disgust, he noticed the moulding loaf on the table, like an island surrounded by a deep red sea. Anger flared up again and he picked the bread up, hurling it across the room. His foot kicked something lying on the floor and looking down he saw it was a long bread knife, its blade no longer shiny metal but dulled with blood. He stooped and picked it up, placing it on the table, loathing its feel, knowing how it had been used.

In an attempt to calm his rage, he forced himself to think clearly. Whoever owned the house was fairly wealthy, for it was large and stood in a privileged position. Could he have been a business rival of Barrett's? Keller knew Sir James had many business interests other than Consul Airlines; he must have had plenty of enemies. But was it possible that someone had hated him enough to murder him in such a foul way, taking all those other lives, too? Or had Sir James merely been used as a carrier, the murderer knowing the director of the airline would use his privilege of boarding with the crew, and thus avoid having his briefcase searched? Had the assassin used this to strike at the airline? No, it was too flimsy; anything could have gone wrong. But Tewson had found the link, and it had meant his death. A sudden thought struck the co-pilot: had it been Tewson's voice that had led them there – through Hobbs? But why hadn't the other spirits done so? Then Keller realized they had tried to tell him, only the other one, the one that seemed to dominate, had thwarted them; he – it – wanted to remain earthbound.

Yet again, the co-pilot wondered at his own acceptance of this other life – this spiritual world. Too much had happened to ever deny it now.

A sudden noise above his head roused him from his thoughts. The man he sought was still in the house. He was sure; he sensed it.

Keller crept over to the kitchen door and stood there with his ear pressed against it, listening for any sound. None came, so he reached for the handle and turned it slowly, easing the door open quietly, first switching off the kitchen light. The hallway was too dark to see anything so he waited, holding his breath, his ears acutely sensitive. A creak that may have just been the house settling sent his heart pounding, his nerves taut. The pupils of his eyes had enlarged and objects in the dark took on a more definite shape. It was a long, wide hall and at the far end he saw the rectangular shape of a window, a less dense shade of grey against the surrounding darkness. A semicircular shape high to its left must have been a window above the front door. The lights from a distant passing car rounding the curve in the road threw the windows into a sharper, yellowish relief, the two framed shapes reflecting off the wall to his right and sweeping round like a searchlight, quickly fading to nothingness as the car sped away into the night. The glow had allowed him to see the doorway to his right and the staircase ascending away from him on his left. He stepped into the hall and peered up, trying to see the top of the stairs through the balustrade. It was no use; everything had become black again.

He wasn't sure how long he had stood there – it could have been seconds, it could have been minutes – but the muffled thump from above stirred him into action again. Keller had taken two cautious steps down the hall before he remembered the knife in the kitchen and went back for it. He clutched the loathsome object in his hand and paused briefly to look at the slumped form of Tewson. Although he couldn't see his face in the dark, he knew those lifeless eyes stared at him across the room, and he felt another voice was asking for vengeance.

Keller returned to the hallway and, holding the knife before him, crept along its length until he had reached the foot of the stairs. Without allowing himself to think further, he began to climb them, pausing at every third step to listen for any movement above. It seemed like an eternity before he reached the top; there were too many shadows, too many deep holes of darkness for someone to hide in. But finally, he was there, crouched low, eyes searching.

And as he crouched, the air grew colder; a cold wind seemed to seep into the house.

There were too many doors to choose from. He could just make out three to his right, two to his left. He quickly stepped over into the shadows of the facing wall, keeping his back to it, the palm of one hand pressed flat against its smooth surface, the other holding the knife to his chest, blade pointing towards the ceiling. Which room, which room? The man was there, he knew. Instinct – or perhaps it was more than instinct – told him he was close. But which one?

There was only one way to find out. Regardless of caution, he stepped towards the first door, twisted the handle, and kicked it open. He quickly moved away from the opening and bent his arm around the door frame, his hand feverishly searching the inside wall for a light switch. He found it, and flicked it down. He was blinded by the light and cursed himself for not having closed his eyes first. He blinked them rapidly until the blindness had gone, then swiftly entered the room, his eyes trying to take in everything at once.

It was empty.

The room smelled musty. It contained a large bed, two soft armchairs and a dressing-table. A wardrobe unit extended along the length of one wall and one of its doors was slid open, revealing its emptiness. The sheets on the bed were stretched taut, the covering quilt neatly folded back. A fine layer of dust covered everything and the room had the air of having been unoccupied for a long time.

He went back into the hall and moved along to the next door, now heedless of any noise he might make. He repeated the process, and found the contents were almost exactly the same, except the furniture seemed to have a younger appeal. There was the same feeling of vacuity.

He moved along to the next door, turned the handle and pushed. Nothing happened; the door was locked.

And then he knew this was the one. The answer – all the answers – lay locked away behind this door.

He stepped away from it and brought his leg up, kicking out at the point near the lock with the flat of his foot. The door shuddered but held. He kicked again, exerting more strength this time, the satisfying splintering sound of wood rewarding his efforts. He kicked twice more before the lock finally gave and the door crashed open. Keller stood just outside the opening, waiting for something to happen, some movement, some sign of life. There was only silence.

He reached around the door and swept his hand up the wall, finding and switching on the light in one swift movement. Holding the knife at waist level, the co-pilot entered the room. It was a bigger room than the others and held much more furniture, was more elaborate. A wide rumpled bed took up only a third of the room; a small writing desk stood in one corner, papers and documents strewn untidily across it, a reading lamp lying on its side, ready to fall to the floor. The furniture, two armchairs and a straight-backed chair, looked old and heavy; an immense, ancient-looking wardrobe stood in the far corner, its deep brown mottled wood dull and unpolished. The smell of staleness in this room was different; it was the staleness of having been lived in too much. He noticed the scraps of food on the floor, the torn wrappers, the empty milk bottles. The bucket brimming over with urine, and worse. Nausea hit him and he almost retched. He clung to the wall to steady himself. What manner of creature could live like this?

He forced his eyes up and quickly looked around the room again. The man – if it was a man – was in here; but where? He fixed his gaze on the bed. The rumpled covers spilled over on to the floor, concealing the cavity underneath the bed, making an obvious hiding place. Controlling the sickness inside him, Keller moved towards the bed, crouching slightly, watching for any movement in the bedcovers, listening for the slightest sound.

In the intensity of the moment, he failed to notice his breath frosting as it emerged from his mouth, the room becoming even colder.

Kneeling, he reached out for the tumbled blankets, holding the knife forward, its point aiming straight ahead. With one swift movement, he whipped the covers away from the bed and ducked low to see underneath. But at the same moment he heard a noise from the other side of the room. Confused, he lost his balance and fell on to his side, the weight of the blankets dragging his arm down. He lay there rigid, but no further movement or sound followed. Squinting into the gloom beneath the bed, he saw that no one lurked there. Then he looked over in the direction of the noise he'd heard. It had sounded like a stifled sob, but it could have been anything, for his mind had been too preoccupied on whatever might lie under the bed. Disentangling his arm, Keller rose from the floor, still shaking from the sudden shock. The noise could have only come from one place, the only other refuge large enough to conceal someone. The wardrobe.

As he approached it, he became aware of other presences in the room, pressing down on him, trying to reach him. But his mind could only concentrate on one thing: whoever or whatever waited for him inside that huge, wooden lair. The key of the wardrobe protruded from the lock and he was sorely tempted to turn it and trap this person – this lurking thing – inside. He didn't, though, for he wanted to confront him, wanted answers. The fingers of his left hand softly touched the wardrobe's curved metal handle, slipping over and round it, his grip tightening, poised to twist and pull the door outwards. His muscles stiffened and seemed to lose their strength; his legs felt weak, almost unable to support him. Without giving himself any more time to think, he turned his wrist and pulled the door open.

He found himself looking into the twin black holes of a double-barrelled shotgun.

The two close-set apertures pointing up at his face had a hypnotic effect on him. It was only with some effort of will that he forced his eyes down the length of the double-barrels, past the finger that trembled around the two triggers, and into the dilated pupils of the madman.

The man rose slowly as Keller carefully moved backwards, away from the wardrobe, and the co-pilot took in his bizarre and unkempt appearance. He was muffled up in a heavy overcoat and short woollen scarf; one arm hung stiffly by his side and he emerged from his hiding-place with difficulty. There was a stench about him that increased the pungency of the room noticeably; he had obviously not cleaned himself for weeks. His hollowed, drawn cheeks and jaw were unshaven, and his grey hair hung in greasy streaks over his forehead. And his eyelids were kept open by grubby strips of sticking plaster.

He stumbled from the wardrobe, but the shotgun hardly wavered away from a position just below Keller's chin.

'So they've sent you now, have they?' The words were slurred, as if the man had been drinking. But among the many smells, there was none of alcohol, nor were there any liquor bottles in evidence.

Keller didn't reply. He continued to back away, the knife still thrust out before him.

'They think you're enough, eh?' Tears had left paler

streaks down the man's face. 'Like the other one. You'll go like the other one.' His snarling lips revealed yellow-stained teeth. The gun shook in his hand.

Keller only wanted to run now; answers meant nothing if you were dead. He forced himself to speak, just to gain time. 'You killed Tewson.' He said it as a fact, not a question.

'Tewson? Who the hell's Tewson? Is it the dead man downstairs?' He seemed to be gaining an aggressive confidence now, almost relieved that he had only been confronted by flesh and blood. What else had he been expecting? Why had he locked himself away like this?

'Answer me!' the man snapped. 'Who was he? Did they send him?'

Keller deliberately kept his voice low and steady, not wanting to excite the man unnecessarily. 'He was with the AIB, investigating the Eton air crash. But you know about that, don't you?'

'Oh yes, I know about that.' A sly look came into his eyes. 'And who are you?'

'Keller. I was the—'

'The co-pilot! The one who escaped. Yes, you're the one they sent. They said they would.'

'Who said? Who sent me?'

'The dead, of course. They said they'd preserved someone to find me. They'd saved someone.' He laughed at the co-pilot. 'Well, you've found me. Now what?'

'But who are you? Why should I want to find you?' Keller had backed towards the door and he risked a quick glance to see how far he was from it. Another six feet at least.

'You know who I am, liar! I did it! I killed them all!'

Keller stopped moving. Despite the levelled gun, his anger began to rise again.

'Yes, me!' The man laughed aloud. 'Barrett had to be

stopped somehow. He was trying to ruin me!' Tears began to well up in his eyes now, tears that could not be blinked away because of the retaining sticking plaster on his eyelids. 'The man was wicked. He tried to destroy me, crush the business I've worked so hard for! Don't you know who I am? Pendleton. Pendleton Jets!'

Yes, Keller had heard of him. He was a pioneer of the jet engine, had joined Frank Whittle way back in the 1930s when Whittle had formed Britain's first turbo-jet company. He must have been a boy then, or early teens at least, and he'd worked his way up until he'd gained enough knowledge and expertise to form his own company. He was almost a legend in the aircraft manufacturing industry.

'That's right, Keller. As a pilot you'd have heard of me. Now do you see why I had to kill him?'

Keller shook his head numbly.

Pendleton spat in disgust. 'Barrett! I had to let him buy into my company years ago, when problems with carbon-fibre fan blades almost wiped me out. It nearly caused the collapse of Rolls-Royce and my company was nowhere as big as that! But dear Sir James came forward, offering money, offering sustenance. In exchange for two-thirds of the company!' His voice had risen to a scream of rage. 'What choice did I have? I had to have the new titanium blades. It was either that or nothing at all. Well, I agreed, agreed to that slimy bastard's proposals. Do you still wonder why I killed him?'

Keller began to move back again, cautiously, inch by inch, his eyes never leaving Pendleton's, waiting for the finger to squeeze one or both of the twin triggers, waiting for the fiery blast.

'No. I don't understand. He saved your company, didn't he?'

'Oh yes, he saved it. He saved it for himself, so he could steal it once it got back on its feet. My company! The company I'd built myself! All those years – wasted! All my people – sacked! That's what he intended. The Americans were going to move in, take over lock, stock and barrel, bring in their own people, their own ideas. We would have been a small sub-company, owned by a major concern. It was just a cheaper way for them to get my engines! Do you think I would have allowed that?'

His face was drained white now, and the whole of his body shook with his rage. Keller prayed the gun wouldn't go off by accident. He stole another inch.

'He laughed at me, said I was finished. Do you know that? I've been ill, all right – but it was caused by him. He said I couldn't hold on to anything – even my wife and daughter had left me! Sneered at me. Said I was so obsessed by my own engines I didn't understand what was going on around me. Well, I understood him, all right. I knew he was flying off to the States to complete the deal. He said if I interfered he'd have me certified insane. Well, I'm not insane, and he knew that. *Myasthenia gravis.* That's what the doctors call it. It's not insanity. Do you know what it is, Keller?'

The co-pilot guessed he had less than a yard to go before he was in the doorway. He wasn't quite sure what he would do then – make a bolt for the stairs, lock himself in one of the other rooms? They were slim chances, but better than being blasted where he stood. He had no doubt in his mind that Pendleton would attempt to kill him. He shook his head in answer to the madman's question.

'A neurochemical condition, Keller. It causes progressive paralysis – sometimes fatal. It usually starts with the eye muscles – that's why I have to tape them open. Looks hideous, doesn't it? But that's not madness, Keller. Not madness! If I'd have been well, he would never have tried to do this to me.'

'How did you plant the bomb?' Keller's rage was still there, but survival played a greater part in his thinking. Only two feet to go. Keep him talking.

'Huh! So easy. I made the bomb myself – it was nothing to a man of my technical knowledge – and bought a briefcase identical to the one Barrett usually carried, one of those wretched slimline jobs. I went to the airport with him, pleading with him up until the last moment. He could have saved himself even then, you see. But he scoffed at me and said it was all for the best, that I would be able to rest, enjoy the money I'd make from the deal, have a chance to regain my health. That hypocritical bastard! I switched cases, gave him mine. He actually smiled and stretched out his hand to shake mine! Can you imagine that, Keller?'

One foot to go.

'I hurried back home and told my driver to leave me. I wanted to enjoy it by myself. I came into this room, drew the curtains, sat in a chair by the open window. Waited.'

Keller was almost in the doorway now.

'I'd timed the bomb, you see? I knew the air routes: Amber One, through Woodley up to Daventry, or Green One, through Reading. Either way, it didn't matter. The aircraft had to pass over Eton, then Dorney. I'd timed the bomb to go off as it passed over here, you see. But something went wrong. The plane crashed before it got here. I saw it in the distance, though – the explosion, the lovely glow in the sky.'

Keller remembered the slight delay they'd had in departure; if it hadn't been for that, Pendleton's timing would have been perfect. He paused in the doorway.

'But all those innocent people you killed with Barrett. Why murder them?' Keller's voice was incredulous, not wanting to believe anyone could be that mad.

'Nobody is innocent, Keller, you should know that.'

'But there were children on board. Women.'

'Children grow up into beings like Barrett. And as for women – even my wife and daughter deserted me. They left years ago; probably don't even know of my ill-health. They left the country. So you see, everyone is guilty, Keller. You. Me. Everyone destroys something in their lives. Haven't you?'

In his own perverse way, Pendleton was right: we all hated at some time, we all crushed something. But his argument was too broad; it dealt only in extremes. Keller had wondered how assassins of this magnitude justified their actions – the terrorists who killed and maimed so many innocent bystanders with their bombs – and now he knew. Their own madness justified it for them. To them, the whole world was guilty.

He prepared himself to leap into the covering darkness of the hallway.

Pendleton was still rambling on, shuffling towards the co-pilot. '. . . My factory. So many men depended on me for their incomes, you see. I couldn't let them down. I couldn't just let my name disappear from aviation history, could I? Don't move any further, Keller, or I'll kill you now. And then, the voices . . .'

Keller froze. Pendleton's tone had hardly changed when he'd warned him not to move, but the menace was all the greater for it.

'. . . Every night they came to me. Taunting. Whispering. Mocking me. They couldn't touch me, though. They tried to. They tried to frighten me into accidents, but I was too clever for them. They couldn't trick me.'

My God, thought Keller. His own insanity had saved him from them. A normal man would have been frightened out of his wits. But Pendleton wasn't normal.

'. . . I dismissed my driver, sent my housekeeper away. They assumed it was because of my grief for a lost colleague – a friend. My executives knew better, though. I sent them a letter telling them I was going away for a while. Of course, they panicked. The remaining head of the company couldn't just disappear in a crisis like this, with the company about to fold and all. They sent people round, but in the end they gave up. They'd always imagined I was eccentric. I couldn't leave the house, you see. It would have been too easy for . . . them . . . to have got at me. So I hid. But they told me they would send someone. It's you, isn't it? The other man was a mistake.'

'Yes, it's me,' Keller answered simply.

'Well then, what are you going to do? Inform the police?' His voice was chiding. It became a snarl once again. 'You can hardly do that if you're dead, can you?'

The co-pilot watched the madman's finger slowly tighten on a trigger, the knuckle whitening with the tension. He raised the knife in futile defence. Was this the end, then? How ironic to have survived the air crash so miraculously only to be blasted into oblivion by a maniac.

Both men felt the icy wind rushing around the room at the same time. Pendleton's head swivelled from left to right as the voices came from all corners of the room, whispering, calling to Keller. Rogan's voice was amongst them, but strangely, the demon's – Goswell's – voice was missing. They were pleading, crying for help. Keller understood what they wanted: Pendleton's death. But what could he do? He was helpless.

The madman's hand was shaking violently now, and his

head jerked from side to side as he screamed for the voices to go away.

Keller took the chance. He pitched himself forward, bending low beneath the raised shotgun, knocking Pendleton back, expecting a roaring blast to take his head off. But the madman's finger had slipped from the trigger, and the shot never came. They went down in a struggling heap, the older man screaming and kicking out at Keller furiously, his stiffened hand now coming to life and clawing the co-pilot's face. Keller thrust his elbow beneath the madman's throat and pushed hard, but the thick woollen scarf prevented any real damage.

The voices in his head urged him on, urged him to kill the man, to end it now. He released his elbow from Pendleton's throat and grabbed at the shotgun, catching it by the barrel and thrusting it away from him. Pendleton's breath wafted over him, almost making him vomit; spittle from the screaming man's throat sprayed him. He raised the hand that grasped the knife and held it over Pendleton's face. The eyes grew even wider with terror at the sight of the poised weapon. 'No!' he screamed, but the voices inside Keller's head screamed for the kill. Suddenly, one of the sticking plasters that held open Pendleton's eyes gave way under the pressure and an eyelid snapped shut. It was that pathetic movement that stayed the knife.

Keller found it impossible to strike. It was just a feeble, insane old man beneath him. A desperate, struggling wreck of a human being. He was evil, but it was the evil of madness, a sickness. He threw the knife to one side and saw Pendleton's remaining open eye glaze over with incomprehension.

The voices inside Keller's head wailed in protest.

But he would not kill for them!

For a frozen, eternal second, the struggling had ceased,

but suddenly, Keller felt a sharp kick that sent him reeling backwards to land sprawled on his back on the floor. Pendleton had managed to get a foot between them and had kicked out with all the strength and fury of a madman. The co-pilot quickly raised himself to one elbow and saw the older man was trying to catch his breath, was struggling to his feet, still clutching the shotgun in his hand. Keller rose at the same time, forcing his body up, and for a brief moment, both men faced one another across the room. Keller gazed into Pendleton's only open eye and saw it was filled with hate.

Then the shotgun was pointed at his stomach and he saw the finger squeeze the trigger as if in slow motion. He saw the flame leap from the black hole, then felt himself falling, tossed back through the open doorway by the blast.

The world was filled with the roar from the gun, the anguished voices of the dead, the laughter from the madman. It spun around him, a crazy carousel of light and sound.

He opened his eyes and looked down at his body. His stomach had been torn open by the explosion. He was propped against the balustrade along the landing, so he could see the blood oozing out on to his thighs. His shirt and top of his trousers had been ripped away, and he watched as his glistening intestines began to protrude through the gaping wound. They began to flow out with the blood, steam rising from them.

He reached down, his hand quivering, and held the warm, slippery organs to him, pushing them back in an attempt to preserve his life, but incredibly, he felt no pain. He assumed it was the shock.

And then, he pushed himself to his feet and walked back into the room, one hand still trying inadequately to cover the hole. Pendleton watched him with new terror and fell to his knees, holding the shotgun to him.

Keller felt no hate. Only an immense sadness. It wasn't the man's fault; he had been driven to it. He could only feel pity for him. And then, a lightness overtook him. A white, blinding lightness. He felt himself rising, lifting from his body, carried by a new surge of strength, strength and potency he'd never experienced before. The lightness filled every part of his being, rushing through him, making him a shapeless, floating thing. The sweetness was almost ecstatic, but it was pure, fulfilling.

He looked down and he saw the room receding from him, saw Pendleton raise the shotgun to his own throat, saw his finger squeeze the trigger. Sorrow swamped his new being, but it passed, never really leaving but becoming part of this strange elation. He saw his own physical body lying on the floor, burnt to a crisp, a black, and hardly human, form, and he began to understand.

He hadn't survived the crash. He had died with the others.

Unholy forces had preserved him, left him there to avenge their deaths, so the tormented ones could be free. They'd got their freedom now, for the man who had killed them was now dead himself. And he, Keller, had not been the cause. Relief now mingled with the elation, each sensation becoming a new, awesome experience, so unlike the muted feelings of life. He soared.

The spirits of the air crash victims were all around him, rising with him, joining; but the evil had left them, the one who had been called Goswell had gone. He reached down for the spirit of Pendleton, just as unseen hands reached down for him, welcoming, helping. Before the room, the house, the field below, left his vision, he caught one last glimpse of Hobbs. Hobbs who stood against the car, looking upwards, knowing what was happening, his suspicion as to Keller's unreal existence now confirmed. The strangely muted aura around Keller had caused the suspicion and now Hobbs understood – not fully, but enough. The dying woman in the High Street, her fear showing as she looked at him. *She had known in her own moment of death.* He felt the goodwill flow from the medium, and he smiled in his new being, his new birth.

He felt their presence. He felt Cathy close to him. It was nothing like their physical love, for everyone *was* as one now. The love was far greater. They reached for him, they consoled him in his apprehension and drew him onward. The first glimpses of understanding touched him; glimpses, but far greater than the sum of all earthly knowledge. This was self-knowledge, the essence of everything. Now he knew why there had been cruelty. Why insanity fed upon itself. Why there was malice. Why there was murderous pride. Why there were wars.

Sadness touched him, but there was no bitterness. There was joy, joy he could now understand, a happiness that spread and bound him even more closely to the others. There was so much more to learn, to understand; the knowledge already gained told him this was only the beginning, the first hesitant step. There were many more, each more significant than the previous.

But if this was only the beginning, how frightening, how awesome, was the journey to be? The trepidation was only momentary and it quickly became another part of him, another part of all of them. He could feel their warmth, their encouragement coursing through him, touching and merging with him. He cried out with the exhilaration and the exultancy of it.

And he went on.

Epilogue

The old man sat on the iron bridge, tucking his scarf tightly around his neck. The night – or early morning – was hazy with drifting clouds of smoke, the grey smoke that mulled around long after fires had been quenched. It was over now, although small groups of people still gathered, slowly making their way back across the bridge to their homes in Windsor, having enjoyed the earlier spectacle of burning buildings. There were not many people around now, for the excitement had died away hours earlier.

The old man listened to their tired voices, their wonder at what had happened. First, there was the fire along the High Street, which started in a photographer's studio and spread until it had taken three other shops with it, completely gutting two and severely damaging the third. They still hadn't recovered the bodies; that would have to wait until morning when it would be safer to search for them. And then the College: starting in the ancient chapel and spreading around the yard until many of the old buildings had gone up in flames. The headmaster was missing, and a count of all the boys was still being made. One boy at least had been found near the burning buildings, but it was said he was still in a state of shock, still unable to speak. Even the town's vicar had collapsed and gone into some kind of coma. Whatever had happened in Eton that night would be a matter for speculation for years to come. The voices drifted away into the night and, finally, the old man was alone on the bridge.

He turned stiffly on the wooden bench, craning his neck to look back towards the field where the aeroplane had crashed. It seemed like years ago now. He grunted silently to himself. The shimmering cloud had gone. He'd seen it hours before, just as dusk had set in over the town. He'd been waiting for something to happen all day, knew the dreadful oppression that had hung over Eton since the crash was reaching some kind of peak, reaching bursting point. And he had been right; it had well and truly burst. Peering through his curtains, afraid to go out, he'd seen the wispy cloud, translucent above the field. But now it had gone, lifted, and the oppression had gone with it.

The atmosphere had altered abruptly, just as the flames were at their worst. He'd felt the change, almost like a spiritual upheaval, a grey veil lifted from his own heart. And the flames had begun to die from that moment.

He turned back and gazed down into the blackness of the river. He had waited in the darkness of his room, waited for the clamour and the excitement to fade. Then, after so much time inside, he had wrapped himself up and left the house, a new lightness in his old steps. It was as if the fires had cleansed the town.

It was over now, he was sure. He'd always been sensitive to such things. Hadn't he looked up at the aeroplane just before it crashed? Hadn't he *felt* something was wrong? Yes, over now. The town could repair the damage and try to forget. The College would never be restored to its former glory – you couldn't rebuild history – but it signified the end of an era, the beginning of the new.

It had been so long since he'd sat here last; it was good to be back. He looked up into the sky. So big. So deep.

The old man shivered as he felt the icy wind rush past him. He thought he heard someone whisper, a low growling sound, then what could have been a snigger. But it must have been his old ears playing tricks on him. It had only been the cold night wind fleeing from the oncoming dawn. His old bones felt the sudden chills too easily now. Still, it was gone, had passed away into the night. Let it chill somebody else's old bones.

He smiled to himself, then trudged back over the bridge, back to his home, back to his warm bed.

JAMES HERBERT

The Number One Chiller Writer

Shrine

£5.99

A little girl called Alice. A deaf-mute. A vision. A lady in shimmering white who says she is the immaculate conception. And Alice can suddenly hear and speak, and she can perform miracles. Soon the site of the visitation has become a shrine, a holy place for thousands of pilgrims. But Alice is no longer the guile-less child overwhelmed by her new saintliness. She has become the agent of something corrupt. Innocence and evil have become one.

'Thrills and chills galore from the bestseller Herbert . . . his best yet . . . The build-up to the horrifying climax is subtle and sophisticated . . .'
Daily Express

REMEMBER WITH FEAR

JAMES HERBERT

The Number One Chiller Writer

The Magic Cottage

£5.99

'We thought we'd found our haven, a cottage deep in the heart of the forest. Charming, maybe a little run-down, but so peaceful. That was the first part of the Magic. Midge's painting and my music soared to new heights of creativity. That was another part of the Magic. Our love for each other – well, that became the supreme Magic. But the cottage had an alternative side. The Bad Magic.

'What happened to us there was horrendous beyond belief. Even now those terrible things seem impossible to me. Yet they happened . . .'

'Beautifully orchestrated crescendo of suspense . . . Herbert has brought the shivers back to the genre'
Washington Post

REMEMBER WITH FEAR